I0891489

THE LUNATIC

GUERNICA WORLD EDITIONS 90

THE LUNATIC

MICHELLE B. SLATER

GUERNICA
World
EDITIONS
TORONTO—CHICAGO—BUFFALO—LANCASTER (U.K.)
2025

Copyright © 2025, Michelle B. Slater and Guernica Editions Inc.
All rights reserved. The use of any part of this publication,
reproduced, transmitted in any form or by any means, electronic,
mechanical, photocopying, recording or otherwise stored
in a retrieval system, without the prior consent of the publisher
is an infringement of the copyright law.

Guernica Editions Founder: Antonio D'Alfonso

Michael Mirolla, general editor
Kulamrit Bamrah, editor
Cover design: Allen Jomoc Jr.
Interior design: Jill Ronsley, suneditwrite.com
Front cover painting: *Untitled* by Euphemia Brock Slater

Guernica Editions Inc.
1241 Marble Rock Rd., Gananoque (ON), Canada K7G 2V4
2250 Military Road, Tonawanda, N.Y. 14150-6000 U.S.A.
www.guernicaeditions.com

Distributors:
Independent Publishers Group (IPG)
600 North Pulaski Road, Chicago IL 60624
University of Toronto Press Distribution (UTP)
5201 Dufferin Street, Toronto (ON), Canada M3H 5T8

First edition.
Printed in Canada.

Legal Deposit—First Quarter
Library of Congress Catalog Card Number: 2024944590
Library and Archives Canada Cataloguing in Publication
Title: The lunatic / Michelle B. Slater.
Names: Slater, Michelle B., author.
Series: Guernica world editions (Series) ; 90.
Description: Series statement: Guernica world editions ; 90
Identifiers: Canadiana (print) 20240447735 | Canadiana (ebook)
20240451910 | ISBN 9781771839440 (softcover) | ISBN 9781771839457
(EPUB)
Subjects: LCGFT: Novels.
Classification: LCC PS3619.L38 L86 2025 | DDC 813/.6—dc23

Contents

Chapter One

Ten years ago, just after the birth of the twenty-first century, one could wander into Café Musil, tucked within the arboretum of Gramercy Park, and lose themselves in Dostoevsky's dream-like St. Petersburg or Musil's early twentieth-century Vienna. This narrator, who liked to frequent the café on rainy days, enjoyed observing readers indulging in discreet glances who reveled in complicit solidarity with those at neighboring tables reading Proust, Faulkner, or perhaps Baudelaire. You might have even caught a glimpse of the interminable novel written by the café's namesake: *The Man Without Qualities.* It was this narrator who overheard spontaneous dialogues that arose over pungent espresso and marzipan croissants, hallmarks at the Musil.

"The Europe of Ulrich and Clarisse was hopelessly decadent, n'est-ce pas?" one reader might have said, dragging a lacquered wicker chair over the coffee-stained oak floor to edge closer.

"Indeed. And I echo Baudelaire's melancholy in *Les Fleurs du Mal* as Paris gentrified."

Literary repartee such as this had kindled friendships at the Musil for decades.

And while there had been no exodus to chain cafés in recent years, eavesdroppers could no longer hear such improvised conversations in 2011. No books were to be found except in a graveyard on the wall, where rows of dusty volumes signified that this was once a bibliophile's café. In their stead, small disk-like devices and thin tablets shimmered on every table, or in the hands of their owners. It was a time when people were mesmerized by the allure of cyberspace. Even the venerable cafés in New York had succumbed. But like this narrator, not everyone welcomed the digital age.

At the neighboring table, engrossed in nostalgia, Nell Harding—who was one such person—sipped at a latte. She considered how the café had transformed since she had first sat there some years ago. It was before an oral exam for her graduate degree in library science, and she'd been absorbed in Edward Gibbon's *Decline and Fall of the Roman Empire*. She wondered when she had last sat in this café and read a book.

She nudged her teal frames farther up on her nose trying to commit to memory every detail of the current environment—the marble counter, the fluid movement of the baristas behind the counter, the crescendo of the frothing machine—as fodder for a future daydream about New York.

"Checkmate." The checkerboard tabletop at the adjacent table was bare. Two men wearing dark jeans, pilled wool sweaters, and matching tousled hair sat hunched across from the table, both staring at their phones with the concentration of mathematicians.

"Which one of you is 'Luzhin' today?" Nell asked.

"Micah. He tricked me again. Why don't you play the winner, Nell?" Trey said.

Both looked at Nell with expectation.

"I'll play if you bring out the alabaster figures like you used to. None of this cyber business for me," she said. But when her own telephone vibrated on the table, Nell pounced on it.

"What's that idiom about taking the log out of your own eye before judging your neighbor?" Trey quipped.

They returned to their virtual worlds.

Nell's screen read: *Res @ Carpe Diem @ 8. Apt. LOL. B*

She cradled the phone between her hands while her thumbs danced over the flat keyboard.

C u @ 8 :) The text was to her childhood friend Blake, and as she pressed send, she thought how like the temporary equivalent of the telegram her message was. She sighed as she banished her phone.

When she was a quixotic teenager enamored with Romanticism, she would have written, *It is with fervent anticipation that I await our farewell dinner at Carpe Diem.* In college, she wrote with a fountain pen when everyone else used disposables. She posted letters to her friends, even though she seldom received responses that weren't electronic. Somewhere along the way she'd stopped. *It's this dratted phone that's tampered with my soul*, she groused in silence. She could feel a small frown on her face.

Nell set her empty mug down and drew her creamy cashmere poncho around her as a waft of chilled air sent a frisson through her. Uncrossing her legs, she adjusted the chocolate-leather riding boots she had dusted off that morning in celebration of autumn's arrival and checked her watch. There was just enough time to pack the last of the boxes into the crammed Volvo and catch a cab to the Upper West Side.

As she prepared to stand, a handsome barista in dark jeans and a black linen apron over his matching sweater approached with a smile.

"Here's a latte on the house, Nell," he said. "We're going to go through withdrawal without you."

"Thank you, Jake. I miss you and the Musil already." She tilted her head up at him and tapped her heart with her right hand. She fiddled with her wound-up bun to brush a strand of hair away from her eyes and bind it back in place, then reached out to accept Jake's gift.

"I was checking you out. We're all guessing why you're here alone on your last day in the city. No book. No journal. I said you were taking in every detail of your favorite things to remember when you start pining away for us." He combed his neatly cut hair back with his fingers, something he often did in front of Nell, as if to hide the electric current in the smile he gave her. She had always found it alluring.

The glow of youth spread across her cheeks as Nell smiled at Jake's hypotheses. She didn't know it, but as she stood, with her chestnut hair in its messy bun and guileless smile, she looked far younger than twenty eight. More like a college student: uncynical, girlish.

He said, "If it weren't for that fateful incident right here, I conjecture you wouldn't be leaving New York."

His words were magnets to Micah and Trey, who paused their game to echo Jake by bobbing their heads.

"Wish we'd been there to stop that creep from pilfering your computer," Trey said. "You never talked about uprooting before then."

The friends sighed in unison before Jake walked off saying: "See you at sunrise tomorrow, Nell."

Nell hugged her chess-playing friends who made sure they had her number in their phones, waved at the baristas, and left Café Musil for the penultimate time.

* * *

As Nell walked her way to an errand, she took a sip of the latte from Jake. She took in the afternoon intensity of the blue sky as she shifted from present to past. She remembered the library scandal and, as she did, felt a ball of mercury roll its way into her chest to sit there, heavy. It had all started when she had been working on the Ephesus exhibit on her laptop at Café Musil, which amused her since the primary Ephesus museum in the world outside of Turkey was in Vienna, Musil's hometown. She left her laptop on her table to use the restroom. When she came out and caught sight of her table across the room, the laptop was conspicuously absent.

Stunned at both her naivete and the audacity of the thief, she heaved the oak door open and ran to the street, but there was no one fleeing. Spinning around, she rushed back in to shout: "Did you see someone steal my laptop?"

One girl looked up from her tablet. "An older guy picked it up, but I thought he was with you," she said.

"Where did he go?" Nell said, panting.

The girl shrugged, nonchalant.

The laptop hadn't even been Nell's to lose.

Monday morning, her chest still taut, Nell registered the theft with Mrs. Hadley, the head rare books librarian who had given her the laptop out of the library's stretched budget.

"It's a shame, but it's not your fault," Mrs. Hadley said. Her kind brown eyes underscored her tone of reassurance. She was an older woman, in her late sixties, with a face that looked authoritative if you didn't know how to look for the twinkle. She had always mothered Nell, who chided herself nonetheless.

"I'll be careful once I get the loaner laptop, but I'll have to lucubrate long into the night to catch up on the Ephesus exhibit," Nell said, shifting subtly into their long-standing game.

"Lucubrate, indeed! You'll write late into the night and forget all about this woeful loss. And on a recondite subject, too." Mrs. Hadley winked as she joined Nell in their frequent game of badinage. Nell felt the knot in her chest dissolving. It was going to be OK. A knock on the door came.

"Good morning, Mrs. Hadley." A young woman in an already rumpled dark suit appeared in the doorway. Willa was a few years younger than Nell, in her early twenties, and she was out of breath. "Excuse me for being a few minutes late, but there was a delay on the F-train this morning. I'm here to get your instructions about the Ptolemy manuscript viewing that I'm organizing," she said. Nell waved at Mrs. Hadley and stood to leave. Willa noticed her then, and her eyebrows came together in an annoyed expression. Nell spoke a polite good morning to her, which Willa returned curtly. She seemed to take note of Nell's pressed suit and coiffed hair, and the lingering smile on Nell's face from the laughter she had shared with their boss; all signs that she had not spent hours on the subway that morning.

A few weeks later, the staff was in the break room cutting a pale-yellow birthday cake for a fellow librarian when two young officers came into the department, calling: "Nell Harding here?" They spoke in a volume the entire department could hear.

"How can I help you, officers?" Nell said. She stepped forward.

The officer with a shaved head stated in a monotone: "You're under arrest for running a big-time hacking operation."

Nell froze. "I … I'm innocent. I would have no idea how to hack." She could hear the surprise in her own voice, how loud she sounded.

The second officer widened his stance, as if he thought Nell would attempt to flee.

"We have enough incriminating evidence from your laptop to put you away for a long time," he said, drawing out "long."

Though she couldn't see her colleagues, she felt their stares at her back. A strange silence hung over the room. Not shock, but resentment, like she had infiltrated their ranks. The two officers approached with handcuffs when Mrs. Hadley brushed past Nell to stand in front of her.

"I attest to Miss Harding's character. She is incapable of committing this crime. Quite frankly, she is fairly computer illiterate for someone of her generation. I could probably hack better than she could," Mrs. Hadley said. Her indignation seeped into the windowless room with every syllable.

No one else spoke. Not her older colleagues, with whom she sometimes had lunch, and not her younger colleagues, to whom she came across as in between generations, for she seemed far more comfortable with Mrs. Hadley than she was with them. When Nell had gone to get coffee one morning, she walked in on two co-workers referring to her as "Mrs. Hadley's pet," as if they were all still in school. Besides Mrs. Hadley, no one defended Nell.

The two officers shifted uneasily. The officer with the shaved head murmured, "Mack, what's the protocol here?"

"We won't arrest you, but you and your boss have to come to the precinct with us and take it to Chief. These are serious charges," the other one said.

Mrs. Hadley assured Nell that they would get it cleared up with the chief, which they did. The chief had thrown his head of curly, hoary hair back and laughed when the officers brought the two librarians in on the hacking charge. He apologized for giving them a scare and explained that a tracking device had been activated on the laptop when the library had reported it stolen, but their error was tracing it back to the librarians rather than to the hacker. Mrs. Hadley patted Nell's shoulder as they walked away down the hall together.

"Dear, take the afternoon off. That was two scares in a row for you about this laptop," Mrs. Hadley said.

"Thank you. I'm too flustered to go straight back today," Nell replied.

"Go curl up with tea and that dog of yours. We'll get back to work on the Ephesus tomorrow."

Nell practiced meditative breathing as she walked all fifteen blocks from the police station down Lexington Avenue back to Gramercy. She told herself to take several steps as she inhaled from her belly to her clavicle, and then to take just as many to exhale whatever wasn't serving her. But she could never complete an inhalation without hearing a beep from her phone, and reaching for it, only to stuff it back in exasperation without looking at it. By 30th street, she caved.

Only six blocks? Time to start a chapter of phone addicts anonymous. I'll be the first to sign up.

There were eleven new messages.

What's going on? Rose from yoga texted. She included a link to a video.

When she pressed the link on her screen, a video loaded. Nell watched herself from the side being charged as a hacker. A member of the library staff must have recorded the scene and posted it under a pseudonym on a major social media platform, tagging her so that all of Nell's friends could see it.

"I am a spectacle, a source of gratuitous entertainment in the most public of places: cyberspace," Nell said out loud to the trees when she turned towards Gramercy Park. By the time she was home, she had decided to depart New York for good.

On that long walk home, she contemplated pursuing a quest that had already been fomenting in her mind. She'd been shaping the contours of it well before the library incident, but now the idea—previously more a longing than a plan—took on definite form. Walking had helped her devise a plan to pursue this quest. For a long while now she'd noticed how the public and private spheres of her life overlapped. She wanted to separate them, place a line back between them. But the internet's omnipresence seemed to make that line of demarcation impossible. While her friends seemed complacent about the digital surveillance that was making a mockery of everyone's private lives, Nell fretted. She had posted recently on the monolithic social media site to her five hundred 'friends':

Why are we so apathetic about digital surveillance becoming the norm? Does our desire to be connected to the internet really outweigh privacy? Has the internet rendered privacy irrelevant? How can we elaborate an ethical position on this?—Over and out on a Sunday morning in New York

Few 'liked' her post or commented on it, though she kept checking to see who did. She posted a few days later after reading an article on mapping and sharing the consumer genome: *The digital panopticon is becoming more sophisticated.*

Only a smattering of her friends clicked the 'like' button. Did they not care if companies tracked their every move on the internet, in stores, and recorded their cell phone conversations only to sell their data? Nell wondered when she thought about her friends posting their most intimate moments. Later that day, she deactivated her account in disgust. That was her first act of protest.

* * *

Nell stared up. Ochre leaves spiraled through the sky towards the sidewalk. One caught in her hair. The New Yorkers passing by hastened while looking down at the metal devices in their hands. She wondered if they noticed the earth was quieting down for the year. Or had their lives been stripped of simple acts like watching autumn leaves fall? *But would I have even noticed a leaf in my hair a few weeks ago?* Nell wondered. She would have been too busy enumerating what she could fit into every last minute of the day.

Bustling had kept her in a state of ignorance so that her interior monologue could not dwell on the raw, unhealed places within. She had bustled so well that she didn't even know what was really inside of her. Nell fell into the rhythm of those who had been walking past her. But at presto pace, coupled with the allure of one's phone, contemplation was impossible. Perhaps this had been by design, and she had chosen speed over the dangers of what contemplation might reveal.

She turned onto a crowded avenue near Union Square to run a last errand, and met jostling crowds of tourists and the illegal claxon of car horns. The disparate noises clogged Nell's chest, where nausea was rising, her recent response to overstimulation. *I'm done with errands in New York*, she decided, turning back onto a side street beyond the fray. Erasing the errand from the elongated to-do list she kept in her mind, she retreated to the quiet enclave of Gramercy Park. Having fed on the stimulation of New York for so long, she had not yet realized that she had been retreating from life for some time.

Hopping up the worn stone steps of the brick building facing the park, she turned the key in the wrought-iron lock and heard the unmistakable sound of dog nails scratching the white-oak floors as Argos raced to meet her at the door. She knelt down on the threshold, greeted by a "Mmmmyawl," as Argos yawned and stretched his forepaws, signs that he had been napping. He caressed Nell's cheek with his cream ruff and reached to lick her forehead, cheeks, and nose until he had washed off Nell's disillusionment about the loud world they lived in. She petted his fur, a mixture of nutmeg and black bear, while he circled her.

"Argos, these separations are almost over. I promise." It was uncanny how Nell's angst vanished when she reunited with him. His molten chocolate eyes drew her into their shared language.

"Shall we go out, my best boy?" Nell lilted in a tone reserved just for him. Argos stood to his full height as a German shepherd before he sat back down on his haunches, panting contentment. She fetched his navy-blue leash and collar from the top drawer of the marble-topped foyer table in the apartment they shared with an old family friend.

"Let's go for our last walk in the city before you become a country dog and frolic with coyotes and deer." Nell fastened his collar, tied a small plastic bag to it, and opened the front door. Having long ago accepted—grudgingly, and only after countless hours of training that irked his independent mind—that Nell was his leader, Argos let her step out of the apartment first before following her down the stairs.

They trotted across the street and strode along the perimeter of Gramercy Park, a pathetic place, for it did not allow dogs inside its exclusionary walls where Calder statues stood alongside prized dogwoods and groomed autumn hydrangeas. Matching strides, they crossed 2nd Avenue and turned right. At 17th Street, they entered Stuyvesant Square Park.

Now they were on Argos's time. She followed him as he meandered, sniffing out a prize spot to mark the grass. "You won't have to walk several blocks just to go to the bathroom anymore," Nell murmured, thinking that this undignified life for a grand dog was going to be replaced by one that smelled like freedom.

Somehow, she felt that Argos already knew this. He had been watching her pack for days, but it hadn't fazed him as it did when she was leaving on the rare trip without him. Rather than pant and pace when wool sweaters and books moved from shelves to boxes, he helped by putting his toys and balls in one of the suitcases. She had been sending him mental postcards of their destination, and she had never doubted his intellect and intuition. Perhaps he did know, for Argos took his time saying farewell to New York that day, causing Nell to be late for dinner.

At eight o'four, Nell stepped a foot clad in a black satin onto the sidewalk in front of Carpe Diem. "Au Revoir, Senghor," she said, waving to the cab driver with whom she had conversed in French about the inequity of once being an engineer in Senegal, before being reduced to carting passengers back and forth on a compact island in the United States. She felt her phone vibrate through the raspberry clutch that contrasted with her sapphire silk dress. Surmising that it would be Blake, she mustered staccato steps, reminding herself to mention Senghor's plight to Blake. Although a cultural anthropologist at the United Nations was not likely to be able to help Senghor become an engineer in the U.S.

"Bienvenue, Mademoiselle," a maître d' in black tie said to Nell. Walking past an architectural arrangement of lavender orchids and cream calla lilies, Nell saw Blake sitting by the window, dressed in a dark suit, as if he had just come from the office. As he watched her approach, he ran his fingers through cropped hair. It was the color of raven's feathers, and she had always admired it. He stood up to kiss her left cheek and then her right, a ritual that they had adopted when they were teenage Francophiles.

"My dear, I thought you might have left for the Berkshires without saying goodbye."

"I would never do such a thing," she said as she slid into the chair that the waiter held for her. With a low "Merci, monsieur," Nell's hazel eyes met Blake's moss-colored ones with an unabashed grin. He looked back at her with a mélange of affection and something indiscernible. It might have been longing.

"Before I forget these relics under the table, here are your going-away presents," Blake said. He passed a cloth tote bag from a bookstore over the table to Nell.

"Mixed tapes! An old-fashioned playlist. Thank you. Where did you even *find* blank tapes in Manhattan?" Apart from the radio, tapes were the only way she could play music in her ancient Volvo.

"They should entertain you between the George Washington Bridge and Stockbridge."

"Thank you, dearie." She reached across the table, fluttering her fingers until he extended his hand for her to squeeze.

Monsieur returned just then with a bottle of Châteauneuf-du-Pape. "Don't look at me like that," Blake said. "I ordered the wine while I was waiting. I told you dinner is unquestionably my treat."

"Thank you."

Monsieur poured a taste for Blake with a rehearsed flourish. Blake swirled the burgundy liquid, observed it slipping down the sides of the glass, and savored a sip before giving the waiter a nod.

Monsieur poured a conservative glass for each of them before disappearing once again.

"I can barely endure the pretentiousness," Blake said. "But the food is good. I ordered a squash bisque and the vegetarian special for you."

Nell cocked her head to the side. "Are you worried there are no restaurants where I'm going?"

"Since you're determined to trade heels for Birkenstocks, and silk for fleece, permit me one last extravagant gesture," Blake said. He raised his glass. "To Nell, the last living transcendentalist."

"To trading Manhattan for the Berkshires," she said, raising her glass not to clink it against his, but to brush her fingers against his in a more intimate toast.

"But are you certain?" he asked.

"This has been a long time coming."

"But the solitude—"

"—is my desire."

"Your life is here."

"I want to pare life down. See if I can read a book again without sending a thousand texts. I know this seems like an act of lunacy ..."

She tried to quote her favorite Mary Oliver poem to dilute the ball of misunderstanding growing between them, but though she had memorized it, she couldn't get past:

"'We will be known as a culture that taught and rewarded the amassing of things,'" she cited, "'not for the quality of life for people (other people,) for dogs, for rivers.' I'm botching this Oliver poem 'Of the Empire,' but consider this: Argos won't have to pee on concrete anymore." She took a spoonful of delicata squash bisque seasoned with nutmeg.

Even before she looked up, she could feel him squinting to understand. She didn't need to see those eyes framed by faint etching to know their expression. She loved that she'd known him in his youth before those lines had first appeared.

"I'm proud of you," he said. "It's so easy to settle at our age, but you're like a young iconoclast. Just one last question. Are you sure that this Volvo is going to make it to Massachusetts from here? I nearly choked when I heard your message that it doesn't have a CD player. What year is it?"

Nell rocked a bit in defense and took her last spoonful of soup.

"1991, but it's new. This lady kept it in her garage in the Upper East Side for years, driving it to Poughkeepsie to visit her son every so often. He put it up for sale after she died, and it only has sixty two hundred miles."

"1991 and *new*, you say. Did you at least have a mechanic look at it?"

"He said she was 'solid.'"

The main courses arrived just then, saving Nell from further interrogations. She looked down at her plate, a still life of vegetables that looked like they had been painted in a studio in Provence: glossy black purple with dark green shading. Blake had ordered the pheasant with a bouquet of sage, rosemary, and thyme, dressed with a cherry balsamic glaze. He tore a piece of baguette and dipped it into the sauce.

Monsieur returned to ask, "Are the plats principaux served to Monsieur and Madame's desire?" Blake and Nell nodded, and Monsieur went on to explain that their signature dessert had to be ordered early.

"Would you like to pre-order the figs baked with honey-infused chèvre warmed by candle light, for a fusion of the cheese course and the dessert course?"

"Should we share?" Blake asked.

Nell was thinking of the new chapter of her life, sans desserts made fresh for each table. Blake nudged her with his foot and she said: "We'd love to try the fig. When it comes, I'll have a decaf coffee, too."

Blake made a "V" with his index and middle fingers to signal for two coffees, and then he reached to take her hand.

"I'll miss you a great deal. I've never had a finer friend."

"Before I drive off into the sunset, or sunrise, since I'm leaving at dawn, let's talk about those ideals you once had in the Peace Corps about saving the world."

Wryly, he said, "My turn to defend my path?"

Nell did wonder about Blake's ambitions. He had been preserving historical sites in war-torn zones since he had finished grad school. She remembered him talking about a moral obligation to heal the world.

Blake paused over a bite of plump fig and a sip of espresso that had just arrived.

"I wouldn't have to save these artifacts if we would stop striking the Middle East. But saving the world the way I once conceived it would mean that people like Senghor would still be engineers in their native countries, and there would be no refugee camps or hatred across religions and races. I see no evidence of that being a future narrative."

The weight of his words silenced them.

"We should get you home to rest for your great return." Blake gestured for the check. When Monsieur brought the tiny silver tray, it already had a credit card with a pen and a slip on it. Nell pretended to swat at Blake's sleeve.

"I have to see you off properly. Besides, I'm working between the New York and Paris office for the next few months, so any visit to the Berkshires will be delayed. But if any old specters visit you, I'll be there," Blake said as they stepped into the chill of the night.

Nell didn't respond, so he put his chin on her head and put his arms around her shoulders. They made one elongated silhouette on the New York sidewalk, but Nell broke their embrace as she always did. He moved to beckon a yellow car for her.

Clutching his bag of mixed tapes, Nell stepped into the back seat.

"It will be your grand homecoming, your great return, your American wilderness experience," Blake said, layering grandiose words on top of one another until Nell called out: "And you'll come witness it!"

He stood staring as the car left his side.

She was already scrolling through her messages, and tapped on her friend Ella's text:

Nightcap at the Jade Bar for a last, last farewell? E+P

10 min away. Yes. Elderflower Gin & Tonic, please.

Will be here waiting for you with a splash of champagne. xx

Before Nell could walk through the chic lobby of the hotel where models didn't deign to glance up and house music hummed, she heard her name called with Ella's unmistakable Jamaican inflections.

Nell slipped through the arched entrance of the Jade Bar, past the elongated pale-pink bouquet of roses on the counter and into the outstretched arms of Ella, burying her face in her caramel and noir dreadlocks. She caught a familiar waft of her friend's signature gardenia perfume.

Peter handed a crystal flute embellished with a sprig of fresh rosemary to Nell as they settled in their crushed velvet seats by the window.

"Our treat. But if we come to visit you in the Berkshires, then it will be your treat," Ella said.

"'If' is quite the operative word, Nellikins. Ell' was just creating variations of your demise. What was it this time, love? Death by wolf pack? This is it. Right here. Tonight," Peter said, thumping the table.

"Thanks for your optimism, guys." Nell let out a happy snort.

"There's something that we didn't talk about last night," Ella said.

"Please. Not more Rodolphe lectures again," Nell said, reaching for her glass.

"He called you a freak and said you were out of context in this world. That is just *not* the empathetic boyfriend that we hope for you," Ella said like the therapist she was by day.

"I broke up with him when he said those things. It was long distance … I have excellent judgment about character and—"

"Nell, you need a gardener. Someone that admires your blossoms, nourishes you, appreciates your uniqueness," Peter said.

"No more Dr. Jekylls and Mr. Hydes," Ella said assertively.

"I never intended to align myself with a verbally abusive boyfriend who belittled me in front of my friends and disappeared on endless trips. That won't happen again, Ella."

"Not if you keep up this obstinate 'no dating' policy," Peter said, "which won't be hard to do in a place where there are more bears than people."

"What is it that you haven't told me about little Nell, I wonder," Ella whispered.

"I can't stay. Long day tomorrow," Nell said, pleading with Ella not to psychoanalyze her.

Peter squeezed Nell's shoulder while Ella held her hand.

Nell stepped out onto a pre-party on the sidewalk in front of the Gramercy Park Hotel. A group of girls with styled long hair and tiny dresses that melded to their bodies debated their choice of nightclubs while the doorman waited to give instructions to the yellow cab driver by the curb. "1 Oak," a few girls chanted, which met with cries for "Cielo!" Nell squeezed by them, and strode to the corner. She peered into the sleek corner window of her favorite restaurant, Maialino, for a moment to see which bartender was on duty, before she crossed the street to join Argos for their last sleep there. She already felt detached from the New York scene, and had looked away from Maialino's windows before any of the regulars recognized her from their counter perches.

She sought comfort from the stars and the moon, but a clouded haze met her upward gaze. Clouds were gathering in her chest, too, as she realized that not even her closest friends understood her need. But she felt driven to cultivate a meaningful life that didn't conform to society's fetish with cyberspace and noise.

Ella had tried probing the night before, at their farewell dinner. "I'm always wary, as a therapist, of those who uproot their lives for abstract reasons," she had said.

But Nell couldn't tell her what lay beyond that need. She couldn't bring herself to probe behind the clouds. She only knew that she had to make this move, as if it were her only way to ward off an intangible checkmate.

Looking through the wrought iron spokes into the park that she had always boycotted because it excluded anyone that didn't have the coveted key—that privilege came only with owning property on the park—she changed course and made for the gate. Taking her keys out of her clutch that she would leave in her landlord's foyer in the morning, she unlocked the formidable gate and carefully locked it behind her, as the draconian neighborhood tenets required.

Alone, she could breathe. Strolling along the pebble path around the perimeter of the formal garden, she exhaled the clouds out of her chest with every step. She inhaled the enchantment the deciduous trees and flowering bushes exuded. She reached out to touch the dark raspberry blooms on the hydrangeas along the path. Blake's parting words echoed in a refrain: "Return … return … homecoming … wilderness," producing a quiver in her.

Fragmented images from her childhood were the only things that returned just then, and though they were muted as a pastel smudge, some of them were far from idyllic. She heard the percussive beats of a fireplace crackling, the silence of snow on a midnight walk. She felt an aged, familiar hand holding her own. Then, there were cumulonimbus clouds announcing a storm, as she had learned long ago from the one with the aged hand.

Chapter Two

As the first rays lent a golden glow to her living room, Nell felt Argos's grainy tongue bathe her cheek. She wriggled out of her sleeping bag. "Time for our fresh start."

From a sartorial perspective, Nell had already left New York. Last night's garb had been traded for a faded pair of jeans, fleece-lined boots, and a loose navy-blue T-shirt that she had picked up at a container gardening event that read: "Plant Seeds. Be Self-Sustainable." She had wound her long hair up and secured it on top of her head, and she was sporting her spectacles.

Picking up her last bag and winding Argos's leash around her left wrist, she turned the key in the lock and sighed with relief when it clanged at the bottom of her landlord's mailbox. Her landlord had been friends with her grandfather since she had been his student at Smith College, and she had offered her apartment to Nell for a price that would have been low even in the Berkshires. Although she had said she would be there on occasion, she never had been. Nell had always felt a little guilty, as if she were a privileged squatter. The clang felt like another step towards freedom.

They stopped at the Volvo to drop off the bag and grab Nell's dented thermos. Argos stopped when they reached the café door and sat. Securing his leash would be a superfluous gesture, for Argos wouldn't budge a centimeter from her on a traveling day.

Two elderly gentlemen were already setting up a checkers game. Jake was pulling a stash of homemade almond milk from the fridge when he saw her enter the door.

"Argos can come in at this time of day; no one will balk at him."

Registering his pun on "bark," Nell could only imagine how many espressos Jake had that morning to jumpstart.

"Argos, come," Nell said.

The young man came around the counter with a biscuit and Argos whipped his tail against the chairs as he circled Jake and licked his hands. Jake stroked his head in return with hands that looked ideal for sculptors to mold clay.

"I better get behind the counter before the NYC health code people show up." He spoke directly to Argos like Nell did, and she always appreciated that about him.

"You get him." Nell nodded as Argos and Jake made eye contact.

"At least I get one of you. Last night in New York, and I bet you spent it with him." Jake shook his head as he washed his hands.

She patted the edge of the counter, getting as close as she could to Jake's side, while Argos watched with interest.

"The Musil is my uncomplicated space," she said. She could never follow through with the subsequent step after whimsical flirtation. She couldn't bring herself to "hook up" even when she was college-age, like Jake probably was. She couldn't even say the term, and called it an intimate interlude. Besides, she didn't like to accumulate weighty traces of those she would leave behind, or who might leave her behind.

"What's complicated seems to be getting a job after college so I can be on that side of the counter with you."

"Any leads?"

"All the acting gigs I get so far involve modeling, which I swore I wouldn't do."

"You don't want to be objectified to compromise," Nell said softly, adding, "I empathize with that ideal."

"And I can't go from playing Alexander Herzen in Stoppard's *Coast of Utopia* to just being a body, a thing to sell things. I can't."

Jake had never revealed himself to Nell before. The way he cleaved to his ideals, foregoing what could be a stable income, resonated with how Nell too desired to live in the world.

"You can't become a commodity. You're a serious thespian; I admire that. I'm leaving New York so I can build my life from scratch, rather than compromise to fit into this world," Nell said.

Jake turned off the frothing wand and looked up at Nell with intent eyes. It was to be their last encounter, and he had nothing to lose.

"I was in this play last year that another student wrote based on a book we read in a philosophy class. It traced a feral child's life into adulthood in complete isolation from society, and maybe that's *tabula rasa.* But you? You'll take whatever followed you to New York with you, and you'll take whatever is bothering you in New York with you." He stopped, as if he was startled by his own forthrightness, and added: "'That and fifty cents will get you a cup of coffee,' one of the regulars here says when he philosophizes. Or, that's me, full of wisdom coming off an undergrad degree in the humanities." This time when he met Nell's gaze, there was laughter in his eyes. He placed her thermos on the counter with the top next to it.

When Nell looked down, still pensive, she saw he had carved a heart into the foam on top of her latte, and smiled up at him. "Jake, I'll cherish this talk. Thank you."

"That's on the house. Don't forget about Jake at Café Musil."

Nell reached across the counter and kissed Jake's cheek artlessly. Argos barked in reply, and she stuffed her coffee money in the glass tip jar when the young man turned to put the milk away. Jake caught her and selected an almond croissant from underneath the antique glass dome, pregnant with marzipan and dusted with fine slivers of almonds.

"I know you never eat these. You only look at them longingly. Here, for the road." Jake handed over the croissant wrapped in wax paper.

"Thank you. And, to keeping our ideals, nonetheless," she toasted in parting with her thermos held up, before walking to the car with Argos.

Nell crawled past the Occupy Wall Street protestors who cheered the old Volvo, a relic in America that once signified a bohemian lifestyle. Wearing backpacks and T-shirts, some looked like college students and some like aging bohemians. They held up signs that read: "Down with the robber barons!" and "JUST SAY NO TO BIG BANKS." They were protesting the corporate corruption of banks that the government was saving, when the hard-working middle-class couldn't pay their mortgages. They were voicing their dismay that the wealthy seemed to get all the perks while they suffered. Their posters traced the wealthy that were now executives on Wall Street back to the robber barons.

At a red light, she reminisced about touring cottages in the Berkshires with her grandfather Waldo. "Cottage" was a misnomer, for they were grandiose mansions rather than simple dwellings. The so-called robber barons had built them during the Gilded Age.

A bit delirious on a diet of caffeine and gluten after a shortened night of sleep, she worried that the vilified one-percent was taking refuge in the Berkshires. *Would it be crowded?* A string of discursive thoughts followed, and she didn't notice the light turning color. Violent honking roused her. She found the gas pedal with her right foot, accelerating through the yellow light, and careening towards the Hudson Parkway.

"I'm a neophyte driver," Nell said out loud, knowing they couldn't hear, and didn't care just as long as she would keep the prestissimo pace dictated by the city.

The sun was casting sparkling light on the Hudson River. She took her eyes from the traffic on the parkway to glance at the small sailboats gliding in an alternate rhythm—an exception to the city's tempo. Runners and cyclists were already gaining ground on the bike path that lined the edge of the river. On a stretch without other cars, she reached for Blake's bag of tapes and fed one of them to the cassette player. The soft voice of James Taylor sang to them about a frosting of snow on the turnpike from Stockbridge to Boston. The music swept her through New York State and well into Connecticut, infusing her thoughts with a blend of escape and hope.

Nell's phone beeped and vibrated. Friends were probably wishing her a bon voyage. She wanted to take her magic phone that could make reservations, check the weather in a nanosecond, or determine the name of an unidentifiable song on the radio, and fling it in the Hudson. But she knew she couldn't relinquish it; she was just as addicted to her device as her friends were. Besides, it was dictating her route through its map apparatus.

As Nell turned off the highway to take the historic route, in defiance of her phone's directed route, the cars thinned. The trees thickened, forming a canopy over the road. Bucolic streams appeared along the grassy edges of the two-lane road lined with fall asters. "If possible, take a U-turn," her phone said out loud in a polite female automaton's voice.

"I can take it from here, thank you," Nell muttered in response, fumbling to press the button that would turn off her guide altogether. Antique shops dotted the edge of the road on both sides, and signs for historic covered bridges cropped up. The inevitable catharsis that road trips catalyze fomented.

A familiar image of the New York Public Library floated into her mind, with its grand staircases and marble floors. How she would miss her Rose Room. She had always watched people writing there while she just catalogued other people's writing. On her last day at the library, she planned to spend her lunch break there. She'd pictured it like a last bit of communion with its high elegant ceiling and thatch of hand-carved wooden moulding. She'd sit at one of the stately wooden tables that beckoned readers, absorbed and reading with all the other students and book lovers.

But on the actual day, as she sat there, instead of hearing the silence that a library had once promised, all Nell heard was *click, beep, click.* Some people had books at their stations, but most of them were alternating between tapping their laptop keyboards and thumbing text messages on their telephones. On the sides of the room, tourists were murmuring loudly in multiple languages as they took photographs of yet another New York landmark. They could check it off from their lists and post the photos to their social media accounts without really reading its architectural contours at all, to say nothing of memorizing them. As she looked down the rows of tables, she grew disconsolate, for no one was reading.

Reminiscing about the library's transformation in the era of virtual life, Nell posed a recurring question to herself: After earning a spot as a librarian in the rare books collection, was she mad for quitting her job? Her country was in a recession, people were out protesting, and she was casting off her stable income as if she had a cavalier attitude to it all.

It was too late to ruminate on that now, she consoled herself, but that thought took her to others when she couldn't concentrate during her last weeks at the library. In the days after the video had appeared online, insomnia had stolen Nell's sleep. Pulling the phone out from under her pillow in the dark, she had plugged her worries into questions on the internet these last weeks, seeking answers about hacking and internet surveillance.

As she drove, she remembered some of the conspiracy theories she had read some nights at two a.m. Hacking sites speculated madly about the world running out of oil, the internet breaking down, and a return to a primitive way of life that would lead to mass-scale crime. Nell's insomnia worsened when she gave into these searches deep in the night. Argos would crane his neck over the bed and lick her forehead when he heard restless turning.

Her night angst affected her days, too. When she nearly let a scholar leave with a rare, illustrated, medieval manuscript that was priceless, on loan to the library, and had to be monitored by a staff member, she took it as her moment to resign.

No one had seen the incident, not even the girl from the F-Train with the rumpled suits, Willa, who glared at Nell at staff meetings with resentment towards her position, her purported wealth, her ease, her camaraderie with their elders. Willa seemed to be lurking, looking for an opportunity to pounce on Nell's inevitable fallibility, and Nell felt the tension it generated. There was the time she had sat on the steps of the NYPL on a warm spring day, just above where Willa was cavorting with Luke, the intern Mrs. Hadley had just hired as part-time staff. "I worked so hard in school, and I do now, but I'll never pay off those student loans living in New York, while she looks like she has no concept of the ninety nine percent!" she said.

Luke bobbed his head while he ate his sandwich, "No clue about the real world, totally," he said.

Nell knew they were putting themselves in juxtaposition with her, and she yearned to go talk with them, but she stayed on the steps with moist eyes behind her sunglasses, sensitive to their casual judgments, to being the object of their discontent.

Nell blinked back to present when she saw a dirt parking spot by a picnic table and a stream that brought her back from those dark reveries.

Giving in to a whim, she pulled off from the road so Argos could have a pee break. She dared to let Argos off the leash, and she sat on a rock eating the rest of her croissant and watching him. Argos looked at her for permission before plunging into the gently rippling stream. She reached for her phone to take a photo of him, but shrugged when she only felt a flat jeans pocket. Following Argos's lead, she crouched on the bank and splashed water on her face, as if the stream could wipe the vestiges of city memories off. Argos bounded over to lick the water from her cheeks and they were off again. Free.

When the Volvo breezed by a blue "Welcome to Massachusetts" sign, Nell cried out: "We are almost theerrreeee. Argos, welcome home!" She cranked the window down and Argos rushed into the front seat, plopped half his body onto her lap, and stuck his head out the window. They flew by fiery maple trees that stoked memories in Nell's chest, but she didn't let them travel up to her mind.

By late morning, the smooth pavement turned into a dirt road. Nell had to take a few detours due to an odd late-summer hurricane that had washed out a bridge, but her internal map knew how to get home. "I know something the phone map doesn't," she said in triumph to Argos. When she turned left onto White Birch Road, the Volvo jumped and veered over puddles and grooves. Argos barked in protest. She took note of the variegated crimson and rust hills rising up on both sides, the silvery, white birch trees lining the road in contrast. The brisk air wafting through the Volvo let her know she was back home in northern New England.

She slowed down to bask in the final mile when she was arrested by a sublime tree. Its branches reached into the sky, belying its elderliness, in an awesome symmetry. Its maple leaves were intact, decorating the sky with their ethereal red pigment. "It's the anti-oxidant anthocyanin that makes them red, Argos," Nell said, repeating a word she had once memorized for the marvel of its function. Nell tilted her head as Argos often did, reading the tree and its colors, for she knew just how ephemeral its autumnal dress was. She felt a familiar moisture in her eyes as she contemplated the finitude of the tree's leaves and envisioned the grey skeleton it would soon become.

As they crested a minor hill, a driveway framed by mature spruce trees came into her sight on the left. Inching up the serpentine driveway lined with pruned peonies that her grandmother had planted decades ago, she saw her family home. The dark brown wood in a handsome Tyrolean style was a cross between a sprawling cabin and a house. The expansive blue stone steps called her to walk up them. Supportive pillars welcomed her home.

Nell swung the Volvo right in front of the knotty wood door for easy unloading. Unwinding herself from the seat with Argos tumbling out behind, she caught a glimpse of her favorite view in the world: the Appalachian Mountains and Grandpa's forty four acres of trails that led to the edge of the Housatonic River. From the house, she knew that she wouldn't be able to see another human soul—just those of coyotes or bears—and that brought a sigh of contentment.

"Argie, how could I have deprived you of being here all these years?" He raced out to the lawn, rolled on his back in the grass, and ran in circles as if he was experiencing freedom for the first time, although he had been there once before.

"I have done the right thing. Manhattan is no place for a German shepherd. Welcome to your new off-leash life, Argos."

Nell hesitated at the threshold once the lock clicked open. Her grandfather, Waldo Harding, had been a giant to her, a beloved giant. When he died six years ago and left his estate to her, every floorboard's creak and fireplace snap sounded the words: "Colossal loss." Nell had closed up the house with Amelia and Fernando, Waldo's caretakers and friends, and they tended to it throughout the years while she grieved in Manhattan, unable to return.

Then Argos had come to her as if Waldo had sent him. A neighbor had adopted an eight-week-old German shepherd puppy, but found it too recalcitrant. Witnessing the puppy being jerked when it pulled against the leash one morning, and overhearing her neighbor say, "Just walk, dammit," Nell had jested that she would take the beast off from his hands if he wanted. She'd only been joking, but the neighbor had handed him over to Nell, saying: "Done. Max is all yours."

Renamed and nurtured under her gentle hands, Argos reminded Nell what it was like to love without limits. His love had helped heal the crater in her heart. Thanks to him, she could think of Waldo without the hollowness debilitating her.

Argos whined, wondering what the delay was. With his nudge in her calf, she walked over the threshold with him. A bouquet of raspberry hydrangea blooms stood on the pine green foyer table.

"Amelia," Nell murmured as she massaged two tiny fallen petals between her thumb and index finger. The house didn't smell abandoned but it looked bare. Nell glided through the great room, quasi-somnambulant, dropping the keys on the expansive island, caressing the sage veins that ran through the powdery greenish-gray soapstone. She opened the chef's refrigerator Waldo had insisted on, because it would last for years, and saw that Amelia had left some blueberries and greens from her garden for her.

Turning the switch on the daunting gas stove, she nodded when blue flames shot out like memories of the dinners it had once cooked. She traced the rustic wooden dining room table just behind the kitchen, letting meals with Grandpa Waldo come out from their resting places in her mind. She sat on the wooden bench for a moment to look onto the living area on the other side of the great room. Rectangular wool sofas stood in front of the stone fireplace, with a guitar on a stand next to them, strings falling off. Her eyes settled on the mid-century modern womb chair in front of the glass doors. She had never sat in it before. It had always been Waldo's sacred reading spot.

Sliding glass doors beckoned. Argos followed her onto the deck. They sat side by side for a moment, she in the dark-green faded rocking chair, and he on his haunches. They peered out at the mountains, painted for fall. Silent. Nell had forgotten that she belonged here, that only New England stoked her fervor for contemplation while walking in the woods. That's what she hadn't been able to explain to her friends while parting. Extolling slowness in an era of speed would have bored them, she thought.

Ready to ground, she stood up to start unloading suitcases, boxes of books, dog beds, and all material contents of her life for the past decade. As she went from room to room, depositing books in the great room, clothes and toiletries upstairs in Waldo's old bedroom, Nell took stock and made a list of things they needed to nest:

- Cedar hangers
- Tennis balls & a new bed for A.
- Journal
- Candles & Matches
- Muck boots
- Firewood? Ask down at the market?

It didn't look like Waldo had purchased sheets or towels since Grandma had died, so linens went on the list. Reviewing it, she underlined "Journal," as if her thoughts were yearning to seep out onto a page.

"Ugh, we are not here to shop, Argos. We were supposed to escape materialism," Nell said. "Just one shopping trip. To spruce up our home."

Nell had saved her grandfather's favorite flannel shirts. She donned a soft navy-blue plaid one interspersed with rust and cream lines, and heard an echo: *The seamstresses just don't make them like that these days.* She nodded her head as if Waldo had said it out loud. When she raised her arm to her nose, she may have dreamt that the sleeve still bore the faint cedar scent of his cologne.

"Argie, can you watch the homestead while I'm gone?"

Argos emitted a half-groan in acknowledgement as if to say, *I don't like when you leave, but I am resigned to the inevitability of your departures.* Nell dug her old suede Birkenstocks out of a duffel bag, grabbed her list, and headed to the Volvo.

Swinging out of the driveway, she paused to dig her phone out from under the seat where she had banished it. She grinned with pride that she had survived hours without it. Plugging in "linen stores," into her map feature, she scrolled down until she found a large department store a few towns away on the edge of the Berkshires. She differentiated America from the Berkshires, as if the 'Shires had seceded metaphorically and its vibrational energy was more at one with nature; less contentious politically, less materialistic.

Just in front of Edith Wharton's house on the way to Pittsfield, she was brought to a halt by traffic. It was at a standstill, as packed as if she were idling at rush hour in Manhattan. Inches from metal friction with the bumper in front her, she hyperventilated as she waited. "*Daahrn leaf peepers,*" she could hear Waldo exclaiming when the hordes showed up in fall. Nell knew she would get her Berkshire solitude fix starting in late fall when the skeletal trees sent everyone home.

* * *

Nell tensed up under the fluorescent lights and nondescript music as she perused the aisles of the department store. When each item on her list was crossed off, Nell rolled her cart over to the checkout line. In front of her were two young women in their early twenties with a toddler and a bulging cart.

"That's spelled out with no caps."

Nell listened as the women supplied their email addresses to the cashier. There was no sign at the cash register saying: "Beware. We Track Every Purchase You Make." They crossed a boundary by stealing information clandestinely. It was Waldo who disabused her of Robert Frost's overquoted line about good fences making good neighbors. The next line in Frost's poem asks what the point of fences is if one doesn't have cows to keep in or out. It wasn't that she had anything to hide, but it irked her that her freedom was at stake. *Boundaries, Mr. Frost, boundaries,* Nell fumed. "Good internet privacy makes for a good society," is how she would have reframed it for the twenty-first century.

"Your email, please?" the cashier asked.

"No junk emails, please," Nell said, shaking her head in a silent "no" as she started filling up her reusable bags.

When the amount she owed flashed on the screen, Nell reached for her cash. She had started this practice after the hacking incident. Now she always carried enough money in her wallet to pay for purchases in places like this store. Between credit card theft and internet surveillance companies selling data to ad companies, she had decided to evade the internet spies and go undetected, especially at national chain stores like this one.

Eager to support the local economy, Nell headed to Great Barrington, where local hero W.E.B. Dubois was born and raised. The first Black person to receive a doctorate from Harvard, he had known about the cost of liberty and worked to advance it through his career, as one of the founders of the National Association for the Advancement of Colored People. Nell wondered what he would think about the liberty of privacy being stolen from all, without their consent or even knowledge of it.

She tapped the steering wheel to one of Blake's road trip songs from the '60s, passing Monument Mountain where she and Waldo had often hiked. Nell could almost hear Waldo tell the story of how Nathaniel Hawthorne and Herman Melville had chatted over a picnic lunch at the top, much like she and Waldo used to do with sharp cheddar cheese and tomato sandwiches on homemade bread with apples from their micro-orchard for dessert, and a shared thermos of black coffee. These reveries took her all the way to the natural food cooperative. "Little Nell's hippie food," Waldo had called it, but he had also been the one to give her Rachel Carson's books about the dangers of pesticides. She had been a member of the co-op here since she was a teenager, so she felt a sense of ownership when she walked in.

Nell loaded the trolley without having to check labels, for the co-op only sold organic produce: Beets, apples, acorn squash, yams, lacinato kale, garlic, coffee, almond milk, wild-caught salmon, salt lamp, chamomile tea, flaxseed bread, soap, raw dog food, and a local environmental magazine that was ad-free.

Feeling confident that she could use her credit card here without having her personal data sold to ad companies, she flourished it along with her member card that had been sitting dormant in the back slot of her wallet. The lady with gray curly hair at the cashier's counter looked quite a few years younger than Grandpa, but she was working well into the retirement years, as many were doing after the financial crises of 2008 had robbed their nest eggs.

"I know that name."

"Perhaps you knew Grandpa Waldo?"

"My memory is working today. I served on the Board of Selectman with your grandfather. He was a stoic man, but not when it came to you." The lady continued to chat as she rang up the groceries. Nell, her throat having closed up at the mention of Waldo, just nodded.

Crepuscules cast a pale pink hue on an oblong moon, highlighting the Appalachians in the background as she came up to the house. It was tucked far enough into the woods that even the United States Postal Service wouldn't deliver mail, a comforting thought for Nell.

She opened the door and Argos came out like a canine whirling dervish. It occurred to her that she had left him in an unfamiliar house, and he might have been unsettled.

"I'm sorry, Argos. I won't leave you for so long again," Nell exclaimed.

From the distance, she heard, "Aaaaaahroooooooo." The coyotes called out to one another, and Argos perked up his shepherd ears in response. The city dog sniffed around the perimeter of the mowed part of the property to determine what territory was his and what belonged to the coyotes, and then circled back to Nell as she made several trips to and from the car.

Nell defrosted a portion of duck nuggets in a bowl of hot water for Argos and set it down. He lay down to eat, and looked at Nell expectantly. "I'm going to eat later, my love. There's work to be done," she said. Argos's eating habits were more human than dog. He liked to break bread with Nell and sync their meals. He communed with her.

She put the new sheets and towels in the washer and set new candles in the row of hand-blown glass hurricanes that were in front of Amelia's hydrangeas. A sudden emptiness in her stomach caused her to stagger as she carried the last box of books to the bookshelves in the great room.

She had had the foresight to pick up a few premade meals from the co-op deli, so she started putting together a plate of ginger teriyaki salmon with beet salad on the side. She chopped Amelia's lacinato kale on the walnut cutting board that had permanent knife grooves in it—making her feel even more at home—and massaged the kale with some of the extra virgin olive oil she had stocked up on. She could probably get by for a month on her provisions, for she would never forget the time she and Waldo had gotten snowed in during October. She was prepared for nature's vicissitudes.

Sitting at the soapstone counter, salmon and kale mixed in her mouth along with headlines about the protests in New York and civil rights activism.

Ding.

You could be at the Wynton Marsalis concert with me at Lincoln Center. Blake was jabbing to see if he could get Nell to text that she missed him and the city. In response, she slid the phone across the island with such force that it fell on the hardwood floor, startling Argos and herself. He went over and touched his nose to the phone and then looked up at Nell expectantly, waiting for her to pick it up. She humored him, but placed it face down on the island.

"I've implicated you, Argos," she said.

When company visited, Argos counted everyone at night by touching his nose to each friend's knee or hand. When Argos started touching his nose to Nell's phone at night and in the morning, she realized that he had begun to see the object as having an ontology beyond objecthood. This act of acknowledgement alarmed Nell even more than her growing awareness of how much she depended on the phone.

Washing her ceramic bowl and hammered metal spoon, she put the heavy, red tea kettle on, and ambled onto the deck to look into the inky night. Argos followed her through the slit in the sliding glass door, and she didn't worry that he would run off with the coyotes. He had it good with Nell, and he knew it. They both gazed out into the night sky, where random white lights swooped down and greeted them.

"Make a wish on the falling star, Argos." Nell knew what to wish for: to be far away from the omniscient eye of the internet. To stop being addicted to it. They heard one owl call out its signature "hoo" series when another owl or two joined. *It's an owl quartet rehearsal*, Nell thought. "Hoo hoo hoo loooooo," Nell joined in softly. The tea kettle whistled, startling them into a bark and a jump again.

As she made tea, she retrieved her phone from the floor to text Blake. *The nocturnal animals are performing a private concert for me.* She then clicked on the weather icon to look up the weather forecast when she gasped.

"What am I doing, Argos? I'm supposed to be embracing this new life off the digital grid. That means no phone."

She looked at her phone settings and noticed a strong connection to the internet. Looking in the corner of the great room, she saw the culprit: a shiny modem by the bookshelves with a note on it.

Welcome home, Nell! Fernando and I thought you would need this, so we set up internet and landline for you, honey. No password. 413.243.1974.—Amelia

P.S. The piano is tuned.

Nell was thankful to Amelia for everything that she had done in the wake of Grandpa's death and in keeping up the house since, but this new life meant no modem. She unplugged all of the cords and wires and put them in a bag by the door.

That wasn't good enough. She flung the door open, beat her bare heels down on the steps, and slung the bag in the back of the Volvo. She stuffed the phone in her glove compartment, and locked it with the key. Heartbeat amplified in her chest, she met an inquisitive Argos at the door. Giving him a pat on the head, she said: "I'm done with all of that."

Nell wrapped a wool throw blanket around her torso and settled in her grandfather's chair with a steaming cup of chamomile tea, stirred with a dollop of raw local honey from the co-op. She reached for the book she had placed on the side table earlier that day, unpacked from one of her boxes: George Orwell's *1984*. She had shuddered when she read it as a teenager, but in light of her recent encounters with internet surveillance, rumors of cell phone tracking, and the incessant news infiltrating people's lives through every orifice, Nell had newfound respect for Orwell's proleptic writings. He seemed to predict the dystopic direction her country was taking.

Perhaps this is only the beginning, after all it was a book that served as a wake-up call for totalitarian tendencies within liberal democracies, Nell thought as she opened the cover and raised her feet onto the matching charcoal leather ottoman. *I would say that monitoring cell phone conversations, if that's true, should serve as a warning to us.*

Reading about the fictional surveillance state and newspeak in Orwell's world, Nell shivered when she came to "BIG BROTHER IS WATCHING YOU," relieved that Waldo never had a television, that her cell phone was locked up, and that she had banished the modem. *Today, it's BIG DATA is watching you*, she grumbled.

Halfway through her chamomile tea, she remembered that she hadn't jotted down the address of the yoga studio her teacher Saraswati had recommended. And she had promised to let a few people know she had arrived safely. *Should I go get my phone?* She shook her head, and sighed as she pressed on. It was the first of many similar predicaments that evening.

"Perhaps a lunatic was simply a minority of one." Her eyes lingered over the sentence. *What were Orwell's influences? I should ask my phone. What time does the sun rise? I should set my phone alarm for the morning. I wonder if Blake texted me back.*

She picked up the book again.

Orwell: *You had to live—did live, from habit that became instinct—in the assumption that every sound you made was overheard, and, except in darkness, every movement scrutinized.*

Nell thought, *Well, I don't have to live like that, because I have no devices turned on around me. Why am I so distracted? This is a profoundly engaging novel and I can't sit still. It's the lure of that devious phone.*

The question Nell had been contemplating came to rest in her mind once again:

Is absorption possible in the great age of distraction?

Nell had been trained to focus on reading for extended periods. What had overcome her? Was it really a smartphone addiction? She wanted nothing more than to retrieve her imprisoned phone, place it next to her, and look up answers to her random questions.

Nell switched off the reading light almost aggressively, and took Argos out one more time before heading upstairs to their bedroom. She liked seeing the clean, white linens with spring-green embroidered vines on the king-sized wooden sleigh bed. By the time she had washed her face and changed into a nightgown, Argos had already nested right next to her pillow.

"We'll probably miss the sunrise, Argie, because I didn't think to put an alarm clock on the list. And no phone also means no flashlight, no chance of making an emergency call. No scrolling through favorite photographs if I can't sleep," she said, lifting her arms up in a 'V' and exhaling them down by her sides. She flowed through a few informal yoga asanas on the mat she had put beside her bed, shaking off the plugged-in New Yorker feeling she had been shedding all day.

It took everything she had to keep from running downstairs to the phone, but she turned to Argos and snuggled against him. Argos released the full weight of his back against Nell. Within moments, he had left her for the realm of sleep. Nell admired his ability to sleep at will, and she closed her eyes with a sigh of gratitude to be home, for Argos, and for Waldo's generosity in bequeathing all of this to her. She remained in this state of blissfulness for a few minutes, anticipating that intangible drop in consciousness when her thoughts would decrease in volume and tempo, and she would enter the oneiric realm.

Nell's patience waned as the minutes increased, and she didn't know how long she had been lying there. She looked at her phone so frequently that she never wondered what time it was. *What time is it? Is it the full moon tonight? Tomorrow?* Scientists may have denied it, but like Aristotle, Nell believed in the notion of *lunaticus,* for the moon's gravitational pull affected her in the form of insomnia and restlessness when the moon reached its fullness in the night sky. Not wanting to interrupt Argos's deep sleep, but craving the answers to the questions preventing her from sleeping—or perhaps the phone itself—she broke down and reached for her slippers. Her attempt at being surreptitious didn't fool Argos, who flew to catch up with her.

The moon adumbrated the pines and spruces, and set the house aglow in otherworldly incandescence. She stared up at it with admiration. *The moon is stable. It's consistent. One knows what to expect from the moon, and one could record the passing months thanks to its cycles. It was little wonder that travelers long ago would journey by the light of the moon*, she mused.

With a measure of disgust that yielded to addiction's desire, Nell unlocked the glove compartment and picked up her cherished yet abhorred metal device. Pressing the cold button that powered it on, she stood and wandered with Argos as he peed one last time. It was only eleven p.m., to her relief. Nell realized that the moon wouldn't be full until Tuesday, October 11th. "Three nights of altered sleep, thanks to you," she addressed the moon. Nell was at an impasse. How would she wean herself from the allure of cyberspace if she couldn't endure one night's separation?

As she paced the lawn with Argos, she vacillated, as she had done innumerable times. The internet provides us with convenience, with the ability to conduct our errands and learn answers to our questions, without having to travel to the library to consult dusty encyclopedias that have lost their currency. Yet, that convenience—the cyber swipe of a credit card on the phone, for instance—creates hackability and disruption to one's fundamental rights to a private and protected life. But the joy of having one's interminable questions answered immediately through a few taps on the phone was immeasurable. How does one reconcile the benefits of the internet with the pitfalls? It was as if the internet had become a trap, that its infinite possibilities robbed one's freedom by creating a gluey attachment to it.

Waldo had always counseled her to write down the advantages and disadvantages to weigh while making a decision. Yet in spite of her multiple attempts to prove otherwise, the advantages column for keeping the phone was far longer on paper.

It had become a philosophical and existential question for Nell. If she chose privacy and anonymity, she would be shutting the door to the modern world. But she could never guard her own anonymity from those who searched her, even if her fierce self-guardedness led her to give out pseudonyms in New York. She couldn't hoodwink anyone in the Berkshires; they would just think she had gone mad. Nell shook her head at herself. She motioned for Argos to follow her back into the house, phone clutched in her hand.

She paused upstairs, glancing at the desk on the landing where her new journal lay. *Should I record these observations?* Nell shrugged that thought off, daunted by the blank journal, as if she didn't trust that her thoughts were worthy of the hallowed white page. She turned towards the bedroom instead.

She stretched one last time, curled into fetal position with Argos's head brushing against hers on the pillow, and closed her eyes, hoping for peace. But her fleeting hesitation about putting a string of her own words, her own reflections on the blank page of her journal, gave way to a flood of diffident thoughts, like storm water rushing over an eroding dune at the Cape Cod seashore on the far reaches of her state. *Perhaps Rodolphe was right, that no one would want me but a dog, that I have nothing original to say because I'm just a librarian living in a world of dusty books that have no relevance to the world.*

Rodolphe's words had seared her to the point that she could quote them verbatim, although she thought she had let them go. They'd broken up nearly a year ago. But now he appeared in her mind: handsome, but with blue eyes that were chilly, and a severe jaw line. *Why have the traces of Rodolphe followed me here? Can I not withstand his scathing comments? Can't I be impervious to the glares of people like Willa who mischaracterize me? Breathe this out, Nell, don't let it seep in. You know it's not true.* An exaggerated exhale sent Argos to the foot of the bed. She sought to distract herself by turning to the phone and tapping every wild query that came to her mind on the phone's screen.

Unable to endure Nell's restlessness any longer, Argos slid off from the bed and groaned for Nell as he nestled on the sheepskin rug on the floor. At an undetermined hour, the mysterious land of sleep claimed her until well into the morning.

Chapter Three

The next morning, groggy, but eager to feel like part of the local community, Nell went into Stockbridge. She turned onto Elm Street, where the local life of the town could be found, unlike the more touristy Main Street, which Norman Rockwell had rendered famous. She found a parking spot right in front of the narrow, white clapboard coffee shop that was still named "The Hawthorne." Although it looked unassuming, it was the heart of the town, for all the locals gravitated there throughout the day. She grabbed her purple thermos and rolled down the window for Argos to take in the breezy fall day.

As if they hadn't left since the last time Nell was here, the old timers sat on tiny metal chairs in front of the Hawthorne, the true early birds in town. Clad in motley textures of flannel and wool, they bantered about the newcomer.

"Isn't that Waldo's granddaughter?"

"Can't be. Brain drain and all. Last I heard she was in New York City."

She recognized one of them as Waldo's fishing partner.

"Good morning, Mr. Butterfield. It's me, Nell. I've come home to stay."

The older man emitted a half-grunt and a half-smile, which meant that he was pleased. He pulled out a notebook.

"N.H. Eight Pounds." He spoke out loud as he wrote. "You didn't become a vegetarian in New York City, did you? You didn't become one of those guppies." He joked like Waldo had.

"I think it's yuppies, Mr. Butterfield, but no, I didn't forget who I am," Nell assured him.

"I've put you down for this year's cod catch. Waldo would want me to do that."

"That's a kind gesture. I imagine Grandpa would want that. It's a nice welcome home to see all of you," she said. The men waved at Nell as she walked up the stone steps and through the narrow door into the coffee shop.

A poster caught her eye on the message board. Black sans serif letters announced a title for a lecture coming up at the local library: "Your Phone is Watching You: Cultivating Privacy in the Age of Cyber Spying and Big Data." The speaker would be a Professor S. Gupta from MIT. Nell dug out her phone to snap a photo of the poster so she'd remember the date and time.

"That will be a sobering talk," said a man in a fleece vest and jeans waiting in line.

Nell nodded.

Before he turned back to face the front of the line, he added: "Cultivating privacy sounds like the kind of idealistic thing an academic would come up with. Just isn't going to happen in this day and age."

"I think that's what they call an 'impossible dream.' Still, it seems worthy of pursuit if our phones are really tracking us," Nell offered.

The Hawthorne coffee shop in Stockbridge was known for engendering spontaneous discussions of note, Nell remembered, pleased to have reclaimed a trace of the Musil. The two coffee shops were named after authors, but it was the liberal-minded, grounded ethos of The Hawthorne that drew her back to the Berkshires.

A lady in black polar fleece and leggings sitting at one of the mismatched tables found an opening. "Who cares about the gravity of data mining when we need to see how many likes our social media post got?" she said with sarcasm.

Nell tried to let them know she was one of them. "Yeah, I couldn't even keep my phone turned off overnight without grabbing it to look up a dozen things. The addiction part makes this cyber hacking issue an ethical morass," Nell said, perhaps with more enthusiasm than was warranted.

A tall gentleman with a shock of ungroomed white hair and a burgundy silk scarf tucked into his camel hair overcoat spoke up: "One can't be addicted if one refuses to consume. I've never had a cell phone. Wisest decision of my life thus far."

The chatter ceased as if everyone were in silent wonder at the gentleman's fortitude.

"There's nothing to it, really. I call my accountant, visit my bank, and call a restaurant if I want a reservation. Atlases and phone books still exist in print, you know. I'm rather afraid of the attention deficit disorder culture out there," he said, musing. His voice was deep and sagely. Nell thought he looked noble. His aquiline nose and distinguished face looked worthy of being remembered, as if someone would make a plaster bust of it one day.

No one spoke. Then Nell lent her voice quietly: "I admire you, sir. I miss the absorption of a day spent with a book. I would choose that over a day spent chasing my every whim on the internet. If only I could break the spell."

The elderly gentleman looked at her. "Rightly so, young lady. I challenge you to do so. Otherwise, you're just one of the sleepwalkers," he said, as if imparting a literary riddle. It was his turn to order, and he turned to the barista.

"Good morning, I'll have my double espresso with a glass of water and a croissant." He had a copy of Hermann Broch's *The Sleepwalkers* tucked under his arm, and Nell thought he looked like a transplant from the Café Musil. Even his order sounded Viennese to her, and he did look familiar.

"May I help you?"

Looking up, Nell realized that the slender, bespectacled barista didn't recognize her. She would have to make her mark here in the community once again, like one of the outsiders who was tolerated with skepticism at first.

"Hi, Bailey. How are you this morning? It's been a long time." Bailey nodded and looked at Nell expectantly. Bailey was still as willowy as she had been when they attended high school together.

"I'll have an almond milk latte with a touch of lavender syrup."

"Oh, Elle?"

"Nell."

"Right. Of course. For here?"

"Here's my thermos, Bailey. I made a commitment not to use throw-away cups anymore." Nell said it a little louder than she had intended and felt embarrassed, as if she were preaching.

A young man looked up from his perch at the zinc counter when he heard that. He caught Nell's eyes, but he didn't look like he belonged in the Berkshires, nor in New York for that matter. He looked like he had come from Baudelaire's Paris. He was wearing a suit of dark purple velvet with a white dress shirt, on a Sunday morning no less. He had been writing in a leather-bound journal with a fountain pen. A lock of errant hair, dark-roast coffee-colored, fell in front of his eye. Nell didn't realize she was staring at him, and turned back to pay Bailey.

"Make it as large and hot as you can, please."

"Sure thing. Are you back or floating through?"

"I'm home for good." Nell underscored "good" with a conductor's flourish with her right hand.

"This one's on me, then, Nell. I inherited The Hawthorne last year, so it's my call to make. Welcome home." Bailey's face stretched out in a generous smile. Nell couldn't help but grin back, admiring the way Bailey had matured into a responsible local business owner in her adult life. She had looked ethereal in high school, but now she had an air of confidence that suited her.

"Thanks, Bailey, and congrats. You'll be seeing a lot of me now." Nell dropped a dollar into the tip jar on her way out.

Argos was craning his head out the car's passenger window looking for her. She got in with him and drove around the corner to one of her favorite walking trails behind town that paralleled the Housatonic River, and let him tumble out of the car. Thermos in hand, she watched the dog cross the wooden suspension bridge over the river, and stand at the other side waiting for her to navigate. One path went up past Laura's Tower to Bear Mountain, and the other meandered along the river. She gestured left towards the river where fragile pine saplings lined the path, and Argos ran ahead with wild joy.

He bounded back to lick Nell's hand—as if to thank her for rescuing him from the concrete sidewalks of New York—and then he returned to his game of sniff and run. The current's soft strains lulled her, sloughing off another layer of tension from the city. Leaves were beginning to accumulate on the path, along with pine needles, and she breathed in the earthy scents and sounds, stopping to pick up a leaf and pine branch to massage between her fingers until her hand smelled like the forest.

The end of the trail formed a circle that inevitably led hikers back towards the trailhead. When they looped around the circle and started back on the trail, she saw the curious young man from the coffee shop strolling towards them.

"You know, we are two of the youngest residents in Stockbridge. We should probably know each other. I'm Xavier Alden," he said. He stretched his arm out for a handshake, but Nell only nodded at him.

"Nell. This is Argos. Either you are one of the youngest or one of the eldest residents here, because you look like you just stepped out of 1860s Paris as a flâneur. Or maybe you're a character in Oscar Wilde's novel, and there is a hideous portrait of you in your attic?"

Argos bent his ears back to lick Xavier's outstretched hand, and the man laughed with a dusting of flirtatiousness.

"You're funny. And you know your literature. I like Argos. The faithful dog of Odysseus. The only one to recognize him after his ten-year absence when he returns home to Ithaka."

"Indeed. And you've read your Homer."

She didn't like being called "funny," as if she was eccentric, just like everyone else her age thought she was. Only, they weren't wearing velvet suits. He wasn't even trying to be ironic; it was clearly his ordinary attire. She had finally met someone nuttier than she was, Nell thought. Xavier strolled along her right side. They chatted about the degree to which they were both locals, until they reached the wooden footbridge and divided into a straight line.

"I think my family has been here longer than yours has," Xavier said.

"Not a chance. My family was among the first to pepper the Berkshire hills," Nell said.

When they reached the Volvo, she and Argos both stopped.

"Lunch, maybe? Next week?" Xavier asked.

"Do I have to wear a bustle and hoops, like a passante to your flâneur?" Nell responded with a parting grin, using the French female equivalent of a flâneur. She decided that she had been right in her first assessment: Xavier had come straight from the 1870s Paris, strolling the urban streets with a nonchalant demeanor, observing the newly industrialized world with detachment. Like a spectator of the contemporary world. That's exactly the aura he gave off.

* * *

As they meandered up the driveway, Nell and Argos spotted a curled-up bundle of russet fur on the sunny knoll by the house. It picked up its head when it heard the old Volvo hum, and unwound itself to form into the shape of a standing fox. The fox seemed just as surprised to see them. It peered into their eyes as they gazed at it through the windshield, before it trotted off with its handsome tail trailing behind it. Argos didn't bark, Nell didn't flinch, and they seemed pleased to share their lawn with a fox that looked like it was accustomed to napping there undisturbed.

Once parked, Nell found the wicker basket and mushroom knife in the garage. She beckoned to Argos, and they set off into the woods to hunt mushrooms for dinner, a historic pastime of the Harding family. The ground was moist under the cropping of white pines, which Nell knew to be prime territory for mushrooms to shoot up in the fall. Argos sniffed the area and was unimpressed with Nell's focus on the soil. She didn't have the tolerance for mushroom hunting that her ancestors had. The excruciatingly slow amble required made her feel lethargic, whereas a brisk walk helped her sort things in her head. Nonetheless, stooped, poking the ground as she wandered, Nell came upon a family of chanterelles. *Make sure the insects have nibbled them, for if they haven't, they're poisonous*, she could hear her grandfather instructing her. It seemed like there were enough mushrooms in hues of sepia with creamy yellow stalks for her and the insects to feast upon, and so she knelt down and took out the knife to carefully cut them. *Preserve the delicate mycelium, that's the root system below the ground, so cut the stalk gently.* But before she did so, she brandished her phone and crouched at various angles to capture her trove.

"Argos?" Nell called out, when she realized that she had lost track of where the path was that led back to the house. And there was a pile of prized chanterelles in her basket to wash. "Argos?" she called again with a note of urgency. And there he was, bounding out from under a thicket of brush, nosing her back to the path that would take them home.

That evening, Nell honored her and Waldo's weekend tradition of Sunday dinner. This time it would be an interspecies dinner party. Sitting back on the rocking chair with her feet up on the railing, waiting for Mr. Butterfield's cod to marinate, she sipped a glass of white Crozes-Hermitage and stared at Goose Mountain. Below the motley treetops, hikers were heading north on the Appalachian Trail to reach Mount Katahdin before snowfall.

She devised a witty riff in her mind to put on her social media page, then frowned as she sipped, realizing not only that would it reveal that she was in the Berkshires and deprive her of the privacy she was bent on protecting, but that she had already deactivated her account.

"I'm living with a conundrum that itches my mind, Argos. Far better to be a dog these days," she said to her dinner companion.

After a dinner of cod and greens marinated in a lemon caper sauce, with sautéed mushrooms in garlic, Nell pulled her worn leather address book out of the desk in the loft upstairs, and then she scrolled through the contact list on her phone. *Ding.*

Nellikins, why don't you answer my texts? It's been two days. I miss you. Xx.

It was Ella, but Nell ignored it, trying not to break her concentration every time the phone distracted her. She copied every number and address that mattered to her in the relic of a book. Putting down the pen, she felt that Harding sense of determination, rising up from the land, settling in an intangible way in her shoulders as she squared them.

Chapter Four

As she dressed, Nell devised questions for the cybersecurity scholar coming from Boston who would lecture at the Stockbridge library that afternoon. She donned a white dress shirt, a sage and cranberry wool suit jacket, and her brushed cotton cranberry jeans that fit like leggings. Reluctant to coax her feet out of the Birkenstocks molded to them, she traded them for the only pair of dress boots she had kept: beige, suede, high-heeled anklets that she would have worn to a special event at the NYPL. "I'll be back soon," she called out to Argos before she drove into town.

Having arrived in town early, Nell stepped into the petite brick building across the street from the library to set up her post office box. It satisfied her to know that she would be reachable in this quasi-anonymous way that didn't reveal her street address. With a fresh set of keys in her hand that fit into a metal box marked 341, Nell bounced across the street, hair swinging behind her in the autumn breeze.

New life, empty box, without a trace, went the lyrical refrain she improvised in her head. In her enchantment, Nell seemed unaware that her hopes for the new post office box's symbolism of renewal were akin to waking up on New Year's Day with naïve intentions. *Tabula rasa*, she added to her refrain, and then stopped. That had been the term Jake at Café Musil had used during her last morning in New York; interpreting the phrase with a skepticism beyond his years, as if it were too late for her to have a new life. She swept that thought aside, consigning it to a cloud of dust from the bustling city she had left behind.

The Berkshires folk lived in these hills to seek refuge, to be unseen at times, but congregate at others. It was a community with respect for solitude. This narrator blanches at intruding on Nell's thoughts in light of her quest for privacy, but she was dwelling on another poem. When Mary Oliver wrote the poem "Old Poets of China," it was as if she had in mind Nell as well as the Berkshires folk at large:

> Wherever I am, the world comes after me.
> It offers me its busyness. It does not believe
> That I do not want it. Now I understand
> Why the old poets of China went so far and high
> Into the mountains, then crept into the pale mist.

The lecture that afternoon might attract those that were skittish about the world's virtual busyness, Nell thought.

Still too early for the lecture, Nell sat sipping a green tea in the café, playing Waldo's old eavesdropping game. She listened to strangers' dialogue and then filled in the blanks when she couldn't hear over the roar of the espresso machine. When she used to come here with Waldo, he'd had the gall to write down the remarks he found particularly striking, but she had no reason to do so herself.

Two middle-aged men in line started an innocuous conversation that turned hot.

"How's work down at the phone company, Hank?" one man with curly white hair poking out from under his baseball cap asked.

"Since we got the contract with the police stations to record cell phone conversations, it seems like business has gotten better," the other man in a wool cap and canvas coat with rough hands responded.

Nell sat still. It seemed too contrived. Two days in a row at the same place with eerie conversations about digital surveillance. As she listened, she opened her journal where she had sketched a rendition of English philosopher Jeremy Bentham's panopticon the night before. It had been her virginal entry, without words.

"I have nothing to hide, so it's fine by me," she overheard the curly-haired man say, as she etched the central observation tower and fleshed out the circle of prison cells around it, trying to make it look as it should: Prisoners would never know they were being watched, yet the guards conducting surveillance could see everything. This dystopic vision immobilized her when she saw her crude rendition on the page.

"That's hogwash, Hank. You shouldn't spread sensationalist rumors like that." A man from a neighboring table put his newspaper down, revealing an indignant face. She didn't recognize him. The espresso machine drowned Hank's response, but Nell had heard enough and didn't want to fill in the blanks. Hadn't she fled New York to escape the digital panopticon?

Ella. She gasped and dropped her journal on the table. Ella had sent follow-up texts to her first unanswered one, and Nell hadn't yet responded. Ella expected immediacy; she thought that was the purpose of texting. Nell dashed off a flurry of apologetic words on her phone screen, joked about the slower pace of country life, and offered to send a real letter soon in the post.

Leaving the coffee shop, she strode to the brick library framed by white columns where she'd spent many childhood hours. She walked through the open door and turned right into the hallowed room reserved for lectures that bore the scent of crisp linen. Light-gray walls shot up and the windows arched tall until they reached a white Greek key molding.

Nell took note of the four computers lined up on one side. "Printing: 15 cents per page," she read. The wooden card catalogs Nell had perused as a child, as if seeking treasure, had vanished. She surmised that the library holdings had been digitized. Children would no longer learn the alphabetical order by searching for books, nor would they experience the palpable pleasure of holding thick, yellowed card stock between their fingers like she once had.

Nell swallowed her nostalgia and took a front row seat in the right corner of the room. She fished out her notepad and pen to start taking notes as if she were a university student again, a role she missed. She jotted the title down along with a few potential questions in the margin, and then she crossed her legs to the left so she could observe her fellow lecture attendees with curiosity, as a newcomer back in her hometown.

Before long, multiple generations populated the room. She had expected an elderly crowd, but a smattering of teenagers clutching their phones clustered together across three rows. Next to her, comfortably wrapped in a wool coat, was an older woman with silver hair. She watched as the woman leaned forward to address a youngish man in wide-wale corduroys sitting in the aisle seat. "I know your mom," she said. "From the garden club."

"For sure, life in a small town, just the way it should be," he said.

Behind her, Nell heard one of the librarians say to another, "It will be standing room only."

I am not an outlier. There are others who grapple with the thorny phone questions I have, she affirmed.

Nell watched as a gentleman dressed somewhat like her in a tweed coat and dark jeans walked through the door wearing black glasses. He was only a few years older than Nell, perhaps in his early thirties, though he had an aura of sagacity far beyond his years. He bore the weight of knowledge that was troubling and had no absolute ethical answers, Nell speculated. As he approached the front row, the head librarian rose from her corner seat, which he took in exchange. She went to the mahogany lectern to introduce him.

Never mind his youthful countenance, Professor Gupta had already built an impressive resume. He had worked at think tanks, for governmental security firms, and for one of the internet firms everyone had heard of. All the while he managed to teach graduate seminars in cybersecurity at MIT, and publish an astonishing array of articles and books. The librarian explained that he specialized in the technical elements of surveillance, security, and risk analysis.

"Books will become obsolete as we progress in this field of study, so I hope that Professor Gupta will continue writing them as this fascinating subject develops in a rapidly changing cyber world," she concluded. The audience clapped for the professor as he settled in at the lectern.

"It's my great honor to speak before you today, where I know I'm surrounded by a group of writers, artists, intellectuals, and independent thinkers, if I recall from a few weekends spent here with friends after I defended my dissertation." He spoke in a vibrant tone at just the right tempo for understanding, not like some lectures Nell had attended where it seemed the scholar wanted to dazzle the audience with linguistic virtuosity.

"The matter at hand is grave, and it will become even more so as we progress into the twenty-first century. How many of you have cell phones with you today?"

Nearly everyone's hand shot up, Nell noted.

"Do you know that they are not just cellular devices that can call Zimbabwe and buy airplane tickets? Though not here in Stockbridge where there is no service whatsoever," he added as an aside and chuckled.

"Do you know that you're carrying sophisticated spying technology in your pockets and purses?" Professor Gupta explained that these devices are employed by data mining companies to track one's every move, spending habits, interests, bank account balances, the recipients of one's texts and emails, one's visits to websites, and where one travels. He counterbalanced the benefit of easily finding one's way with Global Positional Systems—or GPS—by underscoring the tracking element.

"Not only do you know where you are going, but data mining companies, governments, and cyber spies—otherwise known as hackers—know, too. If this troubles you profoundly, it should." He paused, letting the audience shiver at his revelations. Even the teenagers were engrossed (although they still had their phones in their hands).

The internet was lauded as a miracle, he reminded the audience, when it first became popular. It wasn't until addictive handheld devices took root that the ethical morass was laid bare. Convenience and instantaneous communication, access to knowledge, the ability to conduct business and run errands have revolutionized contemporary society. Yet, as the simple old adage goes, nothing comes for free. The tradeoff is the loss of privacy and the commodification of one's life.

The professor took a sip of water from the thick crystal glass set out for him, and continued. He had gauged correctly that the audience could take his detailed and sobering message.

"The F.B.I. and the I.R.S. and even the C.I.A. don't have access to this sort of knowledge about you, but these companies do. They've pored through your every online move and created intricate profiles regarding your age, sex, weight, race, level of education, marital status, and far more. Have any of you ever heard of the company 'Axiomatic'?"

No one raised a hand.

He explained that Axiomatic, based in Tennessee, was anything but what the name suggested—meaning 'obvious' or 'clear'—for they 'obscure' their transparency like double-agent operatives. They'd generated a mammoth database on consumers like them, that was stored on twenty five thousand computer servers. They had surreptitiously become a multibillion-dollar enterprise of marketing consumers' data. Their spies, a.k.a. 'servers,' conducted surveillance on over fifty trillion data moments—like snapshots of peoples' lives in cyberspace from mundane debit card withdrawals to internet searches on terrorism, sex changes, or lasering a mole.

"You've become commodified and you probably didn't know it until this moment. This is a momentous discovery. Furthermore, it is currently legal. You have been sold."

Nell sensed fear course through herself and reverberate to the back of the cavernous reading room, as if they were all one organism. There was no extraneous chatter.

"Does anyone have any questions thus far?"

Nell raised her hand.

"Yes, in the front," he said, gesturing.

Nell cleared her throat. "It seems that the ethical question is unanswerable in existential terms: to be with a smartphone and the internet, or not to be with a smartphone and the internet. Is there any way to use the internet and keep the public and private separate, or is that line of demarcation lost forever?" Her heart quickened in excitement at being able to ask the question out loud that could hardly be contained in her own chest.

He leaned back on his heels and smiled. "You see, I impart the knowledge I have of these systems so others may make ethical decisions on an individual level, but it's not my place to moralize. What I do feel is a conviction to share the inside knowledge I have."

The man whose mother belonged to the garden club asked: "Do the cell phone companies keep the data as well as sell it? That's the rumor I've been hearing."

"The unfortunate answer is yes. Think of cell phone companies as tracking your every move on the phone to the extent that they know whether you go to the gym, if you are engaged in extramarital sex, if you attend church, and if you eat organic vegetables, or purchase drugs that don't come from the pharmacy. Cell phone companies keep this data and sell it to advertisers," Professor Gupta explained.

Character portraits and tracking were the newest phone surveillance techniques, he told them. Cellular systems checked the location of each of their phones on the network at all times, and retained this information for up to a year. Companies like Axiomatic cross-referenced one's geographical data with that of their friends on social media platforms. "This is what they call predictive modeling, for it predicts your future movements as well as your present ones. They then know which companies to match you with for marketing purposes, to send you ads, and the like. We are at the beginning of this clandestine technology, but be assured: if you have a cell phone, you no longer have a sliver of privacy," he said, concluding his monologue.

"Professor, do you carry one of these devices?" An older gentleman in a beige coat and ivory scarf asked. Nell noted that it was the book-carrying man from the coffee shop who had never had a cell phone.

Professor Gupta laughed with delight, and the audience echoed him. His brow crinkled for a moment.

"To elude surveillance, one can use a burner phone or a Trakfone, like drug dealers, conspiracy theorists, and political dissidents. These phones are prepaid with cash, and don't require identification at the time of purchase. Nothing is connected to your name. But they're stripped down to the basic feature of calling without the addictive features we have all succumbed to," he said and paused.

"In fact, this is the type of phone that I have, although I don't fit into any of the above-mentioned rubrics," he said, sharing. "My phone can't find the Stockbridge library, nor can it play Beethoven's Waldstein sonata, but I can call my wife and let her know that I'm cooking dinner at seven." The audience laughed, appreciating the levity.

A young man in the back raised his hand. It was Xavier. The professor nodded for him to speak.

"Do you find, Professor Gupta, that you're able to engage in deeper concentrated work, given the absence of a distracting device in your hands? Are you, if I may, more intellectually productive than your colleagues who choose to use them?" Xavier asked, tilting his thick head of dark hair to the right.

"Thank you for broaching one of my favorite subjects. I hear my colleagues speak about their new procrastination struggles. One colleague said to me last week, 'I sat down to write a draft of my article and found that within two hours I had checked email eleven times, perused my social media accounts, made two plane ticket reservations for conferences, and texted my partner. I didn't write more than a discursive paragraph.' I don't mean to sound arrogant, but I can write with deep concentration."

This was Nell's entrance into the dialogue with the question that had plagued her for months. She raised her hand again, although she didn't want to monopolize the discussion. Professor Gupta gestured to her.

"Is absorption possible in the great age of distraction?" she asked. Her heart thumped as she waited. It was the question she'd been asking herself for days now. It stymied her. Even as she succumbed to the seductive draw of the internet, she yearned for absorption apart from her phone.

"Ahh, I see we have two young philosophers in our midst: the young lady in tweed and the young man in velvet. Have we lost the disciplined concentration we have culled over our lifetimes to be rewired for distraction? Have we become an attention deficit disorder society at large? I can't answer that question, but it veers on a precipice of no return, just like our climate change data. If absorption is of value to you, then I offer these words: cultivate it at all costs. Thank you."

Stockbridge applauded Professor Gupta with an improvised standing ovation. Many stood to approach him. As Nell put her notebook away, Professor Gupta called out to her: "Age of Distraction!"

Nell laughed, and bowed her head.

"Are you a graduate student?"

"I'm a former rare books librarian, trying to figure out how to navigate these modern-day minefields."

"If you ever want to discuss pursuing studies in a different field, one that seems to captivate you, here's my card," he said, and then he turned to the line that had formed in front of the lectern.

Nell put the thick card in the front pocket of her messenger bag, and turned to leave. On second thought, she plunked down at one of the public computers in another reading room to log into her email account. In settings, she disabled the system that forced her to type in a text-generated password that was sent to her cell phone. She checked all of her privacy settings, having learned that they were not affording her any privacy whatsoever. She deleted as many emails as she could, even if they were banal.

Eyes darting about the room as she thought this through, Nell dashed off a few succinct emails to her accountant and to her family's long-term banker. Each one that followed the same format:

Dear Mr. Ali, I hope that this finds you well. I am returning to an old-fashioned system of accounting, and request that you contact me either by telephone at the following landline number: 413.243.1974 or please send all correspondence to P.O. Box 341, Stockbridge, MA. I will no longer be reachable by cell phone nor by email. Respectfully yours, N.E.H.

Nell set up a vacation message: *Unavailable until further notice. Please contact N.H. through the United States Postal Service.*

Back outside, she sighed in relief as she closed the door of the Volvo. It was time to mull this over in the solitude of her mountain scape.

Sleep eluded Nell on the penultimate night of the full moon. Thoughts burned, and visions of Axiomatic stealing glimpses into her life caused her to churn from side to side. Resigned, she reached for the phone in a groggy fury and began searching "Axiomatic. Cyber hacking. Data Mining." The results confirmed what had been revealed in the afternoon lecture. Nell shuddered, turned the phone off in horror, and reached for her new battery-operated alarm clock. If only she could follow through and banish the phone from her bedroom, she thought.

The moon bore through the window and illuminated the time on the clock. Yet another two hours had passed, and she was back to combing the internet according to the whims of her curious mind. Nell rolled out of bed towards the adjacent loft that looked out onto the living room. She sat down at her desk and pulled out her journal.

October 12, 2011 After Midnight, the Berkshires

This must come to a definitive end, the battle between Nell and the Phone. I am unhealthily attached to a tiny, metal device that has revolutionized my own world arguably more than the cotton mill revolutionized the rest. This must cease. I refuse to be enslaved to a crafty cellular device that is robbing me of my identity and transforming me into something I don't want to be.

Nell underlined "to be" and beat the period down onto the page. Argos groaned from the bed, echoing her discontent.

Chapter Five

Nell arose with an eerie silence in her thoughts the following morning. Petting Argos, who licked her face in sympathy for her midnight lunacy, she accompanied him outside. The moon, now on its fullest day, had not disappeared as it usually did in the presence of the risen sun. Quite the contrary, she noted. Wandering back inside, she made Argos a bowl of raw ground chicken mixed with coconut oil and bone broth she had been stirring on the stove for two days. When Argos's needs had been met, she knew full well what she had to do. She could not go deep into the woods and create a meaningful life on her own terms this way. Not with this device tormenting her. When Thoreau retreated to the woods—with similar intentions—he may have had the temptations of town close by, in which he did indulge, but he didn't have anything as magnetic as the perpetual connectivity she faced.

A summons had been made somewhere in her subconscious between the mysterious hour of midnight and sunrise, when she had been in an oneiric state. After breakfast, Nell said, "I'll be back in a little bit." A phrase in their shared lexicon that Argos understood, even if he didn't like the absence that it entailed. She sped out of the driveway in the direction of West Stockbridge.

The pale-blue diurnal sky was a gallery for a solitary object: the moon, so full it couldn't be described without hyperbole. It was one of those rare days when it reflected so much light that it was luminous during the day, as if it were guiding her. As the closest object to Earth, the silvery orb hung low in the sky; its roundness like an exaggerated illustration in a children's book. Nell gazed at it, emboldened, as she drove past fields and open spaces to get to Bash Bish Falls.

Bash Bish Falls was a hallowed place in the Taconic Mountains of the Berkshires, attracting locals and tourists through the summer and fall. It was the tallest waterfall in the state of Massachusetts, reaching two hundred feet at the pinnacle of its cascades before it plummeted into a pool of turbid water framed by jutting boulders that fell into a gorge.

She parked next to cars with New York, Massachusetts, and Connecticut plates, and started up the maple-leaf-encrusted hiking trail that was wide enough for a horse carriage to pass by. Nell passed families and couples, loners, and a group of school children with their teachers. Her pace was rapid in spite of the incline, and she marched through a swirl of crimson, rust, ochre, and orange leaves that came up over her ankles. Her feet were like wooden drum sticks making a percussive symphony on the dried leaves beneath her feet. *Crish. Wesh. Cresh. Crash.*

She looked up at the arched branches of trees that had built an arch over the trail, as if the branches were flying buttresses. *This is what I want to revel in. This is what matters. I want to be absorbed in nature again. No more distractions. That's not who I am,* she thought.

At the apex of the trail, the trees tapered off and she came into a clearing that gave her a full view of the dramatic falls before her. To reach them, she descended the boulders one ginger step at a time, passing the leaf peepers until she stood at the edge where she could see the split in the falls as they became two and churned into an ominous pool. The water's song mesmerized her for moments with its strident tones that didn't pause for measured breaks.

She grasped deep inside for her Harding resoluteness. Standing to her full stature, Nell reached into her pocket, curled her right hand around her phone, raised her arm high, and arched her back in a twist like a baseball pitcher winding a throw. Nell sent the phone flying directly into the churning pool below the raging falls, where it disappeared.

There were audible gasps from above.

Nell stood immobilized save for her breath roaring through her nose, accompanying the sound of the falls. Heart beating a staccato through her chest. Ears ringing to echo her heart. Palms of her hands pulsing like dancers jumping on the floor to Stravinsky's relentless rhythm in *The Rite of Spring*. Cycling through feeling stunned, thrilled, liberated.

Quasi-horror rose like nausea in her esophagus at the loss of the phone she had relied on, cleaved to, adored at times. She had given it an aura in her adoration, created a commodity fetish out of it. The roiling of her thoughts put lyrics to the turbid waters as she stared. The river's water silenced her phone forever; it would guard it from the digital panopticon's clutches and free her from it.

Nell knew full well what her action represented. She had kept the same number since 2002, and had been proud of that stability. Her whole life was contained in that phone, in a sense, yet she resented that her life was contained in such a device. That wouldn't do. Not for her.

Nell moved her hand down to pat Argos, and then remembered she hadn't brought him. She feared that he would have plunged into the dangerous waters to chase after the object that he had confused with a living being. Nell wouldn't put him in that life-threatening spot, as there were signs posted about the dangers of swimming near the falls. Staring at the water's perpetual movement that was impervious to her staggering yet necessary loss, Nell couldn't see the horrified gazes of tourists snapping photos.

When she came to, she heard them muttering behind her: "Must be some kind of lunatic," one man said. "Yeah, a real lunatic," another man said in close proximity. "It's the full moon tonight. Maybe she feels the gravitational pull." The last voice was female, one that decorated the word "gravitational" with sarcasm. The air, chilled by the shadows and the waterfall's mist, bit at Nell's cheeks. She broke her transfixed gaze from the graveyard of her smartphone and the invisible glue that had connected them.

Speculation stopped as Nell clambered up the boulders. When she reached the onlookers that had come for the falls and witnessed a daring spectacle, they parted to make way for Nell. It was like walking between two makeshift rows of people in a funereal march.

As if floating, untethered, unencumbered, Nell looked down and averted eye contact with the onlookers who had dubbed her a lunatic.

One thing she knew was that she was not a lunatic, someone who temporarily experienced insanity during the *luna's* full light. She was simply done with being prey to be tracked, sold, commodified, and stalked. The battle of the phone was over. She didn't know yet who was victorious, but it was over.

The moon, though, had nothing to do with this. Was it futile to resist digital policing in the current age? Maybe privacy didn't matter to anyone anymore? Maybe the Soviet Union won the Cold War insofar as its totalitarian gaze was all-seeing, *novus ordo seclorum*, she thought. That's what the world had become, thanks to the omnipresent surveillance devices in everyone's pockets. She left these thoughts in the maple leaves beneath her feet, left her beloved phone's graveyard, and made her way home.

Argos understood the gravity of Nell's mood when she opened the door. He leaned into her with his full weight to comfort her. He pressed his cinnamon-flaked head into her hand rather than rushing out to relieve himself. Nell then followed his movements as he perused the lawn's scents left by visiting foxes and squirrels.

The moon hung low like a caricature in the sky. "I'm not crazy," she mumbled up to it. "But I'm free. Free from being distracted. Free from the addiction to the device. At least, I will be after a presumed withdrawal." Nell laughed at herself, but the refrain in her thoughts was: *If only Waldo were here; we could parse this out together.*

She found herself walking down the cross-country ski trails with Argos alongside, pensive. With each exhalation, she shed another layer of troubling thoughts. With each inhalation, she bathed in the forest's evening song. The last of the season's insects made a meditative drone. Coyotes took up the melody. The moon lit the pale pink trail before her as the setting sun moved in tandem with the rising moon. She followed the faint light deeper into the forest with Argos.

She had expected it to be a challenge, but the weight of having to respond to messages lifted. The urge to seek answers to random questions on the internet dissipated as the forest lulled her.

Although the air foreshadowed winter, Nell shed the wool coat and wrapped it around her waist. Turning back, she unbuttoned the cardigan underneath it and tied that around her bulging waist, too. Left in her white camisole, she raised her hands so the breeze could caress them. As she circled back to the cabin, she dropped these cumbersome articles by the firepit. On a whim, she pulled off her boots and jeans in one downward whish. Clad now only in white lace-trimmed underwear and her white camisole, Nell threw her head back, giddy with her newfound freedom. Her lightness of being.

Spent, she fell back on the frayed hammock by the fire pit. Argos flopped down beside her, close enough to lick her falling hair. With the hammock gently swaying between the two elderly oaks that held it, she looked up at the sky. The fragment of a poem came to her:

The moon was a cyclops in the sky.

A natural panopticon.

Not a threatening one, merely wise from omnividence.

She gazed in reverence like a moon worshipper, a lunaphile, until Argos pulled at the strap of her camisole and whimpered.

"Dinner time. I know," she said. She ran to the house with Argos and went upstairs to pull a white eyelet wool dress over her head. It was her celebration attire. *Ditched the modem. My laptop broke long ago. Don't even have a tablet. Done with email. I am finally free*, she sang her thoughts silently.

She went to grab her phone to play music, and stopped in shock. The first phoneless sigh escaped her. Waldo had a record player. It hadn't been touched since he died, but she set the needle down on the record already on the turnstile. Beethoven's 9th Symphony, the Ode to Joy, resonated through the great room. She turned up the volume so it sounded as if the orchestra was in the cabin. Waldo must have had a prophetic moment, knowing his music would be there one day to celebrate with her.

Nell descended into the wine cellar to find one of Waldo's bottles of champagne. Her grandfather would have been proud of the gesture she'd made today. He would have toasted the radical stance she was taking. As the leitmotif of joy reverberated through the cabin, Nell sashayed back into the kitchen with a bottle in hand. Argos initiated a game of "chase me around the kitchen island," to celebrate his way before she uncorked the champagne.

Perhaps it was decadent to open a bottle of champagne for one, but this day marked her new life. Nell had gone into the woods to navigate life on her own terms, outside of the clutches of cyber surveillance and smart phone addiction that had become normative. She knew the notion of a blank slate—*tabula rasa*—was idealistic, but this was the closest she could get to it. Her own life's slate could never be truly blank, for the layers of erasures left smudges she could never wipe off. Not wanting to dwell on the chalky residue from the past, though, she returned to her celebration.

She set a checkered tablecloth—meant for picnicking at the venerated summer music festival held each summer close by—on the wood-planked floor, and reached for a fork, knife, and two plates of cod with steamed broccoli rabe and garlic. Argos lay down expectantly, front paws spread, head dignified and upright. Nell wedged the plate between his velvety forearms before arranging her own meal.

"Bon appétit, my dear boy," she whispered. Raising her glass, she toasted: "To freedom. To privacy. To absorption."

She swore she heard him say: "To communing together, eye to eye. To breaking bread."

That night, even though the moon in the night sky shone into her room like a cyclops, when Nell closed her eyes, with Argos nestled into her side, there was an unfamiliar yet blissful quality of weightlessness to her.

She melted into sleep.

Chapter Six

Standing on the stone steps in her underwear, Nell sipped her coffee while Argos nosed the newly white lawn. She watched the snow dance to the ground in circular movements, as if each flake were suspended, like nature was creating a mobile installation in the air. Already the chairs around the firepit had become snowy lumps. Squinting slightly, Nell remembered her spontaneous Rabelaisian gesture that preceded the champagne. Had she really disrobed under the light of the full moon there? She had.

She threw her head back to laugh at herself and the recent memory of the carnivalesque evening before. Argos caught the laughter and grabbed her jeans now frozen to the chair in response. He dragged them around in the snow like a scamp while Nell whirled, mimicking the dance of the snowflakes.

Magical as it was, the snow sobered her as she picked up her coffee again. It reminded her of autumnal obligations in New England. She had to prepare the garden beds with soil amendments, so they'd be ready to welcome new life in the spring. She'd assisted Waldo in this task when she was in high school, but the beds hadn't been sown with spring seeds for years. It would be an undertaking, but as she stood there, her skin prickling against the cold, a part of her relished the idea of it. Spade in hand, her muscles primed to drive it into the soil. Nothing could be more grounding, more unlike wielding a phone.

Nell wished she'd searched "soil amendments for fall gardens," before she cast her phone into the waterfall. "What would Waldo do if he didn't know something?" she asked Argos. Scanning the categorized bookshelves for an authoritative book on gardening, she traced her finger over *The Well-Tended Rose*, and *The Amateur*

Arborist, before landing on *The New England Gentleman Farmer's Guide to Vegetable Gardening*. She could hardly believe such a book existed.

Pulling its thick spine from the shelf, she flipped through the index until she came to it.

"So that's where Waldo came up with all of his gardening quotes. I found him out. 'We know more about the movement of celestial bodies than about the soil underfoot,' or thus said Leonardo da Vinci, purportedly." She scrawled a list:

- Compost
- Bone meal
- Shellfish meal or fish fertilizer
- Alfalfa

Raising her ambitions, she wrote down in her spiral notebook: *Research how to start a compost pile.* "I'll just make my own soil from all these vegetable clippings."

After a morning turn around the trails with Argos, Nell pumped her bicycle tires and set off into town with her messenger bag full of writing materials. Standing in line for a latte and a carrot walnut muffin, she overheard talk about a photo in the paper.

"Must've been a gimmick. You might *want* to do that. But no one actually would," someone said from the room where the used books were stacked. When it was her turn, she fumbled her order when she glanced down at the stack of Berkshire newspapers on the edge of the counter.

There she was on the front page. In the photo, her back was to the camera, and she stood poised like a pitcher next to Bash Bish Falls with her phone in her hand.

Who captured me on camera? Who dared to memorialize me for making an anti-media, pro-privacy, anti-intrusion statement while I am in the midst of the very act? Why is it that I elude freedom at every turn?

Just at that moment, this narrator blanched. Was the narrator's own intrusion into Nell's thoughts a literary panopticon? Was there truly no exit for Nell?

Nell waited for her latte at a corner table without glancing at anyone and set about the task at hand. She had come armed with stamps, note cards, and a pen, which she arranged on the worn wooden table. She took her address book out and flipped it to A. *A for Alden*, she thought, but she wouldn't be writing to Xavier this morning, nor did she have his address. Settling on D, Nell traced her finger down to Davenport. Blake should be apprised first.

Dear Blake,

Epistolary friendship from the days of yore resuming as of now.

She paused. Impulsively, she found a dollar in her pocket, went up to the cash register, and bought the paper just as they called out her order. Folding and tearing meticulously, she put the front-page photo in the envelope, and took up her pen.

I have escaped the digital world. Don't look for me on my phone, nor at my electronic mail address. As of yesterday, I may only be found at P.O. Box 341 Stockbridge, MA 01262.

Ever faithfully, your friend,

NEH

Nell knew she sounded old-fashioned, but she needed to counteract the botched way she had written text messages to him for years with "c u" and "lol." *I'll reach a synthesis,* she assured herself.

A small stack of stamped envelopes grew on the table. She wondered which friends would take the extra steps to correspond with her, and which ones would fall away if she didn't text back. Just as she was nearing the Ts, someone approached her table.

"That's quite an impressive collection of handwritten letters for this era, Ms. Harding. I suppose you'll need to hold those friendships close in creative ways now that you have no phone."

Ever so languidly, Nell turned her head to face Xavier brimming with a knowing smile. He had said it quietly so no one else could hear.

"Why do you speculate about my lack of a cell phone?" she said in the same low tone. She flipped her palm up to question him with a candid face, like an actor feigning innocence.

"A. You would've checked it by now. You've been here for quite a while. B. I saw the photo." He looked like a smug sleuth. Nell wasn't fazed.

"That could have been anyone."

"I know it was you. Not that I was following you or anything."

"Then?"

"I already know what you look like from behind."

She looked down at the table, suddenly warm under his gaze. Xavier repeated her name softly and gently as he deftly sat down in the chair next to Nell and took her folded hands on the table into his own.

"I've contemplated doing the same thing," he said, "Just never followed through with it."

"I had to do it."

"I think we're kindred spirits."

"I'm not used to—"

"What?"

"People being so … close."

Xavier hadn't yet released her hands. "That's it? That's awfully opaque."

Nell squeezed his hands, felt the warm pulse near his thumb. "I'm skittish," she said.

"Old stone wall around your heart?"

Nell nodded. "Come over tonight before sunset. We can discuss all this over wine and tapas."

"What can I bring?"

"I have wine, cheese. Even a guitar."

Xavier stood up. "I'll bring a song."

Still he lingered next to the table, and she could feel his eyes scanning her, trying to read her, as if he couldn't believe he had broken down enough stones in Nell's wall to receive an invitation.

"And where is your abode, anyway?"

"584 White Birch Road."

Be careful with your heart, Nell. Be careful with my heart, Xavier, she chanted to herself before returning to the cards. In New York, she had become impermeable to men's advances after her rupture with Rodolphe. But here, she was her vulnerable self, without filters. Bailey walked by and patted the table to catch her gaze, and when Nell looked up, Bailey blinked what seemed like subtle approval with both eyes. Nell blinked back, to indicate that she got the message, and then she wrote the last of her cards. She deposited them in the blue mailbox across the street before climbing on her bike to go back to Argos.

* * *

Once home, she put on the same eyelet dress from the night before. She put on a record of Spanish guitar ballads and danced to it. She paused before the full-length brass-hammered mirror in the foyer and rose on her tip-toes looking into her unadorned face. She had always felt like a clown when she wore makeup, a persona, and knew she looked wholesome without it. If he thought she was his kindred spirit, then she needed no artifice.

Argos sensed that company was coming as Nell straightened throw blankets and books and set out two wine glasses near the candles on the island. Hand fluttering over the light switch, she stepped away and struck a match instead. She lit the tea candles and scattered them in their flat oval glass holders across the island. She reached up into the cabinets to collect tapas-sized ceramic plates in sea-green and ivory. She created a miniature feast with olives, goat gouda, almonds, anchovies with capers, and massaged kale with olive oil-drenched sundried tomatoes that came from her stock in the pantry.

The one thing Nell did to please Xavier—if she had created the right character portrait for him—was to uncork a bottle of Châteauneuf-du-Pape that she had found in Waldo's back left rack in the cellar. That was where he kept wine for special occasions. Encountering a kindred spirit and celebrating her freedom were good reasons to open one now, she decided.

A rap sounded on the door. Even his *rap, rap* was understated. There was nothing violent about Xavier. Argos didn't rise from his bed, surprisingly. He yawned, as if to say, "You go have fun. I'll chaperone from here."

Nell opened the heavy door to Xavier. "Welcome," she said standing tall. He was holding a bouquet of dark plum calla lilies in his hand, which matched his velvet suit and white poet's shirt. Nell couldn't help but think that faded jeans and a charcoal T-shirt would have been more appropriate for tapas at home, but then she didn't want to judge him, as she didn't want to be judged.

"Your home is … like a sanctuary." Xavier removed his black suede loafers and handed the coat of his velvet suit to Nell. As she hung it, appreciating the sensation of its silky drapery between her hands, they assessed one another with an awkwardness that had been absent in their morning encounter.

"Argos is watching us. Nothing gets by him, but I think he likes me. Can he have a marrow bone?" Xavier asked.

"I can't believe that you brought one for him. That's so thoughtful," Nell nodded.

Xavier offered the lilies to Nell, saying: "From our garden at my parents' cottage." She accepted with a bow. He held up a small cloth bag in his other hand.

"Marrow bone and dark-chocolate truffles." He walked past the kitchen island straight back to Argos's bed, leaning down to pet him. "You give a good name to German shepherds, Argos."

Nell looked up when she heard a tail thumping. Argos licked Xavier's hands before accepting his clever gift. He approved.

"I felt certain that a Côtes-du-Rhône would be just your style. Am I right?" Nell said.

He joined her at the island and grabbed an olive. "Am I that easy to figure out? I do love wine from that region. My parents are oenophiles, and I spent most of my adolescence in France until my father transferred back to Boston," he said. He paused, as if wanting to slow the pacing. "I was always allowed to try the good ones. Educational, they claimed."

"I hear you. I got that education, too. We can toast to that." Nell poured two glasses of wine that lit up like liquid blackberries through the candlelight. She extended a stemless glass to Xavier, and held up her own.

"To two young eccentrics forging their paths in the Berkshires. What are the odds?" They gazed at another in acknowledgment of that truth, and imbibed thoughtfully.

"I know the velvet seems absurd to you. I'm just doing what feels right to me right now, you know?" he said.

There was a hint of defiance in his tone she hadn't heard before, but it wasn't meant for her, she felt. And then he looked at her, as if reading her face to see how she might respond, as if he might be seeking validation.

Enunciating her words thoughtfully, Nell said, "I've had my own share of eccentricities. I only worry that you may be mired in nostalgia. I'm not critiquing you, but nostalgia takes you away from the present moment, and it casts the past in an idealized aura that's distorted by nature. It's always felt like a dangerous indulgence to me."

Xavier looked at her intently. She remembered when she first saw those intense dark chocolate eyes in the coffee shop the morning that she met him. And here they were.

"We just met. Yet you can speak profoundly to me, and I to you. I abhor small talk, and we transcended that at once. How is that?" Xavier untucked his shirt as he spoke and perched on one of the metal stools at the island.

"Uncanny, isn't it?"

"What did make you come back here? Is this your family's house?"

"My grandfather left it to me, but I'm not big on origin stories. And I *don't* like to be looked up." She stared at him to underscore her message.

He nodded wordlessly at her in as he nibbled on a piece of gouda. Nell took a kalamata olive and chewed on it before discarding the pit.

"Wait. I can do better. That sounded like I was cross. Just, just know that coming back here makes it too raw for me to recount yet. How about …" She paused and exhaled. "Disenchantment. Enchantment," she said.

Xavier looked intrigued, like he'd been given select pieces to an intricate puzzle. He didn't speak, waiting for more puzzle pieces.

She said, "I escaped Manhattan to hide out in these woods with like-minded folks and see if I could stop conforming to this technological society's dictates. That's all I can sketch out for you now."

The record had ended, and Xavier gestured to the player. It seemed as if he wanted to listen without weighing in, without judging or lending his own commentary on her life. Nell gave him a nod. "Ah, Rachmaninov's 2nd," he said, browsing through the stack of albums.

"Perhaps not that one. It's so haunting. Too nostalgic for me. Something lighter?" she suggested. He shrugged, and settled for Villa Lobos guitar preludes.

"You know," he said as he walked back and picked up his glass of wine, "we're pretty privileged in this crazy world right now, to be drinking French wine and feasting on tapas." He told Nell about a friend from college who had been laid off, whose parents had also lost their savings. He picked up a piece of gouda, and waited for Nell to weigh in.

Nell nodded, finishing her bite of kale salad. "It feels awkward to talk about it, although I feel guilty, too." She looked down, feeling small. "It makes me feel like a kid who's been misunderstood. As if I must be inherently a bad person if I am not struggling. But my heart hurts for those who have lost so much," she said. "Let's migrate to the floor with our plates and wine," Nell suggested to modulate to a lighter theme. They took seats in front of the fireplace. It was unlit, and Xavier got up to set it. He removed his dress shirt and wrapped it around his waist. Underneath, he was wearing a worn gray T-shirt. This delighted her, and she watched the bend of his back as he crumpled newspaper and placed logs from the woodbin in the fireplace." As he coaxed a match to flame, she asked, "How about you?"

"Fleeing familial expectations and being true to myself. You know, age-old literary tropes. I do have a dream project in the works, but it will be better to have an unveiling if I can pull it off," he added.

They toasted to their equally economical and somewhat cryptic offerings, and looked into the fire as it took over the conversation, popping and spitting light in front of them. Nell didn't want to pry, because she didn't want to be prodded, but he made sense.

He had been perusing the bookshelves throughout the evening, and asked suddenly, "Who was the literary genius behind this collection?"

"That would be my grandfather. Although, I've made many additions," Nell said.

"Who was his favorite author?"

She gauged him.

"Montaigne," she said in three quick syllables.

He seemed to perceive her unease. He motioned towards the guitar on the stand in the corner by the piano.

"May I?"

Xavier sat on the piano bench and tightened the loose strings before he tuned the guitar. He started to play a song for Nell against the backdrop of firelight. His voice sounded like honey. He sang about a swan standing on pavement when its habitat was paved over. It was about wistfulness for things that could never exist again, and feeling lost in the chaos of a new and unfamiliar world. It was about Xavier. He was narrating his reasons for being in the Berkshires through song, like one did in times of yore, but his voice sounded like a modern singer-songwriter's. It produced an ineffable feeling in her.

Nell clapped with raised hands and an encouraging smile. Xavier bowed his head in acknowledgement, but he wasn't finished.

"You're a literary girl. What are the origins of my song?" Xavier said while strumming a chord, quizzing her.

Nell peered through the window at the luminous waning moon, the cyclops, as if to ask for answers, when she had an epiphany.

"Baudelaire," she announced triumphantly. Xavier laughed, and strummed a chord in major to reward her.

"That's my kind of girl. Tell me more."

"Well," she said at the pace of her thought, "it was my initial analysis of you—casting yourself as a flâneur with existential angst about brushing up against a changing world. It's not that you want to be old-fashioned; it's like you are a retro déjà vu modernist experiencing the same angst Baudelaire did when he was writing the poem 'Le Cygne,' which functions as the literary influence for your song. The Parisian boulevards were changing, and the old world disappearing." Nell stopped. She was in her element, happy to have someone to engage with this way. Still, she refrained from divulging that she had once been a graduate student studying French poetry until her advisor counseled her to switch to library science, since jobs in poetry were obsolete. She yearned to add that if she were nostalgic for anything, it would be for analyzing Baudelaire's poetry, but her cheeks were roasting, and she was afraid it wasn't from the fire. Self-conscious, Nell worried that she had gone off on a pedantic tangent during a light-hearted evening. Her self-consciousness had an origin story, and its title was *Rodolphe*. She rose to put another log on the fire, stepping back as the fire cast orange sparks out at her in response.

Xavier put the guitar down in its stand without taking his eyes off of Nell, approached her, and cradled her face between his hands, moving them so slowly, so lightly against her cheeks that it felt like a feathery caress. He leaned in and pressed his lips against her forehead. Leaning back and sliding his hands down to circle her shoulders, he frowned fleetingly.

"I have been waiting for you," he said, enunciating each word so that it stood apart, had heft.

Nell looked up at him with lips that couldn't stop quivering to form the smile she felt. Teardrops populated the corners of her eyes.

"Are you sure you're real? You're not a hologram? Not a figment of my idealistic imagination?" he jested.

Nell reached her arms around his neck, though her fingertips couldn't quite join, and she nestled her head against his chest.

"I promise I'm real. In the present moment."

Argos rose to investigate, brushing up against their legs. They parted but held hands as they went outside for a midnight stroll. Nell started dancing by herself, like a modern dance to the moonlight, and Xavier joined in at a distance, humming his song. Argos observed them.

Nell yawned and slowed her swaying down.

"I should probably go. That's my cue," Xavier said. They went in to gather his things. "Will you give me your number?" he asked on his way out.

She took a pen and notepad by the rotary phone and scratched out her landline number. Then, after a brief hesitation, she added her P.O. box number.

"Here you go. I don't have voicemail, but you can always drop a note in my P.O. box," she said.

"You can find me most early mornings at the coffee shop. But here, let me give you my number, just in case." He reached down with her pen and wrote something out before waving farewell and seeing himself out. "Night, Nell." Nell looked down and saw: "Zavs," followed by a Boston cell phone number and an address.

She bounded upstairs with Argos, sounding out his nickname as she went, "Zav, Zavs, Zavvv," tongue tickling her mouth's roof.

Chapter Seven

Nell's hibernation began in earnest the following day. Retreating from the outside world had been her dream when she devised it walking the streets of Manhattan. When she imagined what it would be like to arrive in the Berkshires and leave behind the scene that had become increasingly frightening to her, she hadn't counted on stumbling upon cybersecurity lectures and a dashing kindred spirit. And she hadn't practiced narrating the dramatic phone throwing moment. Yet her plot was unfolding in a far more interesting way than she had imagined it would.

But now this was her moment.

She had anticipated each logistical need and attended to it, for even traveling to Stockbridge village would interrupt her seclusion. Besides, needing to appraise the intensity of her evening with Xavier from a critical distance, she intended to avoid the coffee shop for a while. The Volvo wouldn't be budging.

Nell poured her inchoate emotions into churning the soil in the expansive vegetable garden. Waldo had always done it before the first frost. The earth seemed to be on the cusp of frosting over as it prepared for its own hibernation. If she was too late, she wouldn't be able to till it, nor could she nourish it for spring planting. As she plunged the rusty pitchfork into the soil and hefted earth over, browned leaves rose up with their pungency. The sharp smell of fermentation grounded her. And as she worked, she burned off a restlessness that the unusual young man had stirred in her. He had wanted to know if she was real, but she was beginning to wonder the same thing about him.

Nell tilled and raked every day until the moonlight reminded her it was time for dinner. Massaging her hands with coconut oil, she noted small blisters forming around the crooks of her thumbs where she had grasped the rake. On the deck, she contorted her back to assuage her muscles, and rolled her hips in circles, startled by the creaks her body made after unfamiliar exertions. In the evenings, she observed the sky and listened to the animals' songs. The full moon seemed to extend nearly five days, creating a pop-up festival of lights in conjunction with the stars each night.

She had rustled in the gardening shed until she found rolled-down bags of organic compost, bone meal, and fish fertilizer; remnants from a time before the garden's lengthy dormancy. One morning, as she mixed them in the red wheelbarrow with naked hands, Nell felt as if she had shed everything that had urged her to seek refuge: library scandals and tensions, Rodolphe, the phone's magnetism. She grunted with contentment as she folded her soil amendments into the earth as deeply as she could.

The wooden rake handle had rendered her librarian's hands raw. Harvesting spring lettuce would reward her labor, she reminded herself. When the last corner of soil had its winter meal, Nell fell back on the grass in her stained overalls (Waldo's actually) and let her weary shoulders sink into the grass, throbbing from their exertions.

It had long been Argos's dream to dig in the dirt at will, a longing he had never been able to fulfill in Manhattan's parks without stern admonishments from Nell. He had jumped in the garden while she worked, uninvited, casting the soil back with his front paws furiously until he had made a deep rut and Nell chased him out. Argos bounded back over to pee on the garden while she looked up at him, too weary to protest.

"Thanks for your contribution to the fertilization process, Argie." Nell rolled over to bury her face in the soil, rub it between her fingers, and inhale it some more. It smelled like life, like it was primordial. She was far away from the glistening grocery stores of New York where the shiny vegetables piled high in their bins were stripped of soil, glossy and gleaming. They looked like someone had robbed them of history and put makeup on them.

Amelia had left the organic seed catalog for Nell, which came with a printed ordering form, to her relief. Each day, she added to the list. She would coax a field of vegetables to grow the following spring, with the help of companion flowers and plants. There would be no pesticides like the ones that were killing off the cherished bees that pollinated the earth's crops.

Nell started sketching and writing about her gardening in her journal under a section that she called: "From Seed to Compost: The Life Cycle of an Organic Garden." She made a diagram with arrows pointing to pictures of the plant's cycle of life that included the compost she would make and the seeds she would plant from vegetables already harvested—the seeds inside green beans, cucumbers, and acorn squash, to name a few. She started collecting her coffee grounds, vegetable odds and ends, apples cores and the like, and dumped them into her compost barrel that she churned every week. She had cordoned off a place to deposit her first batches of soil. There was something that excited her about helping create a cycle of life with the soil. She had heard the locals talk of the hawks stealing their chickens from time to time. People in the Berkshires shrugged their shoulders and said: "Hawks need to eat, too. It's part of the circle of life." Now she got to take part in it, rather than glibly grab decontextualized apples from the bins at the city markets. These tiny triumphs brought the quiet hum back to her chest, and she hoped to record them in her journal soon.

Still lying in the grass, she watched as the moon rose over charcoal-etched outlines of spruces and pines. By now, it looked like a gargantuan bite had been taken from the southeast curve of the moon. Without her phone, she didn't know the precise day, but several moons had come up at night and she hadn't even counted them. She had no idea where they were in the sidereal cycle.

What she did observe were the subtle changes in her. Between her labor in the garden and her phonelessness, she slept deeply through the night. When she sat down in the leather armchair to read, her mind didn't concoct pressing questions for her to type in the phone. Instead, she kept a small, spiral notebook where she recorded questions to research later, the old-fashioned way. She adhered to no unspoken moral code that dictated she dash off an immediate message as soon as she received one—for there were no instant messages in her enclave, apart from Argos's cues. When she closed her book each night, though, she marveled at how many pages she had read in one sitting. Nell didn't intend to become a recluse, no, that was never the dream. But an initial hibernation as she recalibrated, that was as necessary as the act of throwing the phone in the falls.

At the last light, as her back grew damp, she pulled herself up and went inside with Argos to scrub off the soil and partake of a hearty meal of vegetable stew that she had been simmering all day, as if to anticipate the following year's harvest.

* * *

One morning, traipsing through the crisp grass that had frosted overnight with her coffee in hand, Nell watched Argos run his patrol of the perimeter to her right. Movement distracted her, and then she saw their resident fox conducting his own patrol to her left. They would surely meet. The fox saw Nell and paused to take her in. His signature tail brushed out behind him, and he held his head steady, with inquisitive eyes. Argos, coming into her peripheral vision, stopped. She could only surmise that he was taking in the fox's presence, too. They all held eye contact, calmly—if she could dare to speak on the fox's behalf—until he turned and trotted down the path to the woods instead of towards Argos. They had made an interspecies acquaintance, to her delight.

The earth told her that it was her last day of fall gardening. As the sun defrosted the soil later that morning, she set out the tools and seed envelopes for the mustard, peas, and clover she would plant as a cover crop that could be folded into the soil come spring to nourish it. She would also be planting garlic that afternoon to harvest the following summer.

As she drew her soil-stained fingers through the soil like a trowel, making an indentation for the seeds, she thought about how tending to the soil was nourishing her, adding nutrients back that had been stripped from years of being glued to her phone instead of to the sunsets, sunrises, and moon cycles. It was symbiotic, she thought, as she started to plant seeds with Argos close by.

As she put the last of the garlic in, the waning light told her it was dinnertime. She had prepared in advance, placing yams in foil under the fire she set in the hearth on her late afternoon break. As had become her custom, she fell back onto the grass to rest and feel the ground's vibrancy beneath her. She indulged in visions of broccoli and marigolds thriving alongside one another come next summer, and smiled in hopes that the weather, pests, and crops would coordinate to make it true. *I'm taking stewardship of the land, Grandpa,* she whispered silently.

"Aloha, ma'am!" A foreign human voice drawled out mere feet away as Nell lay on her back embedded in her reveries. Argos emitted a low growl that rumbled through her, warning her of the intruder. Like a vulnerable beetle on its back, she rolled over in Waldo's earth-stained overalls, remnants of soil smeared across her face, and stood up. Dizzy in her modulation from daydream to unanticipated human interaction, she coughed as she tried to speak.

"This is private property. Unless you've broken down on the road, and need me to call a tow truck, you must leave at once," she mustered between coughs. Was it anxiety? Was it soil from the garden that got into her throat? Argos had accelerated to full-throttle barking, unimpressed with Nell's attempt to talk off the intruder.

"Pardon the surprise, ma'am, but I've been doing some digging. I'm doing a human-interest piece on the girl that threw her phone in the falls, and some people thought it might have been you. They gave me this address. Also, I'm researching a writer that might have lived around here ..."

She barreled towards him. She could feel her arms swinging beside her in rage.

"Get the hell out of here and don't come back. I'm calling the police."

Beside her, Argos barked and advanced. He looked and sounded like a police dog.

She saw the reporter's mouth open, then close. Then he turned and sprinted down the driveway. She jogged after him to get his license plate number. Argos followed behind, still barking, only stopping his pursuit when the man crossed over the seam to the road.

A silver sedan was parked on the street. It looked new and nondescript, a rental. The reporter went to it, and once the door was safely open and he behind it, he yelled, "Can you at least admit that it was you, and you just don't like being found out, or are you really that mad at me for barging up your driveway?"

She spotted Georgia plates with numbers she couldn't make out since the sun had left the Berkshires.

"If you want to dig, try gardening, but don't come here again. We'll be even less welcoming." Nell snapped her dirty fingers and cocked her head left to motion Argos to join her. As they walked back up the dark driveway, Nell could hear the loud thump of her heart, her pulse in her ears. It palpated like a thumping orchestra, she thought with alarm. Who would have outed her? Who knew?

For the first time since she had been home, Nell turned the cumbersome bronze lock to the right. Argos yawned with skepticism, as if to say that the lock was superfluous in his presence. The old lock made an eerie click that sounded definitive.

She scrubbed the dirt off in the shower with the water turned all the way to hot. "From public to private to prisoned," she grumbled as she scrubbed and scalded her unsuspecting skin with a stinging lavender salt scrub. "Even if I had my phone, I couldn't look him up. What would I search for? 'Slightly rotund reporter in mid-thirties harasses females in Massachusetts for human-interest stories'? I should have asked for his name." An errant doubt about the wisdom of her phonelessness wafted through her turbid thoughts. She was troubled by him looking for a writer that used to live around here, too. She didn't like any of it. Not at all.

"I burnt the yams because of you, Georgia," Nell muttered as she unwrapped what looked like chunks of burnt orange charcoal and dumped them in the trash. The incident had taken her out of her concentrated state, so that even her readings were interrupted by thoughts of his audacity that night.

"Absorption is a fragile state, Argie," Nell said as she stomped up the stairs to bed, eager to bid the day goodbye.

When they woke up to a white blanket on the hardened earth the following morning, Nell put the gardening tools away. The timing was almost too neat. She turned to indoor creative pursuits. The longer she lived in the cabin, the more she found her past stowed away in boxes. There were her watercolors, her paintbrushes, and even a box of blank cards, as if she had anticipated this moment. She found a wicker basket of Icelandic wool yarn, along with her grandmother's wooden knitting needles. She wanted to make handcrafted Christmas presents to send Blake in Paris, to her friends in New York, to Amelia and Fernando, and the Butterfields, among others. She could ignore the consumerist spirit that took hold after Thanksgiving.

With the fireplace romancing her, and Argos napping like a hibernating bear, she knitted scarves and painted cards. She painted each one in the phases of the moon with sunsets in the background. She tied each bundle of cards with a strand of the Lopi Icelandic yarn once they had dried.

Nell found that, like walking, knitting made her delve into her thoughts. With the wooden needles dancing in a swift rhythm between her fingers, the bundles of Lopi wool loose on her lap, she thought about how fortunate she was to engage in the mere act of knitting in the middle of the day. She knew she wouldn't be without a larger purpose indefinitely, that she wasn't an indolent passante—the idling equivalent of the male flâneur. But she was grateful for this pause she had taken from life's linearity.

Willa floated into her mind. Willa, who had judged her without finding out who she really was. But Nell didn't blame her. Her gratitude shifted into guilt when she thought of Willa back in New York, working overtime to pay her college loans and the rent at the same time. Nell felt a softening spread through her as her fingers continued to knit and purl the yarn.

And the more she interacted with nature, the more awed Nell felt by its mystery. It made her feel more compassion for those she came in conflict with. Like Willa. It reminded her of something Dostoevsky had written, that a literature teacher had shared with her: "Love the animals, love the plants, love everything. If you love everything, you will perceive the divine mystery in things. Once you perceive it, you will begin to comprehend it better every day. And you will come at last to love the whole world with an all-embracing love." It's a humbling way to see each other, she thought. Even the reporter was doing his job, looking for a good story, and he probably hadn't thought of those he might hurt along the way. She set her knitting aside that had made her so pensive.

In between painting and knitting, she would mix batches of oats with hearty toppings, drizzle them with Vermont maple syrup, and spread them on cookie sheets that she baked in the oven. The baking experiment went less well than the cards. The cabin smelled like burnt almonds and cranberries, as she fumbled.

"If I could just look this up on my phone, maybe I wouldn't have ruined the first three batches," she said out loud. Within a few days of experimenting with the alchemy of baking, though, glass jelly jars brimming with granola lined the island alongside the cards. She cut an old checkered cloth napkin with zigzag shears, and covered the tops of the jars with pieces before wrapping strands of red yarn around them. When her hand cramped from knitting, and the scarf fell in emerald and plum drapery onto her knees, Nell put her crafts aside for the day and snuggled up with Argos before dinner. Her busy work had displaced her desire to journal, yet she felt the twinge to write all of a sudden.

The following morning, she sat at her desk and stared at the journal she'd bought in Great Barrington. Even after the past weeks of writing in it, the remaining blank pages still daunted her.

I wish to record epiphanies and thoughts worthy of being recounted in this journal. Allergic to clichés, I fear I'll write them on accident, for lack of experience. For, as my childhood hero, Henry David Thoreau wrote: "A written word is the choicest of relics. It is something at once more intimate with us and more universal than any other work of art. It is the work of art nearest to life itself." Now, Thoreau was thinking of Alexander the Great carrying the Iliad with him on his quest to conquer all known lands, and this is a mere journal before me, yet I wish to do justice to its blank pages.

Nell looked up to pause and waited for her next thought, relishing the weight of her fountain pen. She dropped the pen as she peered out the window in astonishment for what seemed like minutes. Then, she wielded it again.

A red-tailed hawk just made an elegant landing on my windowsill. It displayed its brown and pale yellow flecked back at first, and then it turned to face me with its eyes set wide to accommodate its impressive hunting beak. I felt as if it were welcoming me to the wild, acknowledging my presence among the beings that roam freely here. I have read that hawks symbolize not only courage in Native American culture, but also the creative spirit. Should I take the hawk's presence to mean that I should let my thoughts flow onto this page?

I remained still, calm, silently thanking it for visiting me, when it lifted off with its powerful yellow talons and glided through the sky before me. May I be free, courageous, and creative like this hawk that has graced my morning.

P.S. That includes the freedom to write. The freedom from my angst about producing combinations of words that might sound foolish.

Nell set the pen down and wandered through her bedroom, pensive, massaging her hand, hoping her muse would keep churning thoughts. She picked up the pen again.

I can handle this phone-free existence. Sometimes I reach for it, to take a picture or ask the internet a question, but then I just smile at myself for having forgotten. I don't feel that addict's urgency to be gratified. What I feel is a mischievous exuberance with the accomplishment of having gone days without the phone and not having craved it. I could only have done this by going to the woods.

[I fret that by citing Thoreau's Walden Pond *too frequently, I am a cliché, since some of his choice words are quoted so often. But they are apt.] This is my version of wishing to live deliberately in the woods because I could no longer live a life of quiet desperation and angst. I could no longer keep the pace of my companions—to rephrase Thoreau—because I heard the music of the wild calling, and it was not as a ringtone. And here I have been welcomed by no one less noble than a hawk. What else has the wild to teach me? I believe its lessons have just begun.*

Nell sketched the hawk's contours that were lingering in her mind, trying to represent that probing look in its eyes. She blew on the pages for a moment, before taking up her crafts for the day.

Some nights, if the air's bite didn't send her straight back into the cabin, she bundled up on the hammock to study the constellations' choreography. She thought of it as moonbathing.

What about Xavier, though? She was hiding out in the woods but he hadn't sought her out either. *Good fences make good neighbors, but do they make good lovers?* She startled herself with that word and shook it off, standing abruptly and walking back inside.

Thoughts of Xavier propelled her towards the spot on the bookshelf where her volume of Baudelaire poems stood. She slid the short hunter-green volume with a gilded spine out. Waldo had gifted her with the authoritative version in the original French, holding all of Baudelaire's musings on melancholia and modernity, a gift given before she lost her capacity for absorption. She fell asleep against Argos's back with visions of Parisian arcades flitting through her dreamscape.

In the morning, when she went to get more raw meat for Argos from the chest freezer in the garage, and found just a lone bag standing there, she knew the hibernation was coming to a close. She had resorted to frozen vegetables from her dwindling stock of provisions the night before, and they had exhausted Mr. Butterfield's cod. It was time to visit the outside world again. She was content with her self-imposed exile from society, but reason reminded her that she had to venture out.

Taxes hadn't been done yet. The accountant had filed for an extension, and she had sent him the last batch of documents before hibernation began. This would be a test of Nell's ability to function without electronic mail, but she presumed there were documents waiting for her at the post office. Grabbing the notebook by her knitting and reading chair, she petted Argos, who looked up in consternation at her impending departure. He had acclimated to a life without separations.

Chapter Eight

The steering wheel felt cold and alien on her hands as she drove into the village to the post office.

Turning the key to open her box, Nell was greeted by a torrent of mail that spilled into her arms. Pink slips notified her of packages, too.

"Is that 341 there?" The postmaster sounded perturbed.

"Yes, sir. I have a few parcels to retrieve," Nell said.

"A few?" The harrumph she heard was meant as an admonishment, but she felt no guilt.

"I'll just need to see your I.D., 341."

Nell brandished her Massachusetts driver's license. In exchange, the postmaster, a gaunt man with graying hair and brooding eyes, handed her a stack of thick envelopes with the name of her family's accounting firm marked on the return addresses.

Nell groaned. "Taxes," she said, and then regretted it.

She headed across the street to The Hawthorne, hoping Xavier would be there. He was sitting at the counter facing outwards as he usually did, feet crossed, head bent over a staff notebook, in which he was writing out a musical composition. He didn't see her, so she plunked her messenger bag on top of her usual table.

From behind the counter, Bailey said, "Haven't seen you lately. I wondered if you had headed back to the city already."

Xavier looked up, puzzled, as if he, too, didn't expect to see her. Nell smiled at him before responding to Bailey.

"Never. I was hibernating."

"There aren't that many young folks up here that stay through the winter. Glad to have you here, Nell," Bailey said, setting her hands on her slim hips for a moment as if to add weight to her comment. Xavier nodded a little to that. He regarded the pile of mail spilling on the table with what seemed to Nell like relief, as if an unstated certainty had been resolved.

"How about a touch of my pumpkin pie spices in your latte?"

"Sounds delicious."

When Nell stepped near him, Xavier said, "No chance of texting you. No chance of calling and leaving you a message. And no chance of even being your epistolary friend, it seems."

Now it was Nell's turn to look puzzled, but she impulsively put her hand over his pen-wielding hand. "I'm here now. Just needed to be a woods nymph for a few days," she whispered, wondering what had prompted her to be so forward.

Bailey was busy at the espresso machine, but Nell saw her eyes flicker over towards her and Xavier's hands. The people at the two nearby tables also seemed to take notice. Their silence was the sound of true busybodies. Xavier relinquished his thumb from the fountain pen to wrap it around Nell's hand that was holding his. He didn't look at her. Still, the tempo of her heartbeat increased. She left him and took her coffee back to her table.

Taxes. Bills. An angry message from her accountant saying this foolishness could result in her being late to file. A letter from her family banker expressing similar discontent and requesting a meeting at once. Wincing, she knew she was breaking the trust protocol that had enabled her to try out this new life. She addressed those letters first.

Then, there it was, a thick cream envelope with an embossed return address on the back. Xavier P. Alden. Of course, he had taken the old-fashioned approach. As she felt the weighty paper between her fingers, a burst of delight made her smile. Although she didn't look up, she thought a young composer nearby may have taken note.

Dear Nell,

I write to thank you for the meeting between two kindred minds that we shared with Argus at our feet. I offer the first stanza of a poem written by Percy Bysshe Shelley:

The fountains mingle with the river
And the rivers with the ocean,
The winds of heaven mix for ever
With a sweet emotion;
Nothing in the world is single;
All things by a law divine
In one spirit meet and mingle.
Why not I with thine?—

I would like to invite you to a cello recital in Lenox. One of my compositions will be played on October 15th at 8:00 p.m. in the Round Barn recital hall.

Affectionately yours,

Xavier

Her eyes lingered over the page. *Had they stepped on an accelerator?* she wondered. They were both on unconventional journeys, but neither of them seemed to care much about matters of the heart. She read the date on Xavier's invitation with curiosity. How many days had she had been hibernating with Argos? Bailey was passing by with a refill for the elderly gentleman sitting in the window who seemed to live in the café.

"Do you happen to know the date today?" Nell asked. She was worried she had missed his recital altogether. The last she knew it had been the full moon in early to mid-October.

"That's what happens when you don't have a day job," Bailey quipped. "It's the 21st today."

Nell stared at her with chagrin at the thought of missing Xavier's concert, forgetting to say thank you. "Are you suuure?"

"I have a business to run here. Paychecks to write. On time. Ya know?" Bailey then bent down and whispered, "I kind of thought you might be the one wearing the velvet suit, what, with those Romantic ideals you always had."

Nell was still shaking her head at herself in dismay. Bailey laughed at her ignorance and walked away.

Xavier was staring, too.

Nell grabbed the letter from the accountant with her taxes enclosed for signatures: "Please return with a postmark by Friday, October 21st," it read. She stopped a bout of hyperventilation from starting. Doubt crept into her serene state.

Nell stepped outside with her mug of coffee to take stock of her happenstance at having chosen today, the tax deadline day, to come into town. *All of my privacy measures will be overturned if the Internal Revenue Service audits me. Waldo would not be proud. I don't get to ditch my faculty of reason.*

She inhaled from her lower abdomen up into the crown of her head in the durga pranayama breathing practice she had been taught in her yoga classes. She released her tension with an exhalation that had a rallentando built into it. She repeated the cycle until the ceramic mug had grown cold in her hand.

"What day did you think it was?" Xavier had stepped out behind her.

"I'd stopped thinking in calendar time." Nell shook her head at her folly. "What am I thinking? Or not thinking. I could end up in a Kafkaesque quicksand if the IRS doesn't get my documents postmarked today. And I'm out here doing my yogic breathing," she said, letting out a "Ha." "And I missed your recital. I would've really enjoyed that. I do want to be part of the community, too." She rambled when she was flustered. It hadn't occurred to her that this was the first time she was speaking in dialogue with another human in quite some time; another factor causing her sudden loquacity.

Xavier gave a wry smile and stepped closer, but his eyes remained on the street in front of them.

"Do you know how many thousands if not millions of people today would like to forget what day it is, for over a week? I should have asked how often you check that box, or I should have stopped by. I'm also a little worried about intruding on that space of yours that you guard."

She was still shaking her head so he kept going.

"I was hoping to share the recital with you. You would have liked it," he added quietly.

"I'm so sorry. The cello is my favorite instrument, too. It narrates emotion like no other instrument does. It's so soulful," Nell said with remorse.

"I have a recording I could text you."

Nell laughed. "Not anymore."

"I will play it for you if we have another evening in our future." He studied the micromovements on her face.

"Oh, we do," Nell said. "And I would like that. I hereby waive my invisible 'no trespassing' sign only for you."

They had both been looking out towards the street side by side, but then his eyes met hers. Their fledgling bond deepened in those sustained moments.

"I have important correspondence that won't wait, Zavs."

"Wait. Shall we make a plan?" Xavier said.

"What day is it again?

"You're a miracle. It's Friday, Nell, Friday," Xavier said, shaking his head.

"Friday is a good night to go out. I always went out religiously in grad school on Fridays. Fridays only. All the other nights were for studying." As Nell spoke, she realized how eager she was for his company.

"Do we have to go out? How about we cook dinner together so we can avoid the stares of our local elders? Argos would surely prefer that."

"You got me. Argos and I go together," Nell said.

"I'm bringing food and wine this time. How about a little bit before sunset again, so we can watch it together?" Xavier sounded as if he had imagined such a scenario.

"That sounds perfect," Nell said.

Together, they went back inside, returning to their respective spots. At her table, Nell signed her documents and organized the mail in her bag. There were still cards to read, presumably from friends who were reaching out in response to her audacious news at being phone- and internet-free. But there was no time to read them.

She gathered up her bag, and hesitated. Walking to the counter, she asked Bailey, who was wiping the counter in between drinks: "You haven't heard anything about a reporter nosing around here, have you? With a southern accent?"

Bailey frowned and shook her head. "I would have remembered that and chased him away. What happened?" she asked.

"He showed up at the house, and it's been pestering me how he got there," Nell said.

Xavier had also looked up. "We'll keep an ear out in case he comes back," Xavier said, reassuring Nell as she waved to them.

She crossed the street and went into the post office to mail the signed tax forms back. Relief spread through her shoulders as she watched them being stamped at the counter with that day's postmark. Nell then left the post office and headed to the library with her notebook in hand. She vacillated on the library steps, wondering if she wanted to tamper with her routine. Did she want to allow the internet to creep back into her life at all? What if she couldn't keep it at bay?

Nell sat down at one of the library computers intended for public use, and reluctantly pulled the keyboard towards her. Opening the notebook, she scanned her index finger down the first page:

- Transfer funds to pay taxes
- Knitting store. Lopi wool.
- Moon phases 2011
- Co-op: Dog food. Human food.

Nell logged into her online banking account, only to find that it required a secondary code that would be generated on her cell phone text messaging system.

"You've got to be kidding me," she gasped.

"Shushh." A lady with a perfect silver bob was sitting in a leather recliner with a stack of books in her lap, and she scowled at Nell, who mouthed a silent "Sorry" in reply.

Nell was nonplussed as she stared into the screen. Hitting the keys hard, she clicked off the page and pulled up a search engine—the contemporary version of an encyclopedia, only it wasn't crosschecked and verified as fastidiously as print volumes were. She found answers to her questions and jotted a few things in her notebook. Then, she marched out of the library and down the street to the Bank of the Berkshires.

Determined to bypass the internet's attempts to lure her back in, she set up a new account. Nell arranged for the local bank to transfer funds from the bank in New York that wouldn't let her conduct her business without using every device connected to the internet imaginable. She wouldn't be thwarted by the omnipresent force that had seeded itself into every aspect of people's lives.

Paperwork was the one thing she had dreaded about adulthood. She had watched Waldo disappear into his writing studio from time to time after announcing that it was an administrative day. Then he'd go off for a long hike when the documents were in order. She thought those duties of adult life had sapped his creativity. It was as if he had to work to get his zeal back for the ordinary beauty of everyday life. The dread had been warranted, but she was no longer a child. Her thoughts settled on Bailey and how she seemed to have mastered the art of everyday adult life. Nell realized she couldn't live entirely off from all grids.

She ducked into the wine store to collect ingredients for Kir Royale: Kir, Chambord, and a modestly priced bottle of champagne. Moving expenses and the lack of a day job were stirring up her frugal side, but she had Waldo's trust to fall back on. At the co-op, she found the same goat gouda with the quasi-cheddar taste from their tapas night. Xavier had liked that one. She added smoked salmon and eggs to her cart, in case they lingered, in case the moon turned its duties over to the sun before they parted. She loaded the cart with raw, frozen dog food and frozen vegetables in case she lost her grasp on linear time again. On the way home, she pulled off at the farm stand and picked up a bunch of lacinato kale and two acorn squashes, leaving five dollars in the glass ball jar according to the honor system.

Putting the groceries away, she heeded Argos's whining, and ran out of the house behind him, spreading her arms out in the wind. After seeing shoppers staring down at their phone screens while shopping for groceries, she was reminded of just how giddy she was to be phone-free. *How else could one go deep into the woods and listen to the songs of the forest?*

"Yahhhooooo. 'i thank you god for most this amazing day ...'" Shouting e.e. cummings verses to the sky, Nell ran down the wooded path with Argos. He raced ahead, weaving in and out of the trees, mapping out the local animal kingdom's comings and goings. They ran a long while, the young woman and her dog. As they came to the copse of white spruce trees that formed a canopy over the trail, Argos sniffed at the spot where Nell had seen deer sleeping through her binoculars. They curled up next to one another, in peace with their bedding and feeling safe enough to sleep with nature around them. Out of breath, Nell flopped down on her back in the pine needles as Argos inhaled the scents of the forest.

As she panted, she looked up at the elegant green pine needles against the afternoon sky. She listened to her heart as it slowed pace. She emptied her thoughts so she could hear the subtle music of the wilderness. The nearby bushes snapped, probably from a hopping squirrel. And she could hear Canada geese overhead. Closing her eyes, she basked in the earthy pines. When Argos came over and nudged his nose into her chest, she got up and scampered off with him.

She usually stayed on the path while Argos meandered at will, but she could tell that he was beckoning her. He paused, looking back at her, until she followed him into the woods off the trail.

Although she had to separate brambles to forge her way at first, as they rose upwards, Argos showed her a trail. It was like he had found a hidden path up the knoll. The way he kept pausing to wait for her made her think that he had been there before. It was as if he was guiding her. As they approached the crest of the knoll, she saw a small cairn of stones piled up. She paused to catch her breath while Argos waited, still standing, as if to say that they hadn't arrived yet.

But Argos led her up to a tiny clearing at the crest of the knoll. Seen from the house, the knoll seemed to be covered in a dense thicket of trees with no view, so she had never explored it. This was foreign to her. In the center of the clearing sat a stone bench with moss embroidered on its seat. Faded mulch in front of it indicated that shoots from spring bulbs might push through the soil here in several months. Daffodils, perhaps, Nell thought with wonder. The bench was encrusted with pine needles, which she stooped to brush off. Then she realized that Waldo had been there once, too.

C'est une vie exquise, celle qui se maintient en ordre, jusque dans son privé, Nell read words etched into the stone.

The handiwork of Waldo. Stupefied, Nell sank down into the bench, tracing the etching with her fingers as if it would bring her closer to Waldo. She read it out loud and then translated it, as if for Argos. "It's an exquisite life that maintains its order in private." She continued reciting the verse from memory, as if rubbing the stone was bringing it back to her. "Anyone can play his part in the farce … but inside … where all is hidden … to be regulated there is the point." Like Montaigne, Waldo had been a master of regulating his private life. This phrase had been so important to him that he even had his teenage granddaughter memorize it. Autonomy, she thought. Like grandfather, like granddaughter.

She looked up and saw that from this vista, Goose Pond Hill was framed in the sky. The Appalachian Trail ran through there. Was that the reason he'd created this secret spot? All these years and she'd never known about it, never heard him mention this hideaway on his land. *I thought we had no secrets,* Nell pondered. Secrets were part of what bonded them, what they kept from the world, not from one another. They were beyond secrets. That's what Nell had always thought.

Waldo had thru-hiked the Appalachian Trail and many other long-distance trails from Patagonia to the Himalayas. *Was Waldo paying homage to the mountains here? Was it his secret place for pondering?*

She glanced down at the traces of old mulch and saw that they covered a granite plaque embedded in the ground by her feet. She rubbed off the mulch with her hand and read: *Requiescat in pace,* etched in dark charcoal. They had scattered her grandmother's ashes, so she surmised that this was a personal memorial that

Waldo had created for his wife. "Rest in peace," she whispered to Argos, taking her thoughts away from the message on the plaque. She sat back on the bench, staring at the mountains, but seeing her grandmother's image in her mind. Nell could see her walking with that lively movement in her steps, taking a fresh fruit pie out of the oven, and offering a warm slice of it to Nell in that lilting old Boston accent of hers that was so endearing. Coming up close to Nell, she would whisper, "We'll have it with a dollop of vanilla ice cream," in a conspiratorial tone. Grandma was like a warm hearth, offering pie and witty humor that comforted her clan right up until that winter when Nell was in junior high school, and a severe bout of pneumonia had claimed her. Nell blinked her tears back and smiled at Argos to thank him for bringing her there.

"You're a treasure hunter, Argie. Thank you. What a good boy you are." She praised him and he leaned in to receive her caresses on his ears, his head, and the nape of his neck where his hackles rose sometimes when he was wary.

Argos sat on his haunches looking proud for facilitating Nell's discovery. He had been trying to show her the clearing for some time, but she had always been too distracted to follow his cues.

"You should listen to me more," Nell thought she heard him say, and she cocked her head at him the way he did when she spoke in long sentences.

"Indeed, I should," she answered.

It had an aura to it. The curation of the clearing was an invocation of nature's power. "Waldo had a mystery." She could feel herself smile as she said it. Admiration spread through her as she realized that Waldo had spaces in his life that even his beloved granddaughter wasn't privy to. Perhaps it had been his place to grieve and remember her grandmother, as she had just done. She understood that some of his emotions were not meant to be shared with the little girl he cared for; he had been her mountain.

A perennial autumnal stirring of melancholia weighed on Nell's chest just then. Argos sensed it. He leaned in closer and nuzzled her.

Chapter Nine

As Nell followed Argos out of the clearing and back down to their customary trail, a cold wind blew across her heart. Wrapping her arms around her torso, she called out to Argos and knelt down for another hug before they went home. She was relieved that Xavier would be coming over later.

When they were in the thick of the forest, the sun started to lower over the horizon of October Mountain, casting a dark-pink hue on her hundred-foot pines. "The sunset! Argos, we need to fly!"

Nell accelerated nimbly into a run, but Argos surpassed her. Racing, he disappeared from her sight as he climbed up to the cabin. She panted and slowed down, knowing that Argos would play host until she crested the hill.

And there, sitting on her stone steps, clad in faded jeans held up by a brown leather belt, and an oatmeal cable-knit sweater, Xavier was surrounded by a whishing Argos. They both stopped and admired Nell.

"Jeans? Welcome to the twenty-first century," Nell said.

Xavier's dark-brown eyes twinkled at her. "Your words resonated with me last time about being steeped in nostalgia for a world that no longer exists. I'm really more about preserving the land in this world for the future, but more about that another time."

Nell clapped her hands in playful approval. "I hope you haven't been waiting for long. Argos had a new trail to show me, and we were engrossed in the stories of the woods," she said.

"It's very special here, so I didn't mind. You can see mountains from all sides and no other signs of civilization."

"Yesss," she exhaled in a whoosh, hinging at the hips and hanging in rag doll, her favorite yoga pose for letting it all go. "I can breathe here," she said with her hair hanging on the driveway.

"I know. I can, too," Xavier said.

Argos scratched at the door, their cue for the evening to begin. Xavier slipped his shoes off by the door and walked straight to the island. Some of her bags were still on the counter, and Xavier added his own cloth bag full of provisions. He started to unload groceries, looking as if he felt at home.

Nell plunked on the floor and splayed her legs out, beating her thighs rhythmically in a sign for Argos to come. Argos stood between her legs, submitting himself for inspection, as she said, "Let me perform a thorough tick check on you." She deftly combed through his thick, black fur, and then patted his hips to release him.

"It's like you guys have your own secret language," Xavier observed.

"You can't possibly imagine. Our working lexicon blows the theory that dogs don't have the faculty of speech right out of philosophy's archives." She confided in Xavier because she knew he believed in the faculty of intuition like she did. Argos was more than just a dog for him, just like he was for Nell.

She fixed Argos his customary dinner and set the bowl down on his placemat on the floor. "Here you go, love," she told him. Argos didn't wait for her that night.

Xavier called from the other room. "I'd like to cook for you. Why don't you curl up and I'll do all the work?"

The discovery in the woods had sapped Nell's inner reserves. *Did Xavier see the new shadows in my eyes?* In a platonic gesture, she stepped behind him as he unpacked groceries on the island, wrapped her arms around his waist, and stood there for a moment. Her eyes moistened, signaling to her that she missed having a human connection that wasn't superficial. He reached a hand back to pat her outstretched arm. The kindness that lay behind what was not spoken softened the mass in Nell's chest.

Nell said, coming around him: "I'd like to share something. I've been loosely tracking my attention span without the phone. It's astonishing what I've been able to achieve. It's exactly what Professor

Gupta was talking about, regarding the difference between him and his colleagues. The implicit irony of it all was that I was a librarian who had lost her attention span to read." She flung her arms out to underscore the last point. He was still listening, and she couldn't stop unleashing her pent-up thoughts.

"Over the course of two days I sat in my armchair and read Dostoevsky's *Brothers Karamazov* from cover to cover without thinking of five things I wanted to look up on the internet, or stopping to check email, social media, and text messages. It's truly happening for me."

"It's laudable that you're pulling this off," he said.

Remembering that she still needed to take a shower, she said, "Let me freshen up a bit after the hike, and perform my own tick check, and then I'll make a Kir Royale for us."

"You warn me about being nostalgic, and then you make my favorite French cocktail. How is that fair?" Xavier said, laughing. Already wearing Waldo's red-striped apron, Xavier had his arms outstretched. "Luxuriate up there. I got this," he said as she left the kitchen. As she went up the stairs she heard him call, "And one fire, coming up!"

Nell set the needle down on the Bach cello suites—she had unearthed another ancient record player for the bedroom—and stripped down to exfoliate her still-sweaty body. Trail running with Argos was far more rigorous than her classes at the gym in New York. She stepped into the steaming shower and washed off all the fall emotions that were creeping back in as they ineluctably did each year. As she raised her underarm to scrub it, her nose wrinkled at the smell that reminded her of the underbelly of the leaves she had unearthed in the garden. Taking on a certain quality of earthiness was something she wanted to write about in her journal when Xavier left.

She stopped in front of the mirror. Her hair was damp and her cheeks still ruddy. She went to the wooden box on the dresser and pulled out a necklace with a single pearl on it and put it on. She pulled out the pearl so it rested against her sweater, which was in the same fisherman's style as Xavier's. As she zipped up her jeans, she said to the mirror: "Here we are. On our own terms. That's the privilege I fought for. That Waldo created for me. Finding Xavier is the surprise gift some intangible narrator must have manifested for me." She thought her hazel eyes looked happy.

Downstairs, Xavier had the fire crackling already, and the faint smokiness resonated with the earthiness she was already sensing. It was as if the outdoors was edging its way inside.

"My lady, one Kir Royale for you. And I have many more treats in store."

Nell accepted her glass, her fingers like natural magnets to his. She raised the thin flute, then hesitated with it in the air in front of her.

"And I have been waiting for you, too. I just didn't know that I was," Nell offered, shy yet willing to articulate her burgeoning truth to him.

Out of a deepening respect for Nell's solemn attempts to remain behind the curtain, this narrator will refrain from commenting on whether midnight's inkiness or dawn's first rays framed the back of Xavier's old Land Cruiser exiting onto White Birch Road.

Can you content yourself with imagining that they shared Mediterranean delicacies inspired by a young man's travels? Songs were sung by the hearth. And the fire reflected the way they illuminated one another.

Chapter Ten

Nell had always respected the structure of time. It gave her a frame in which to accomplish her goals. Yet now, her disregard for time seemed equally important. Existing in a sort of timelessness that was only loosely governed by the rising and setting of the sun, Nell's capacity for absorption was growing every day. To reach her synthesis, though, she felt that it was necessary for her to have first led an ordered life. Nell's Philosophy of Everyday Life was a mingling of the two that she thought she was reaching.

The following afternoon, she wiped the island's soapstone down with a lavender spray and dumped out the contents of her messenger bag. With a cup of turmeric and ginger tea that she had steeped by slicing their fresh roots into hot water, Nell wrapped herself in a throw blanket and set down to work. There was the trust executive to deal with—a character in her life that she kept concealed, concerned that people would disdain her for being financially well-off. She wrote a brief letter to him, requesting that he visit at eleven on Friday, November 11th. Then, she moved towards the stack of unopened letters.

About half of her friends had responded to her brief letters. As she read through their responses, she was gratified that most of them used words like "admiration" coupled with "envy" at her ability to go off the digital grid. Amelia and Fernando wrote that she reminded them of Waldo, and wouldn't pop by until she was settled in her new life. In her letter, Rose indicated that she understood Nell's decision based on what had happened in New York. Many of her friends who had written cards hoped for a visit, but she knew that few would actually make the trek.

Peter and Ella were absent from her mailbox. It didn't surprise her. She knew that they both lived on the electrical current of the moment. Nell drank deeply from her earthy tea, reminiscing that during her road trip from the city she had thought that their parting speech was just that: a final farewell. She was no longer part of their culture of immediacy, especially now that she couldn't even respond to their texts, so she didn't exist for them any longer.

When she reached for another envelope from the stack, a postcard glided out in front of her. The reading room in the St. Genevieve library in Paris with its dazzling arches and wooden ceiling stared up at her. The library had been designed by architect Henri Labrouste, who had—Nell happened to recall—also created the initial designs for the Eiffel Tower. The same mustard-brown tower that Victor Hugo had instructed his carriage driver to avoid at all costs, because he was allergic to its ugliness. And, Nell mentally added, to its modernity. Surprisingly, Nell didn't make the connection between Hugo's aesthetic judgment of the tower as ugly, and the cell towers that she had observed peppering the local hills. Her distaste for them echoed Hugo's.

The St. Genevieve library was on Nell's list of cherished places. She had studied there in the afternoons after school at the lycée where she spent a semester in high school. The glossy image transfixed Nell, starting to turn the reel of an old movie in her mind.

She'd been fifteen. Young enough to still whimper when she fretted.

"I don't want to go abroad, Grandpa. Please don't insist," Nell told Waldo.

"I don't want to raise you to think that the entire world revolves around American exceptionalism." Waldo wasn't a disillusioned liberal, but he had hoped Nell would become a young citizen of the world under his tutelage.

"But I'm a homebody. I want to be here with you," she explained.

"America is isolated, my dear girl, and you're at risk for developing monolingual complacency, for thinking that everyone should speak English. I don't want you to become a nationalist. This is the

Age of Globalization." Waldo's tone wasn't condescending, but it did verge on being professorial.

"Grandpa, we speak and read in French together. You make me study Latin. It's too late for me to be monolingual. I'm in no danger of becoming a nationalist either, after all those history books you make me read on the Native Americans being robbed of land," Nell had argued. "Besides, I come from a line of anthropologists!"

"One semester. If you're homesick for your old grandfather, then I won't insist that you stay through the year." He tapped the soapstone counter with his palm, like a judge pounding his gavel with the verdict.

"Deal." She wrapped her arms around him until his scratchy tweed coat itched her nose, but he didn't let go of her until she was ready.

"My dear girl, my dear girl, there now." He lulled her in a soothing tone as he patted her back.

Recalling this conversation so many years later, Nell unconsciously wrapped her arms around herself in the flannel shirt that had once belonged to Waldo.

Still hugging her arms around her torso, she peered at the postcard as if she could see into it. Scanning the long wooden tables in the reading room, she picked out her favorite one. She could see the domed green light she used to read by, and the elongated arched windows she used to peer out of. What fun it had been to peruse the volumes of books that lined the expanse of walls when she took a break from studying. She had even fantasized about writing one that would eventually be housed there. Startled by what her reverie was uncovering, she realized that she had forgotten about ever having thought of writing a book.

She had walked the streets of Paris in search of hidden beauty every day for months. Winding up the spiral staircase at Gustave Moreau's atelier to take in his Symbolist paintings delighted her—far from the crowds at the Louvre. Stumbling upon the mosaic-tiled arcades in the Galerie Vivienne with intricate Art Deco glass ceilings stoked her budding aesthetics, and birthed her love of cafés. Studying at A Priori Thé, while savoring a pot of tea and a basket of currant scones became a weekly ritual. Yet, her affinity for Paris couldn't compare with her love for Waldo. Her attachment to him couldn't withstand the ocean separating them.

So, as per their negotiations, Nell boarded an Air France plane bound for Boston just before Christmas and never went back, to Waldo's chagrin. She had tucked neatly wrapped parcels from French boutiques—mostly books, but also packets of coffee, and macarons—that she knew would soften her news. He let her be a global citizen in philosophy, if not in practice. When Waldo had asked her if she wanted to board at the prestigious Shire school starting the semester after Christmas, Nell paled and stated she would be a day student.

Only one person in the world could have written this postcard, and that was the young man with whom she had studied at the library: Blake Davenport. Exchange students at the same school, they became friends who studied together at the library next to the Panthéon. They kept their pact of only speaking French with one another. After his study abroad, Blake had transferred to the same boarding school Nell attended, though he had always assured her it was true serendipity. She had always been skeptical about such a seemingly manufactured coincidence, as had Waldo.

Acknowledging receipt of your note. Bon courage off the evil grid. Come to Paris for New Year's. Meet me under the Arc de Triomphe at 9:00 p.m. on December 31st.

Nell wondered how a note that started off like a business memo could end with such a bold, even mysterious proposition. Nell read the crisp message four times. Each time, she fleshed out her interpretation. Understated at first, perhaps slightly disdainful with the descriptor of "evil" for the grid, as if Nell was exaggerating in her stance. Blake had used the imperative twice. And meeting under the Arc de Triomphe wasn't a platonic decree. Blake was finally making an amorous statement by sending this card. Her final analysis was that his intentions were romantic.

When she looked up from the postcard that had enthralled her, the time on the stove shocked her. Nell had been transported into the disembodied space of memory. She had let the old reels roll forward in her mind as if she had partaken of Proust's madeleine. "I would never have taken that journey just now if I had a cell phone sitting by me on the kitchen island." Nell spoke the truth out loud to Argos.

She ran upstairs to spike the postcard to the corkboard above her desk. She skipped back down and took an unappealing sip of cold turmeric tea before signaling to Argos. They went out into the frigid air and meandered through the yard, one sniffing and one contemplating.

Blake had been patient and kind since she had first met him, like Waldo in a youth's body. And Waldo had taken to Blake, she ruminated. *He had known him and invited him to family dinners. That's how Blake knew to order Châteauneuf-du-Pape for our special farewell dinner.* She could only depict Waldo to others, yet Blake understood her references to the iconic figure that had anchored her life. He saw Waldo through her words, where others might not. And he loved her.

She couldn't imagine her life without Blake in it. Yet to love Blake romantically would mean sacrificing herself and her ideals. He thrived on the charge of New York City and Paris. He was as plugged into the digital grid as anyone Nell knew. If they were to be a couple, then perhaps his patience for her would diminish, for she could not be Blake's idealized version of herself and retain her ipseity, her Nell-ness.

The leaves from last night's rain drenched her bare feet as she paced. Argos was nudging Nell's ankles with his red ball. "Play will do you good," she heard her boy whisper through the ether. She picked the ball up with gusto and threw it as far as she could towards the hiking trails. Argos catapulted after the ball, curling and stretching his legs. She clapped, as per their rules of the game, and he raced back to deposit it at her feet. "Good catch." She praised Argos each time he retrieved it. As she watched him run, she thought about how he was her model for unconditional love.

"My love for Argos is what Gramps would call agape love—Aristotle's term for an absolute love not based on any conditions at all," Nell proclaimed out loud. She had made a rational choice to love Argos from the morning that she had rescued him from her impatient neighbor. "Argos, you win the prize in knowing how to love and be loved."

The dog bounded back to her.

"You saw all of me, you got me. It's easy to love you," she heard the silent words reverberating in her mind and knew they were his.

"You could sure give humans lessons in how to love, Argie." He lay his ears back and licked the hand that patted the creamy-colored fur of his cheeks. Nell had gone out farther than she meant to anyway, and though she had a high tolerance for cold, her feet were becoming numb against the boggy soil.

As they walked back towards the house, Nell honed in on a lion's mane mushroom clinging to a beech tree along the trail. She paused to gently separate the cartoon-like white mane off from the tree bark and put it in her pocket. There would be more foraging days to come in the spring, when they would go on treasure hunts for spring ramps. *I wouldn't have seen that lion's mane if I was still under the enchantment of my phone*, Nell thought.

In their letters, her friends still referred to Nell's disconnection from cyberspace as an "experiment."

"You're depriving yourself of new inventions," Rose wrote in her last letter. Rose described how she discovered new places throughout the globe, from cafés to sculpture parks, thanks to a new magical button on the phone. Only photographs were allowed. No lengthy expositions in words, but they could be categorized with special signs, and one attracted followers with them. Something about a hash, Nell recalled. Rose used words like "dazzled" and "glamorous," as if she had been seduced by the spell of this new place to spend time.

Argos's hackles rose into a sleek black mohawk and he hurled forward. Slipping on the wet field grass, Nell ran after him, wincing at every step as the field tore into the soles of her naked feet. Nell realized that it wasn't their acquaintance, the fox. In the distance, a sinewed gray coyote stood staring.

"Argos! He's a seasoned hunter." Then, to the coyote, she growled, "Get back."

"Raughrrrrrrr," Argos roared, jumping at the air some paces from the coyote, who wrinkled his muzzle into a grimace in reply.

"He kills for dinner. You don't! Stand down!"

Nell made an instant decision to fight the coyote with her fists and feet if it attacked Argos, who was structurally bigger, but who had never killed before. Although its tendons and muscles looked as if they were always ready to encounter prey, the coyote didn't seem to view the two of them that way. It stared as if it were curious, and kept its gaze. Then, astonished, she watched as the coyote turned and trotted back into the woods.

"Don't follow, don't follow …" she chanted quietly.

And Argos didn't, but it was clear that he had come to think of Waldo's acres as his territory. He looked just as astounded as Nell had been to see the coyote. It didn't appear that Argos wanted to fight, but Nell had noticed that he seemed worried about her sudden vulnerability, as if he were more attentive or protective of her than he had been in New York.

When she dried off inside, she had to blot the sides of her feet where bloody etchings had formed. Toes throbbing, Nell paused at the island and wrote "Coyote-dog fights?" and "Photo Gram" in her spiral bound notebook, under the heading "List of questions to ask the internet."

* * *

The following morning, while stamping her outgoing letters, she saw the thick, handsome envelope she had been about to open when Blake's postcard slipped out. The return address was from the Berkshire Land Conservation Group. That was the council Waldo founded with fellow preservationists back in the late 1960s. The envelope contained an invitation to a cocktail party in honor of those Berkshire residents who had donated land or helped purchase acres to conserve. Waldo would be proud that the BLCG had conserved thousands of acres to date, whether by outright ownership or conservation restrictions on private land. It was an organization that she wanted to join, too. It would make her feel like she was carrying a torch for Waldo's principles.

The party was to be held on the afternoon of Saturday, November 5th, at the Lenox estate that Frederick Law Olmsted had landscaped. She squinted at the invitation and held it up to the new calendar on the side wall of the oak bookcase. She'd tacked it up after she'd nearly missed those tax deadlines. Each day, she crossed off a line to mark her days. She hadn't missed it. Retroactively discovering an appealing event was not a habit she wanted to cultivate. Besides, she had a reason to remember that date. Xavier had called on the landline to say that he had been summoned back to Boston for family obligations that week, but that he would like to come and see her on the evening of November 5th.

She had kept her hand on the receiver after she placed it back in the cradle when they had said farewell, as if his spirit were still lingering there. They were like two independent streams that converged into one healthy brook, with no stagnation, no festering pools of algae, just water naturally smoothing down rocks in a clean flow. He was at ease with himself, and he appreciated her without wanting to alter her. And they had found each other here away from the city. She hadn't forgot those last words she had heard in New York: "Just don't forget about Jake at the Musil, OK?"

Her last conversation with Jake had been so reflective, so honest, that she regretted not having given him a chance before. She had wondered that day, as she drove, when she would have another conversation as profound, but Xavier hadn't made her wait long. And maybe she would tell him one day that he had already restored the confidence that had ebbed from her when Rodolphe eviscerated her character and values. She couldn't sit still in the house with these reflections. She, like Thoreau, had always valued the art of sauntering.

* * *

She and Argos walked the mile and a half to the hamlet post office just before Stockbridge that had never seemed like it was necessary given the proximity to town. She held her letters in hand as they walked past a thicket of blue spruce trees where a red cardinal observed them. Electric-red shone from its wings, and it looked back at Nell as they passed, as if it were somehow encouraging her as she walked the path.

The familiar sorting and shifting of thoughts took place as she walked, and a few things fell away, as they often did. When they crossed the rusted bridge over the Housatonic River, they came to the petite white clapboard building. A man named Jack was still postmaster at this little outpost. She had already seen him a few times since she had been home. His friendly banter differentiated him from the gaunt postmaster in Stockbridge who disapproved of her mail collecting habits. As she opened the door, defying the explicit "No Dogs Except for Service Dogs" sign, Jack called out: "Mornin', Nell. Would Argos like a biscuit?"

"I'm sure he'd love a biscuit from you, Jack." She grinned in appreciation of his mild rebelliousness.

"… wood chopped. Two cords, I think."

She'd missed something. She looked up at Jack, mentally skipping to catch up to what he was saying. Argos was lying on the floor with his paw over her hiking boot.

"What was that, Jack? That's what happens when you live by yourself; you start to block out dialogue," Nell said..

"I was saying that I had extra wood chopped and wanted to know if you needed any out there at Waldo's place. I could give it to you for seventy five bucks."

"I'll take a cord."

"Prob'ly bring it 'round tomorrow afternoon before the turkey supper."

"Thanks, Jack. It's kind of you to think of me."

"Better to stock up now then to run out in the dead of winter." He gave her an affable wink.

"Is the supper at the Congregational church? Maybe I should go?"

"Should call Evelyn for a ticket. She heads up the Women's Fellowship Committee."

"Maybe I'll see you there, Jack."

That settled, Nell handed her envelopes to him.

He said, "Say, Nell, I'm transferring over to the Stockbridge post office next week because they're closing down this little outpost. More emails, less letters, I guess."

"I'll see you there. That's where I have my box," Nell said, unsurprised at this development. She waved Jack farewell.

She wondered if there would come a time when the post office was obsolete altogether, and electronic correspondence prevailed.

On a whim, since they had no more adventures that day, she and Argos walked two more miles into the village of Stockbridge to check Nell's post office box. She wondered if Jack would be able to express his quirky humor there, or if there would be stricter rules in a larger post office where he wasn't the only employee. The gaunt postmaster who usually scolded her pursed his lips when he saw Nell coming, but he gave her a courteous nod as she walked to her box, keys in hand.

A lone card stood diagonally. Wishing to savor reading it with a cup of tea by the fire, she slipped it into her bag without noting the origin. She chose to walk home on a trail by the river, so Argos could go off-leash. They watched another wave of migrating Canada geese. The black skeletons of trees against the offing of the gray sky reminded Nell of the necessity of their flight.

Argos had gone off-trail, but he trotted up when Nell encountered the white-haired man from the coffee shop who had been carrying the Hermann Broch novel. He was walking towards them. His tall stature lent him a sense of grandeur, and his dignified posture made Nell elongate her spine as she watched him walk. She was awed again by the aura of wisdom that emanated from him.

"Please, meet Argos." Nell gestured and Argos extended a paw, as if he respected the gentleman, too.

"Argos. That's a good one. My favorite dog is Karenin," he said, patting Argos's head with affection.

"Right. Terezas's dog in the Kundera novel. After *Anna Karenina.* We can share literary dogs," Nell said, charmed.

"One must be named first, like the dog. And my rigid designator is Hugo," he said with a flourish of his hand to prompt her own introduction.

"Nell," she said, shaking his hand.

"Nell, the super-reader, or so it seems. 'Books are the treasured wealth of the world and the fit inheritance of generations and nations.'" He spoke as if to make clear he was quoting.

"Thoreau again. He's one of my oldest friends. But as much as his iconoclastic ideas resonate with me, I fear I make them hackneyed since I cite them so often." Nell spoke the way she thought, unabashedly earnest in Hugo's presence. "I do agree with his assessment about books—now more than ever as books compete with smartphones in a losing bid for attention," she added.

"Cultural decline in the presence of technological advances has long been a theme to lament, my dear girl," Hugo said.

"But I'm going to prove that I'm not one of the metaphoric sleepwalkers from your Broch novel."

"You saw me carrying *Die Schlafwandler* through town? Perhaps we can talk about that on our next walk. I'm not as pessimistic as Broch was about the state of culture," Hugo said. "But please do excuse me, I have a dinner engagement presently." He waved and bid her farewell as he continued to walk.

Nell paused and turned to watch his noble stride. From his burgundy and navy silk scarf tucked into his long black wool coat, to his polished leather boots, it seemed as if aesthetics were innate in his identity. It wasn't only his appearance; it was his agility with cultural and literary history that made it seem as if he was a keeper of beauty. There was a verve to the way he articulated his ideas that made them come alive. She felt a stirring, as if she had met one of the great humans. It was so imperceptible that it flickered through her thoughts like a sense of awe until they reached home.

Later, at home, as she prepared to nestle under her throw blanket by the fire with a volume of wilderness essays that had Waldo's notes in the margins, she took the card from her coat pocket over to her nest. She had been saving it, but the conversation with Hugo made her nearly forget it. Once she was tucked in her spot, she turned the card over, but it had no return address. Curious, she opened the envelope to find a single sheet of matching paper that read:

Dear Nell,
Thinking of you. Missing you. Sending warmth to you and A.
Affectionately yours,
X.

The little pool in the center of her chest felt warm. And stimulated. She noted the difference in the verbs that Blake and Xavier had used. Blake had commanded her with imperatives, while Xavier demanded nothing of her. He stated how he felt without wanting anything in return. *Succinct, yet effective.* She pressed it to her chest as if there were a trace of his vivacity left on the page—an impulse that was becoming familiar in regards to Xavier—before she slipped it into the pages of her book on stewardship of the land.

* * *

Nell spent the next few days in her Age of Absorption.

The Latin etymology for absorption revealed a deeper meaning from the eighteenth century that was becoming obsolete, but that pertained to Nell. Like the past-participle stem of *absorbere,* or "swallow up," she had literally disappeared by assimilation into something else. Nell was swallowed up, just as the nominative *absorptio* indicated.

With each passing day, she was folded into the words she read, yet not so much as to ignore the moon's cycles. Nell was charting its orbits, and the moon told her that the late autumn days were waning as winter neared, bringing the holidays with it. She deliberated about attending the community turkey supper, but thought better of it. All the old timers would be there, and they might bring up things she wasn't ready to talk about now, if ever. It threatened to awaken ghosts in the form of questions about her family's past that Nell was not keen on answering.

Chapter Eleven

This time alone, in a world where other voices have been muted, brings me to expose my interior world. But even here, I shall not divulge all of my reveries. I posit that there is more that will surface.

Nell was becoming more confident in placing her pen tip on the pages of her journal without having to share ideas in public that might seem foolhardy in today's age.

In French, the autobiographical writing in a diary is called a journal intime, an intimate journal, and this is how Nell conceived it.

In the city, wisps of thoughts wafted into my mind, fleetingly, that could have led me on a pensive inner journey. Yet, here, far from that fray, I often have thoughts that startle, fascinate, or nudge me into pondering.

I have become fond of observing animals' quotidian habits. I speculate that the same wiry coyote who stood stoic before me and an agitated Argos is the one who curls up to nap under the white spruce trees. I watch him with my binoculars from my writing desk. [Though, I fret that I am violating him in some way by turning the knob to focus on him as he sleeps. I didn't do it a second time, out of respect.] In my animal medicine book, I noted that coyote magic is found in their resilience in an ever-changing world. Perhaps that's why the coyotes appear before me so often? Must I grow more resilient in response to this loud world that I have succeeded in keeping at bay? It seems like a distant land, as I cultivate wildness.

"Life consists with wildness. The most alive is the wildest. Not yet subdued to man, its presence refreshes him. While almost all men feel an attraction drawing them to society, few are attracted strongly to Nature."

[This may be one of my last references to Thoreau in these pages, for I feel that I have developed my own reflections and need no longer reread

his.] If the most alive is the wildest, then I feel truly wild and alive! I smell the earth's pungency and revel in it as I walk, taking it home with me in my musky sweat. When I wash it off, I see my body morph into a sinewy shape, like the coyote who naps nearby.

Epiphanies of thoughts are connecting and unfolding as Argos and I join the wild woods here. I feel a greater responsibility to the earth as I walk through alder and ash, and wonder why my fellow humans ever thought to subjugate it, to make it tractable to the point of decimating it.

But like Thoreau, who walked into Concord from his rough-hewn cabin on Walden Pond for dinners with far more frequency than his readers can imagine—thereby breaking the spell of his mythologized solitude in the wilderness—Nell was ready to engage with society once again. She didn't believe that Thoreau had pulled off the solitude he venerated either. Therefore, she didn't believe he was an authority on the subject when he said that there was no companion as great as absolute solitude.

* * *

The evening of the cocktail party, Nell took out her floor-length plum and rust-plaid flannel dress that flared out as it swept to the floor. At the top, it looked like a fitted dress shirt with a collar, but the buttons continued to the bottom of the hem. She cinched it at the waist with a dark brown leather belt. She dusted off her brown suede heeled boots, and chose pearl earrings and her pearl necklace to go with it.

Before she left, she consulted the atlas to find Hawthorne Road. It was curiously faded, as if Waldo had run his fingers over this spot many times. It was adjacent to the summer music festival where they had spent many nights listening to the Boston Symphony orchestra while picnicking with friends on the lawn. Now her own finger traced the map. The route lines had smudged to white, but she thought she saw a faint pink line that indicated what road she should take.

But soon she was lost. The road she planned to take wasn't where she thought it would be. She saw a winding hill that looked promising, and turned up, but it took her past inns, farms, and bed-and-breakfasts on the backside of Lenox that she had never seen before. It hadn't been a short detour. Nell pursed her lips and tightened her hands on the steering wheel. Feeling ambivalent for the first time in her short phone-free existence, she reminded herself that the radical choice she had made was the right one. Just as she was about to give up, she saw the thin, rectangular sign for Hawthorne as she circled back onto the main road and passed the yoga center Saraswati had been coaxing her to visit.

Further on, she saw a sandstone manse rise from a green hillside. Its portico was lined with elegant columns. As she rounded into the circular drive, a suited valet stepped forward, bowed, and motioned for her to park.

He helped her from the car, and she rushed up the steps. The foyer was vaulted and grand but empty, and she could hear an introduction being made from a nearby room. As she hurried on, she caught a glimpse of stone fountains gurgling outside the windows, and the naked branches of the tall trees in the high panes of the hall's upper windows.

A stately lady in an emerald silk gown stood behind the podium speaking: "The chairman of the board ensures that our founding fathers' and mothers' vision of protecting the land will always be honored. Please join me in welcoming Preston Alden." She clapped her elegant hands, and stepped down from the podium.

The room was filled with smartly dressed people. The faces above the formalwear, though, were affable. It was an infrequent combination at the cocktail parties Nell had attended in New York. Observing them made her want to write the scene, or even sketch it. A man with excellent posture took the podium with a "Thank you." He exuded dignity, and his demeanor made Nell think he was accustomed to being admired. His charcoal suit with a navy silk tie looked more Boston than Berkshires. Perhaps he was a weekender.

Something about him was familiar. As he started to speak after the clapping diminished, she knew who he was.

"When I was a child, my family spent time not only in the Berkshires, but also in Vermont and New Hampshire. I witnessed land being sold off near ski areas. Sadly, it was turned into commercial strips where animals once roamed in their native habitats. When I asked my father what could be done, he shared what was happening right here in these hills.

"A movement sprang up in the late '60s under the aegis of my grandfather, Prescott Alden, and his friends, Waldo Harding and Sylvia Booth. Along with others, they espoused the radical notion that land ought to be preserved during a time when people wanted to pave it and put up parking lots." He paused, letting that thought settle. "Today, I'm proud to hold the torch that our forefathers lit." He explained that the Berkshires could boast more hiking trails than ever before, because hundreds of Berkshire landowners had donated land so that these hills would always be home to wildlife and hikers.

"This gathering is our way of thanking you. Aldo Leopold's land ethic, as he outlines it in his iconic *Sand County Almanac*, calls for moral responsibility to nature. Thanks to your help, we can uphold his high ideals. I look forward to raising a glass with you in celebration of our joint efforts. Thank you."

The room boomed with clapping, and Nell joined in, inspired. She stood a little taller to scan the smiling and nodding guests. She was looking for Mr. Alden's son, who had told her on the phone that he had an event to attend that afternoon with his father. She was certain that Preston had begot Xavier Preston, for their honey baritone voices could make a duet sound like a solo. Ruling out the majority of heads that were white, silver, and gray, she disregarded the blond men, and then she saw a head of dark chocolate hair.

Dressed not in velvet, but in a dark chestnut wool suit, Xavier stood clapping in support of his father. She decided to let him discover her, so she turned to the gentleman next to her and murmured, "That was a fine speech."

"It was, indeed. Jeremiah Rawls. You don't have a nametag," he accused her gently.

"I was a bit tardy since I rely on an atlas to find my way. Nell Harding."

"You would be Waldo's daughter. I was hoping that you would attend when I heard that you had returned home." Mr. Rawls gave her a good old boys' club smile.

"Please forgive me, Mr. Rawls, but I don't recall whether we have met. How did you know Waldo? I'm actually his granddaughter."

"Right. My apologies," the older man said, patting her back as if offering condolences. "We hiked together. We built trails together. Waldo and I liked to picnic up on Mount Greylock on Sundays after my wife died. I suppose you were away at college then. I was very fond of Waldo. Miss him a good bit."

"What I would give for one of those hiking picnics with Waldo," Nell said. Her gaze strayed towards a window where the mountains were framed, and her fingers raised to rub the locket that held a photo of him.

"Champagne, miss?" A tuxedo-clad server raised his eyebrows at Nell.

Nell accepted a crystal flute and joined hers to Mr. Rawls' as he said, "To Waldo. Say, I'm a poor substitute, but I'd like to drop by and hike his trails with you. We could reminiscence about him."

"Please do come visit, Mr. Rawls," Nell said far more earnestly than she would have a month ago. He shook her hand and turned to introduce her to other guests.

A voice whispered in her ear. "I'm looking forward to dropping by for a spell this very evening," Xavier said. She spun to face him, causing the drapery of her dress to swirl. He brought her inches away from his chest for a conservative hug.

"I'll hug you better later, but my dad is probably watching us right now," he murmured.

"I can be discreet for now, but I'm wildly happy to see you," she whispered as she stepped back.

As Xavier had predicted, his father was walking purposefully towards them.

"Son, I don't believe I have made the acquaintance of your friend," Mr. Alden said. His tone was cooler than it had been when he was speaking to the crowd of supporters. Nell felt that he was assessing her worth. Judgment raised Nell's hackles but she stood tall and put on a courteous smile. He stepped up to place his arm around Xavier's shoulder. Mr. Alden appraised her with steel eyes that chilled. Nell could feel him critiquing her in just the few moments they stood triangulated. *How had Xavier come from this?* Like a masterful actor, he shook her extended hand and patted it with his other hand.

"Father, I am honored to introduce you to my belle, Nell Harding. Nell, please meet my father, Prescott Alden," Xavier said in a formal tone.

"It's an honor. You must be about the last of the Berkshire Hardings. I wonder if you're related to Waldo Harding," he said. His entire demeanor changed on hearing her last name.

"I'm delighted to meet Xavier's father as well. Waldo was my grandfather, mentor, and dearest friend," she said.

"Your grandfather did more for the Berkshires than any of us will ever fathom. If it weren't for him, we could have high-rise apartments and major cities here. You're a very fortunate young woman."

"Thank you," Nell said, holding her head with dignity, while placing her hand over her heart.

"We must have you to dinner one of the weekends we are at the cottage. Please see to inviting Miss Harding, Xavier."

"I would like that, but do please call me Nell." She could tell it had been the wrong thing to say, for the crevice between his brows crinkled. This man favored formality as if it were a defense.

"Or Miss Harding is fine. I'm just unaccustomed to that name now that I am no longer a rare books librarian at the New York Public Library," she explained.

This seemed to appease him, and he raised his eyebrows with either interest or condescension at her former profession. She couldn't tell. Someone addressed him from the side, another elder in the organization judging from her nametag, and he excused himself.

Nell felt her shoulders slump when he left, glad that the dress rendered the movement invisible. She was drained from this transient encounter. She just wanted to go home to Argos, where her worthiness was not at stake.

"I know," Xavier was already saying apologetically, nearly empathetically, though she hadn't spoken. "Shall we?" he asked.

"I'm ever so ready to be with you and Argos alone."

Xavier placed his hand on her lower back to guide her through the clusters of chatting conservationists. He was already pulling at his knotted tie when the valet opened the weighty oak door for them. Xavier looked down at Nell as if he was going to embrace her right there on the steps, but she knew that he wouldn't. They both had enough of the New England stoicism running through their blood to make them refrain.

"I'm going home to change, get some groceries, and then I'll be right there," he said, massaging the palm of her hand with his thumb for a moment. He bounded down the steps towards the distant parking lot where he must have evaded the valet. She felt certain that his father, on the other hand, had valet-parked his car and that it was one of the sleekest.

Nell drove down the elegant driveway lined by maples stripped down to their winter bones, pensive as she retraced her route. There was a psychological component to Xavier that she hadn't surmised, and that was his father issue. She wouldn't probe, nor would she be judgmental if he shared what his childhood was like.

Idealism ran in the family, just in divergent ways. *What had this done to Xavier's psyche, these early childhood expectations that Preston must have imposed on him?* Perhaps that was the true reason Xavier sought escape in the hills, but she stowed this thought away, so it wouldn't surface that evening with him. Unsolicited psychological advice about family from a layman seemed like a sure way to drive any love interest away.

The sight of Argos replenished Nell at once. Their reunion ritual on the threshold was even more affectionate than usual, as if her companion sensed that Nell needed him. She changed into an ivory sweater with leggings. They were the most comforting clothes she could find apart from flannel pajamas, and she was not at that stage with Xavier, she thought. The wind swooped down the chimney through her open damper, and she turned the teakettle on in response. It was a good night to nest, but first there was Argos to attend to, and the angst to cast off.

Together, they went outside. Nell stood on the stone steps in her shearling slippers. She needed to commune with the trees and wind for a few moments after the flurry of chatter. As she let the wind's force vanquish the stagnating angst she felt, she noted the grayness permeating the night sky accompanied by what Waldo always called an Arctic wind. She said it out loud with his crisply articulated lilt: "Ahrc-tick." She breathed in the aroma of the prominent pines and bent into Ardha chandrasana, or half-moon pose as it was called in Sanskrit, and exhaled the tension that had crept into her shoulders from having to meet so many people all at once.

She stayed in the shape of the half-moon, arms extended up with fingers clasped in steeple position, until she saw the headlights of the Land Cruiser coming up the drive. Xavier opened the back door, but didn't take anything out. It looked like his pressing priority was to see Nell. He had replaced the suit with a sweater and the same faded jeans he had worn last time.

"Now I can hug you properly," he said and bounded up the steps.

"That's what I was thinking," she whispered as she tucked her head against the softness of the cashmere on his chest. Some primordial sensations were running through her body, and she kept her torso melded into Xavier's. Nell felt a ringing sensation as if they were emitting a vibrational pulse when they finally parted. He held her hands, saying: "You know, tonight I wished you hadn't thrown your cell in Bash Bish," he stated, tense.

"Why?"

"When I was at the gas station filling up, the old-timers were talking about a storm coming in, first big snowstorm of the season. I wanted to text you and see if we should get some extra provisions. I figured you had no clue about the storm. Then, when I got home, I decided to throw my snowshoes and ski pants in the truck, just in case. Lastly, at the market, I couldn't remember if I have seen you eat steak. It always seems to be wild-caught fish, but I couldn't text you and see what you wanted for dinner. I tried the landline, but you weren't home yet. So, I got everything." His arms gestured in the air as if to express just how helpless he had felt. Nell noted that in spite of his frustration, he didn't bear the slightest hint of anger. It made her want to reassure him even more.

"I get that. It sounds frustrating. I had my own first moment of skepticism about the cell-phone-free life this afternoon when I was driving to the party. The atlas was too worn for me to see the turn, so I almost missed your dad's speech."

Xavier frowned at that. He had dropped one load of bags in the foyer and started to walk back to the car. He paused, and then stopped to say, "Let's just look at the ramifications for a second. It's one thing if you're here at home, but what if you were driving to Boston or somewhere where you couldn't easily find the way? What if you needed help and couldn't make an emergency call? If you went away for the weekend with no phone, I would worry about you." He stopped as he reached into the back of his car. She rubbed her arms on the threshold, listening, while hopping from one foot to another.

"I think you're channeling Waldo," Nell called after him. "I get what you're saying. It's duly noted, and I'll think about it, but I would just like to decompress from all that right now."

Xavier was lifting multiple bags out of the car and setting them on the driveway.

"Hey, do you need help?" she asked.

"I got it. You're shivering."

Nell scurried into the house to the whistling teakettle. She turned it off and mixed two cups of hot water whisked with raw cacao and almond milk. From the plunking sounds of bags accumulating in the foyer, it sounded as if Xavier was moving in. An eerie frigidity spread through her core as she put her feet up on the rungs of the stool at the island, mug nestled between her hands for warmth.

"There's a cup of my hippie hot chocolate waiting for you if you want it."

Xavier came into the kitchen. She saw he was wearing gray wool socks.

He dropped onto the stool at the counter. "Thanks. Long drive from the city today and then the party, and worrying about provisions. My energy is waning like a half-dead cell phone battery."

They both sipped hot chocolate without words for a time. Provisions. Fathers. Days without speaking to another human. It all ebbed out, like it did when she was alone with Argos.

"As much as I just want to hang out, too, can I share an inner monologue with you that I've been having?" Nell asked.

"Of course." Xavier said. He squeezed her shoulders before mimicking the way she cradled her mug with both her hands clasped around its warmth.

"Mmmm. That's liquid comfort," he approved.

"Something about this new life is transforming me, bringing me closer to the earth. I get lost in the woods with Argos," she added an emphatic "figuratively," when Xavier's eyes stretched in wild alarm.

"And it's as if I am touching into this primeval union between human, animal, and nature. I'm in a pre-verbal, pre-linguistic space about describing it, but Argos and I hiked a section of the Appalachian Trail last week, and it was as if we were listening to the music of the trees, as if they were speaking to us. Something subtle is waking up inside of me that I couldn't hear before. I am bashful about discussing this, because it sounds so otherworldly."

Xavier was frowning at her.

"What is it?" Nell queried, waiting for feedback.

"That's my listening face. I want to understand, and it's fascinating. I mean, have people really forgotten what it was like in the pre-internet era? Have we normalized distraction? That's what I'm thinking about as I listen to you," he said.

"Xavier, that is exactly the question I have been posing. I think we have. But you look tired, and so am I. I just … haven't seen another human to speak to about this. And I would rather do it with you. Let's do a part two later." She rose to prepare dinner.

"You're here now, so no need for cell phones to connect us," she assured him.

"Right. Only I see some couples out at restaurants who are probably texting with one another while they are at the table."

"Are we a couple?" Nell raised her eyebrows in a flirtatious smile without really needing Xavier to answer.

"I would be half of a couple with you any day, Miss Harding. I just hope that you like grass-fed steak, or wild-caught salmon, or one of the things that I picked up at the market for us," he said with a grin. The hot chocolate and musings had reignited his spunk.

"I haven't eaten meat for ages. Ethics. Climate change. Greenhouse gases. I wonder if I'm missing iron or B12 or something, and I'm trying not to be too draconian about my diet, so I'll try it," Nell said.

Xavier snorted.

"Not be too draconian? No, you'll just be draconian about the no-cell-phone policy," he joked. There was no sarcasm in his voice, and they both laughed and started sorting out dinner.

Xavier was marinating fish and steak, and when he seemed satisfied with the concoction he had ground and squeezed, he walked over to the porch.

"Does Waldo have a grill out here?" Xavier cupped his hands over the glass doors leading to the screened-in porch that Nell resisted using because she didn't want a screen to separate her from nature.

"Yeah, but it hasn't been used in *yeeahs*. I'm practicing my old New England accent and sound ridiculous, I know."

Xavier knew just what she meant, and started riffing to sound like an old-timer. "I reckon we could *fiahh* up that grill, but I'll use the newfangled oven to broil them. OK. We suck at this," he said.

"That's the least anachronistic thing I've ever heard you say. What would Baudelaire think? Slang and jargon from your own generation," Nell teased.

"He'd love it. Modernism. Slang and all. Though sometimes anachronistic feels safer to me than today's world," Xavier said.

He sounded vulnerable, as if these words hadn't left the unspoken realm of his thoughts before.

"You have my empathy as you break trail. The Xavier Trail." Nell said, reaching up to pat his shoulder.

They moved in wordless rhythm together. Without needing to allocate duties, they made a fire, chopped vegetables, and uncorked wine. Xavier looked up.

"How about eating on the floor at the coffee table? By the fire?" he suggested.

"Sounds cozy, or *Hygge*, as my Danish friends say." Content to let conversation diminish to logistical banter, Nell went back to dicing mushrooms on the cutting board, Argos's head on her feet. Xavier put the pillows from the sofa on the floor and lit the pillar candles in their glass globes on the coffee table. The steaks started spitting, a sound that interested Argos, and Xavier slid on his socks back to the stove to flip them.

"Done at medium rare. Maybe we just load up here?" Xavier suggested.

"Yes, otherwise Argos might be too tempted to graze from the coffee table. He has probably never seen steak before." She laughed, handing him a plate.

"Argos does have his own steak. I anticipated that." Xavier sliced Argos's steak in pieces and fed it to him by hand before plating his own food, which Nell observed with an appreciative awe in her eyes.

"The way to my heart is definitely through feeding Argos's stomach," she said.

At last, they were nestled with their dinner plates by the fire.

"This steak comes from a cow that was grass-fed, antibiotic-free, hormone-free, humanely raised, and ethically slaughtered right here in the Berkshires. I hope it meets your approval," Xavier said.

"And on the side, we have lacinato kale sautéed with miso, pine nuts, and mushrooms that I foraged myself. The acorn squash came from the local farm stand. May it be the last year I have to purchase squash before I start harvesting my own."

Xavier raised his glass of pinot noir and toasted: "To the fledgling couple and Argos."

The perfunctory eye contact that one makes while toasting turned into an entire non-verbal conversation in seconds. They acknowledged that a symbiotic bond was forming between them and that they honored it.

They took first bites, tentative about the other's contributions at first.

"Kale and miso with steak is a hit. You know what? I would rather be cooking with you right here than be at any restaurant," Xavier proclaimed, smiling and tapping the coffee table.

"I'm with you," Nell affirmed.

"About my dad ..." He looked down at his plate.

Nell squirmed from one side to the other.

He kept his eyes on her face. "I was watching both of you. Your face told me: 'I don't think he likes me,' 'He's judging me,' and 'Now that he's heard my family surname and deems it be respectable, he has changed his opinion of me.' Lastly, I watched as you played courteous and respectful on my behalf. Yeah, that's what I got from reading Nell," he said, concluding.

Nell's eyes widened. "You're an excellent reader, Zavs. I was taken aback. You weren't planning to introduce me to your dad today, so if you don't want to talk about Dad Alden, I understand," she said.

"He does judge everyone, which tells me he judges himself the most severely."

"I perceived that. I liked that he's idealistic about preservation. But from our fleeting interaction, he seems like a perfectionist about upholding societal ideals, whereas you shirk conventional ideals in favor of your authenticity. I'm struggling to land on the right word," she said.

"Your psychological portrait is sound. I'm embarrassing the family by not making anything of myself," Xavier said. He looked away, into the fire. "That's what my trip to Boston was about. Dad threatened to evict me from the pool house here if I don't make serious inroads with my future career."

She considered this, thinking that he sounded less brave than he had when he had strolled through Stockbridge in his velvet suit, as if the boldness of his attire amplified his confidence. There was that aspect of the flâneur that was criticized: indolence in society, and wasting one's time, but she wasn't going to bring that up. She then said, "This just sounds so stereotypical: 'Wealthy white boy experiences travails with father concerning his lack of success.' I'm not downplaying what you are going through, though."

Xavier smirked for the first time since she had met him. "Dad appreciates profit and loss, but I'm overhead right now in a time when the markets are not doing well. Musical composition and poetry are not acceptable pursuits, but he knows I have a major project in the works that should please both of us. I want to wait until it's finished to show you."

"I worry about being fiscally responsible, too, Xavier. There's an urgency to not be the Marie Antoinette in the room," she said in a husky whisper.

He gave a somber nod.

Nell put her fork down and lifted her hand towards Xavier. He did the same, and she held his hand up in the air for a moment in between them, massaging his palm gently before letting go.

"I also hate that he treated you like a commodity with the way he looked at you, assessing whether you had value that could enhance his standing. I know that's what he was thinking and I hated it."

"I'm so sorry, Xavier. You're so kind to me, and you don't play games. You always say what you mean even if it makes you vulnerable. I can't imagine you having a father who isn't kind to the marrow," Nell said in a soft tone.

"I get that from my mom," Xavier said between bites of steak. "Dad and Mom are still together, but I know that he doesn't understand her. I watch him belittle her, and I decided early on that I wanted to emulate Mom, not Dad."

He took a sip of wine, and Nell met his eyes. She wanted him to go on. She tilted her head and nodded slightly.

"That being said, I do respect my dad. He's a conundrum because he can be kind and generous, but then he can flip and speak in this abrasive voice intended to produce friction. Mom dragged him to all kinds of couples' workshops, and he has these new tools to use, but he chooses not to. I've cut my losses about ever having the ideal dad." He sighed.

Xavier stood to add more logs to the robust fire. He didn't posit reciprocal questions to Nell, which would have been the natural trajectory. Instead, as he was pausing to grab another log, he looked at her. "I see clouds move across your eyes sometimes. I decided not to ask you questions and let you come to me. That's not as eloquent as I meant it to be, but there it is in ordinary language," he said, turning back to position one more log among the flames.

Nell said, "I've razed a lot of my walls with you naturally. But some remain, and, well, the Berlin wall didn't come down easily."

Xavier sat down next to Nell on the floor, put his arm around her, and leaned back. Argos crawled close enough to put his head on Nell's lap, and she stroked it. Nell leaned her head on Xavier's shoulder. He brushed her hair behind her ear, and stroked the top of her head with his hand in a gesture that asked for nothing in return. They sat like that for a time, like musicians with several measures of rest.

Nell felt stirring in her heart again. She craved an inestimable bond, yet she feared the equally incalculable loss it had the power to incur. To lose another loved one would topple her. But finding one to bond with was equally challenging. Such a rapport had been elusive. It had been hard to connect with those who didn't understand her eccentricities. With Xavier, though, it was as if the bond had already been woven naturally between them, and they only had to acknowledge it, deepen it. The wind reverberated through the wooden beams on the ceiling, and the fire danced in response.

Nell reached for him first. In an unspoken agreement, Xavier deferred to her as if to say: "I honor your boundaries, your vulnerability, yet I am eager to be with you, if you are ready." Hail beat on the roof. Argos padded upstairs to his bed—that he rarely used—in Nell's room.

Nell cupped her hands around Xavier's face, drawing him towards her as she caressed his lips.

"This is my invitation to you," she murmured when they paused in the midst of their improvised intimacy, a significant event marked by the first snowstorm of the year.

Chapter Twelve

The morning landscape was black and white. Snow salted the air in a quick rhythm. Flakes piled up on the deck over the rocking chairs; only the backs were sticking up. Black skeletons of pine stood highlighted in winter white against a pale gray sky.

Nell came tearing back up to the bedroom after she saw the snow on the deck.

"Nature left us magic!" she cried out.

Argos swished in excitement as he stared at the mountain of snow against the glass doors. Nell clapped her hands for Xavier to wake up, and he ran down after her. Nell tore through the coat closet like a child, unearthing hats, mittens, and ski pants that she pulled on haphazardly in her zeal to get outside. When she opened the door, snow came gushing into the foyer. Argos waddled out first.

A certain giddiness took hold of all three of them. Argos plodded through the yard, snow spilling onto his back. Nell followed in his footsteps, stumbling in drifts that came up to her thighs. She bent down to roll the sticky snow into a ball that she threw for Argos. He leapt and chomped down on it just in time. Just then, she caught one on her coat. Xavier hooted with laughter behind her. The three of them tangled in a rolling frenzy when she fell back into the snow to flap her arms and legs, leaving a lopsided imprint. Argos fell on top of her and Xavier was close behind. Nell crawled to get up, and shuffled across the driveway to the garage. She found her old cross-country skis hanging up with laced boots. There was an old wooden pair of Waldo's skis, too, but Xavier opted for his metal snow shoes.

Nell broke trail, and they trudged along the looped trail. The pores on her face sprouted sweat as she herringboned her way up the hill to the cabin at the end of their trek. Everyone was panting, but Nell was first to shed the gear and clamber up the steps to make breakfast.

"This is the perfect day. I didn't know they could exist like this …" She trailed off.

Xavier whistled on his way in through the door. He reached for her guitar and started to strum a few chords, while she bustled around the kitchen making smoked salmon toast with avocado to go with cacao stirred into coffee. She handed Argos a marrowbone from the freezer after his breakfast. Everyone was tended to.

Xavier sang, "*Ohhh, let the more loving one be me.*"

He paused and tuned, then continued:

"*How would we like it if the stars burned with*
A passion for us that we simply could not return?
If equal affection cannot be,
Ohhh, let the more loving one be me."

Nell clapped her hands between spreading avocado on the toast.

"Hey, not fair, Zavs. That was definitely a riff on a W.H. Auden poem. You can't slide one past the librarian lit girl."

"I didn't claim to write it. I just modified the lyrics. I'm saving up my original songs right now. There's one about you, but it isn't ready yet," he said with a shrug between retuning strings.

"I can't wait to hear it."

They sat at the kitchen island and set up a modern version of Scrabble in which each player creates an autonomous Scrabble board on their own with tiles of letters. The first player to finish using all of the tiles wins. The individual pace and board suited the independent thinkers, and they played while scarfing down the open-faced sandwiches and sipping more of Nell's mocha coffee. Xavier had added chili powder and honey to his, and Nell copied him, licking a dribble of honey from her finger.

"I'd love to get bees here. Have to support the bees these days," Nell said randomly.

"Part of my project is planting local wildflowers to give the bees and other pollinators refuges from pesticide-laden areas," Xavier said, adding, "but I have to stop foreshadowing for you."

"I hate that people still use glyphosate on their lawns," Nell said, ignoring his slip.

"Well, the more people that create pesticide-free corridors for the bees, the better. We just have to spread the wildflower seed and the word."

"I like that. That could be a slogan for the bees," Nell said.

They concentrated on the game in silence for a while, Argos snoring on his bed.

"Done."

Xavier clapped his hands when he was the first to use all his tiles. Nell peeked at his grid, suspicious.

"'Xylophone'? How did you get those letters? 'Itinerant.' A+."

"Look at your 'exacerbate' and 'fastidious.' We're just a couple of logophiles." He laughed.

"There was a logophile I adored in New York," Nell shared, bringing her city life into their dialogue. Xavier looked at her as if he were keen to hear if this lover of words had been a love interest.

"Mrs. Hadley. She was my department head at the library, but she also seemed like a great-aunt who had adopted me in some unspoken way. We used to exchange favorite abstruse words, like 'abstruse.' I miss her." She looked up.

Xavier said, "I think she would approve of me as her Berkshires stand-in."

Nell smiled. "I know she regretted my sudden departure. I do feel wistful about not seeing the Ephesus exhibit I had worked so assiduously on with her." Nell added a word she and Mrs. Hadley had included in their word game to soften her serious thought. Continuing on, she said, "We even had some rare artifacts shipped from Vienna on loan." She felt the excitement of it swell in her again. "After all, Ephesus did hold one of the Seven Wonders of the World, the temple of Artemis."

"It sounds fascinating, Nell. I'm sure she appreciated your hard work. We could take a field trip to see it, but I have a feeling you wouldn't leave the nest."

Nell nodded in affirmation.

"But speaking of libraries, how about a little reading?" Xavier asked.

Snowed in for now, they migrated to the leather armchairs and sat reading their respective books, side by side. Xavier borrowed a volume of Mallarmé poems. Nell, meanwhile, was far away in the Heian period of Japan from *The Tale of Genji.* She didn't look up from the book for hours.

Xavier's eyes flitted from the page, to Nell, to the snow, to Argos. He got up to take Argos out and putter around. When he came back in, Nell was still reading. He sat back down and extricated his sleek metal device from his pocket. Nell didn't notice as he tapped on it. Then, she looked up at the unmistakable sound of distraction and gasped. "Hey. This is a cell-phone-free zone. We have principles to keep, velvet-suit-boy."

"Yaa, I can tell, because I have virtually no signal here." He rolled his eyes and put his device away to comply.

"Do you have that instant photo button that everyone keeps telling me about?" Nell asked.

"Of course, I do, but that's not even what it's called." He chortled.

"I'm kind of curious, but I don't want to see it," Nell said.

"We'll see how this plays out," Zavs said cryptically.

Their dialogue paused for a time. Nell retreated upstairs only to take shy steps back down with her journal clutched to her chest.

Timid, child-like, she stood in front of Xavier and opened it. He looked up with a smile, as if he were intrigued.

"You know how you had a song for me? I might have something for you. I'm not a writer, it's just a journal entry." Nell said, looking skittish, as if she were about to change her mind and flee upstairs. Xavier rolled his head to the side and gave a welcoming flourish with his hand, waiting for her to begin reading.

"*A sprite alive solely in the labyrinth of my mind?*" She stuttered and paused to swallow.

"*The ghost of a flâneur who touches dormant emotions*
within the shell that houses my heart?
Has he already shattered its brittle covering?
Are my diaphanous wings free to be wild, unfettered?

Il occupe le rôle principale dans mes rêves."

The sound of a plow truck scraping the driveway drowned out Nell's soft tone over several passes. It was Fernando. She stopped, and with that metallic sound, they knew that their weekend party was coming to a close.

She looked up to see the literary analysis forming behind his eyes, as he smiled in encouragement. He patted his hand over his chest, similar to the way Nell did, as if he had picked up on her gesture. "I'm honored that you shared. And its fairy-like. You're a writer."

Xavier pulled her to him as she closed the book.

"It isn't finished," she mumbled, to which he replied, "Let me show you that I'm not a ghost."

They went upstairs to her bedroom with Argos, and she nestled closer to Xavier, knowing a morning farewell was coming in a few hours. It was as if their bodies hummed when her head lay on his chest and her torso turned into him.

* * *

Monday morning, Nell followed Xavier to town in her Volvo, where they had agreed to have breakfast before their paths separated. Slipping as she went with her rear-wheel drive, she noted that Xavier's Land Cruiser didn't budge in the snow. She wondered what Waldo would think about her careening around in the snow.

She slid into a spot next to Zav in front of the coffee shop, relieved that she didn't hit the Cruiser, and jumped out to join him.

"I saw that. Maybe at least get some snow tires. Some good Scandinavian ones," he said.

"I was thinking that, too."

The door to the coffee shop was locked.

"It must be a snow day. We would have known about this had we had a cell signal," Xavier said.

"Would we? Perhaps we would have been too engrossed in each other to find out?"

The general store was open next door, and they sat down at the counter. Ed was standing with his back to them, frying hash browns that sizzled as he turned them.

"Hey kids. What can I get you this morning? You're my first customers brave enough to venture out." Ed entertained them with tall stories about epic snowstorms from his childhood while he made eggs for them and poured black coffee.

"Saw a few slick cars off the road as the city folk hightailed it back to Boston. One was a fancy European sports utility vehicle half on its side; looked like a Porsche or something. That will teach them to respect the frosting when it comes."

Xavier blanched and muttered, "Dad." He hopped off the stool and went outside to pull his phone out and look for a signal in the village. Stockbridge was notorious for its refusal to install a cellular tower. He stomped the snow off from his boots before blustering back in.

"Ed, may I use your landline?" he asked.

"Sure, son. Just don't forget to dial one before the area code. We're still in the olden days here." Ed gestured to the phone with his free hand.

Xavier punched numbers. Nell observed from her stool as she quietly cut her scrambled eggs with knife and fork, nervous for him.

"Dad? Dad! Are you OK? Did you have an accident?" His dad's voice projected so clearly that Nell could hear his side of the conversation from her seat: "I left the Berkshires after the party Saturday to avoid the storm; I guess that means you haven't been home yet." His tone was cool. In spite of it, Xavier's body sagged with relief.

"Good to know, Dad. That was smart. We got snowed in."

"I have to take this call, son." That was the extent of the conversation, which Nell would have ended with an "I love you, Zavs," but then she wasn't his father, nor did she know how his father had been treated as a child. Xavier set down the receiver. He smiled at Ed and Nell and walked back to his seat.

"Sorry about that. He drives so fast that I thought it might have been him."

"You're a good son." Nell patted his hand.

"It's November, Nell. I'll be going home to Wellesley for Thanksgiving week soon. I hope you're going home to your parents. You can't hide out here forever." He used a casual tone that sounded as if he had rehearsed how to be nonchalant while delivering this message, one that she thought he had promised not to deliver.

He went on: "I'm sure your family misses you, and it's indulgent on your part to stay here and bask in your own solitude." He rephrased the words as if they would be helpful to Nell, as if he were a mediator. *Whence had this come? They had made a pact that she would come to him. Did their increasing intimacy open a portal for him that remained closed for her?*

Nell could feel her eyes turning like an old slate roof: gray and impenetrable. As Xavier chided her, she felt cold as stone.

Neatly, she placed her fork and knife together diagonally on the plate, folded the napkin in her lap and placed it to the left of the plate, took twenty dollars out of her pocket, placed it wordlessly on the counter, nodded at Ed who had been quietly observing, and looked down.

"That's my Berlin Wall, Zavs. It has rusty barbs on the inside and outside. Please don't try to knock it down."

She walked briskly to the Volvo before he could follow her. Jerkily slid in. Slammed the door. Spun out of the snowy spot. Disappeared.

Chapter Thirteen

Maybe I should never have left New York? Nell thought. New York had been her escape into perpetual movement, distracting her from her inner landscape, whereas coming back to White Birch Road was returning to her homeland. Nell had felt lonelier in New York than she did in the woods, partially because she never allowed herself to be seen, to be vulnerable with her friends there. But the homelands were fraught. Coming back held its own risks, for it was the country that contained her specters, her sadness. The black hole of sadness that she had kept at bay in New York, she had kept from falling into, lest it devoured her. But here, the residents of her homeland expressed their knowledge of her past through their kindness towards her.

She had admonished Xavier for his flagrant nostalgia, yet what about the unacknowledged nostalgia that she had been harboring for years towards the Berkshires? But she had appeased her yearning to return. Xavier didn't even seem to know what he was nostalgic for. It was as if he carried a sadness for something he couldn't describe, whereas Nell could have written a dissertation on her own pain. She just chose not to.

How dare he intrude like that. Hadn't he promised not to posit questions? Didn't it occur to him as odd that she didn't talk about her dad after they discussed his ad nauseum?

Loneliness settled in Nell's chest for the first time since she had returned home. On the drive up from New York, she'd marveled at the possible relationship she might have had with Jake. Had she learned nothing from that parting lesson? The chance to connect with a profound soul was rare and no one should be complacent about it. Had she squandered the pure love and ease she had with

Xavier since the moment they first spoke? She was already feeling nostalgic for the untainted love between them that seemed lost since those parting words.

As she turned into her driveway, she wondered if Ed had said something to Xavier back at the diner. She doubted it. In her country, people protected one another's secrets.

When Nell opened the door, Argos smelled her anguish. Instead of going outside, he stayed beside her. His eyes searched hers and he licked her hand as if to lick a little of the sadness off.

"I am grateful for you, my dearest companion. The one that understands me best. But go pee."

She watched Argos release a stream of urine onto her fragmented snow angel from the day before. The symbolism wasn't lost on her. Argos's eyes never left Nell's as he continued his business. He skipped mapping the animal tracks in the snow and zoomed back to where she stood. When she closed the door behind them, Nell locked it, as if she could shut out the outside world for good.

She walked straight back to Argos's bed and dropped down on it, bringing her knees into her chest, hugging them with her arms. He curled up next to her, edging closer until her nose was buried deep in his fur. She thought they must have looked like a yin and yang sign. He licked the locks of hair off from her face, licked her forehead and cheeks, and put his paw over her neck, diagonally. She closed her eyes under his care, feeling his protection as the black hole's gravity pulled her light into its center, taking her back.

Turkey was in the oven. Grandma's gingham apron protected her cinnamon-velvet dress as Nell rolled out her pie crust for the dark chocolate pecan pie she had challenged herself to make in honor of her parents' return on their favorite holiday.

Having come on the Mayflower in 1620, Nell's family never failed to celebrate Thanksgiving with reverence for the indigenous Native Americans who had helped the pilgrims survive that first winter. They always read a passage from their family member's diary of the voyage, but they also read a passage about the abusive treatment the Native Americans endured at the hands of ungrateful white settlers. Nell had chosen the readings for that year, bookmarked them with the envelope from the private high school's admissions office, planning to surprise her parents with her acceptance over dinner. Waldo had prepared the celery and wild mushroom stuffing that he took up making after Grandma had passed a few years before.

The door jiggled, jostling Nell to the present day, but the lock prevented it from opening. Argos touched his nose to Nell and leapt from the bed with an unleashed "Ruhhhrrrrrrr." *It's my day to protect her heart,* he thought.

Stamp. Stamp. He heard boots leaving. Argos growled a last warning, and returned to his bed where he again touched Nell with his nose. He lay down to resume comforting her when he heard steps crunching through snow, coming from the wrap-around deck.

The sliding glass door jiggled until it slid, when it should have been locked in place. The sliding sound jostled Nell, but she kept piping the pie crust, rolling up her velvet sleeves as she worked.

Immobilized. Little Nell alternated with Big Nell.

Xavier must have left the sliding glass door open when he measured the snow on the deck. Funny that the person didn't knock, she thought, but she couldn't open her eyes or budge. The dormant dragon of grief had woken up inside her again. That was where Argos came in on their strong relay team.

"Guurough! Ruuf," Argos growled as he lunged at the door. *Argos could be at risk if he charges someone wielding a weapon.* Argos stopped in surprise. Conflict rippled through his muscled haunches as he sat back down, deliberating.

Nell ran her pinky finger along the edge of the bowl, collecting a dab of the dark chocolate pecan filling. She brought it to her lips, and sucked her finger until the sugar hit her empty stomach like nausea.

The face before Argos was familiar, but his priority was Nell, and this may have had something to do with her dysregulated state. He didn't like that protocol hadn't been followed about coming through the front door and being announced. His instincts told him that this backdoor entry was not authorized. Following this logic, he resumed:

"Gruough! Raaarouh."

"Nell! Nell!"

As Xavier's anguished voice called her, she smelled the turkey and heard Waldo mumbling about it nearing Thanksgiving perfection at a hundred sixty five degrees.

"I am so sorry. I understand how much I must have hurt you. I'm an incomparable idiot." Snow was clumped to his jeans, and it was melting, staining her floors. He tried to approach her, but Argos bristled, and Xavier couldn't get past him.

Nell hadn't moved, hadn't opened her eyes, but heavy ropes were hauling her out into the present. Her sudden somnolence weighted her tongue as she spoke.

"Understand? I didn't give you that opportunity because I wasn't ready to share." She hurled the words out of her mouth like boulders rolling. "My favorite philosopher says you can never understand another's pain." She was shocked by her own eloquence, by her ability to use ordinary language to say precisely what she meant.

"I just want to acknowledge your hurt. I never intended to disrespect your boundaries. I respect you so much," Xavier said, drawing out his words.

"But to even say that, you must have looked me up! If you care about my boundaries, then how dare you stalk me on the internet? Because that's how you found out, right? My tragedy is my private history, but the bad-mannered internet has taken that dignity from me. You promised you would wait for me to share." She surprised herself with her powerful feelings of distrust and anger.

Argos repositioned himself by her side, leaning into her, facing Xavier.

"I'm ashamed, Nell. I respect you. So much. I honor your losses. Please forgive me," Xavier pleaded. She saw tears in his eyes.

"I let myself be vulnerable with you. I let you in, not only because we get each other, but because you respected my principles. Then you violated all of them in one day. Just go," she said, parts of her still residing in separate decades at once.

Xavier stood frozen. It was as if his tongue was too numb to speak.

"I'm existentially tired. Please, just go," Nell said, insisting.

But he held his hands out to the side, looking as if he couldn't get enough balance to risk moving his feet.

So, she moved first. Standing up—dizzy, groggy—she went to the front door, eyes still mostly closed, pulled on her boots and coat, and walked right out of her house with Argos heeling at her side like a professional canine. If emotions were rendered visible to the human eye, then Nell would have been surrounded in angry coal-burning clouds with jagged strikes of lightning emanating from them.

She tried to break through her own cloud cover into the light as they trundled through the snow towards Waldo's writing studio, a sacred space she hadn't entered since his death. She had never really entered it, except to leave a tray of sandwiches and a thermos of coffee for him when he was away in foreign lands that he created with his fingers and a typewriter.

The field stone chalet in the shape of a triangle stood before them. Standing under the overhang that had protected the threshold from snow, she opened the door (astonished that it was unlocked) and let Argos in before she locked it behind them. She felt her clouds disperse in the presence of Waldo's world.

Once up the spiral staircase, she flopped down on the white oak daybed still made up in oatmeal flannel sheets. She imagined Waldo used to lie there to edit drafts or read. Argos leapt up to take his place beside her. She pulled him close. He licked the sweat from her forehead and cheeks, and she wiped crust from the corners of his eyes.

"My faithful boy. I love you so much. You are my best friend in the world," she chanted in her softest voice. He placed his head on her chest until both of their heart rates slowed. She pulled the beige merino wool blanket at the edge of the bed over them, and closed her eyes again, unable to keep from going back.

Waldo looked at his wristwatch in consternation after he pulled the turkey out of the oven. While the turkey stood resting, Nell slid her pie on the hot rack in the oven, turned up the temperature, and set the timer. Waldo dialed the operator and asked for the telephone number for Logan Airport. Nell looked up at him, undid her apron, and straightened a stray fork on a place setting.

"Good afternoon. I'm calling to check on a flight that my son and his wife were on this morning that should have landed several hours ago. It was coming from Baku with a layover in Istanbul. I, uh, must have the … what's that?

"I beg your pardon. Let me get the flight number. Maybe they had a connection in Paris or Frankfurt. Or, maybe there were two flights today from Turkey.

"Oh, the name's Harding. Bradford Harding and Vivienne Berger. Yes, I'll wait."

Waldo looked more flustered than Nell had ever seen him. His once-tall back had started to hunch a few years ago, but now its curve looked pronounced, even covered by his brown tweed coat.

She migrated to the piano bench, listening in, digging circles into the pad of her thumb with the nail of her index finger. Rehearsing the bars of the Rachmaninov excerpt in her mind that she had practiced to play for her parents.

"All of them? Every single one? Are you certain?"

Waldo turned towards the wall, and Nell saw his shoulders heave. The shoulders that had always looked invincible to her.

"Thank you. Arrangements? Right. The phone number is 413.298.1207. Waldo Harding. One daughter. Nell Eleanor Harding."

Waldo's voice was crackling like the fire. The drop of nausea from the cloying pecan pie climbed against gravity up her esophagus as Nell ran to her grandfather.

"Thank you. Thank you," he said.

Ashen, the ridges in his handsome face appearing more pronounced, or as if there were suddenly more of them, Waldo stumbled to place the phone receiver back in its cradle. He brushed a lock of silver hair from his forehead, as if to displace the news a moment longer. He turned to Nell with waves of tears crashing from his ocean-blue eyes that she hadn't seen since Grandma Eleanor died.

"My darling little girl," he said as he stepped back to the sofa, where he sat, patting his thighs, adjusting his brown wool trousers. He drew her down on his lap and put one arm around her back.

"My darling little girl, we have—" Sobs afflicted his vocal cords. He continued, his voice gentle, "We have lost our beloved ones, Dad and Mom." He patted her folded hands with his free hand.

Nell sobbed with him—wordlessly—as he held her, the living remains of his son and his daughter-in-law. She was now the last of his kin.

They walked as if in a trance to the door, and headed for the woods together—walking it off, moving it out, giving it to the earth—forgetting all about the pecan pie that would blacken in the oven, leaving a burnt aroma that would haunt them for days.

A faint rumble in Nell's ear called her back. Yawning, she felt Argos's stomach under her head, vibrating in a low roar. She had no idea how long they had been sitting there. They stretched together, and he yawned, endearingly, releasing an "Eeeehhhhowah." He padded down the stairs first, by the light of the moon coming through the triangular window. They followed their morning tracks home through the snow by the light of the waxing full moon.

The outside lantern shone for them as they approached the house. Xavier must have turned it on for them. He had closed the door, too. Flinging her coat on the floor by her snow boots, she saw that he had turned the lights on over the island for them. He had locked the sliding glass door, too, and wiped the traces of his snowy boots from the floor.

Perhaps she should have told him about her parents, she thought. Everything seemed to come to a head during full moon week. *Only look what happened last month,* she thought. *I have nothing else to throw in the falls. My memories would bounce off the water back to me if I tried to cast them in.*

There would be no dinner that night. When she was sad, Nell fed off from the pangs of her hunger. Her hunger echoed the emptiness of her heart, and she gave in to it, just this once, for the first time in years. She set Argos's bowl down and waited for him to finish before she took heavy steps upstairs to peel off the leggings that were wet to her thighs. She turned the bath on, and dumped Epsom salts laced with Siberian fir oil into it. Argos curled up on the bath mat she set out as she wound her hair in a bun, lit a candle, put on the cello suites, and lowered herself into the womb-like bath. The pine's scent brought her a trace of the night forest outside.

She glanced out the window into the opaque shades of charcoal, muted white, and black. Closing her eyes, she felt as if she could become one with the stars. She wished that she and Argos could morph from their physical bodies into a constellation.

Chapter Fourteen

Nell woke to the old heaviness that sapped her. Argos was sitting on the floor by the bedside with his paw on the pillow next to her face, urging "Fight for your light." But it was as if her pilot light had gone out.

Nell could hear Waldo singing to her on those early mornings after the tragedy. *"Wake up, rise up, like blueberry muffins in the oven."* Although the pain from losing his only child numbed him, Waldo bolstered Nell, for he knew that she had always basked in his steadiness. If he was an oak, she was his sapling, drawing strength from his nearness.

Waldo would make her favorite blueberry pancakes with Vermont maple syrup, and let her have coffee, something her mother would never have allowed ("Nell's little heart," she'd have protested). After breakfast, he would pack ham and cheddar cheese sandwiches, apples picked from their own trees, and flasks of water into the rucksack. When she'd loiter on the kitchen floor with unlaced hiking boots on but no further will to get up, he'd prod her. She could still hear the way he would sing to her: *"Move it out. We have got to move it out."* He would hold out his strong hand and pull her up. It was as if she were being whisked into the air, like a leaf in the wind. They'd walk together to the car, he'd belt her in and they'd drive to Goose Pond Reservation. She stared out the window. Even now, much older than she was then, she remembered how heavy with sorrow she felt, how listless and not like a child, but like an aged old woman. One particular hike stood out as the most poignant of all.

Waldo led while she trailed behind him up the mountain. She took in the emerald velvet decorating the rocks, the sage lichen growing on the birches, and the peeling paper of the birch trees themselves. The rust-colored leaves underfoot contrasted with the variegated greens, and in spite of herself, Nell found them sublime.

She rubbed her sweat-dampened hands against the cool papery birches, and paused to brush her cheek against a birch branch that jutted out into the trail. When Waldo stopped for water, they didn't speak. They were both listening to the forest. She hugged one of the birches and cried with her cheek pressed against it.

"You're safe here. Give us your sorrow," Nell thought she heard the trees whisper to her. She would form a lifelong bond with them that day, one that led her to speak directly to them from then on. Snow hadn't fallen, but the sodden leaves underfoot matched the heaviness in her heart, which she kept giving to the forest as they hiked higher and higher.

Waldo had told her to keep bringing in the light every day, that it would help vanquish the darkness, so she made little lists of things she was grateful for.

Nell was grateful that the weight of the leaves matched the weight of her heart, like a sort of solidarity that she couldn't explain out loud, not even to Waldo.

Lichen. Moss. Birches. This bosky trail and its forest songs. And then the grandfather in front of her, moving surefooted, guiding her with his might and kindness.

But she would never see Maman's hands again, grasping a pen as she wrote out lectures. Her mother had had alabaster skin that never seemed to wrinkle.

Dad would never read to her again in his baritone reading voice. Its infinite intonations matched the characters he embodied for Nell, as he recounted narratives from their adventures. She would lean against his chest, nestle against a cashmere sweater, and peer at the book he held with the arm that was wrapped around her. How warm she felt there, how safe in that crook, with the shared book in front of them. "Weren't you very afraid, Papa?" she'd whisper when his narrative frightened her.

"Enthusiasm and trust in human nature are good antidotes against fear, little one. Blood is a common denominator. We all have blood coursing through our veins and there's no reason to fear anyone," he would

say. He put the book down and looked over at her with his eyes that held cosmopolitan wisdom. His broad face looked solid, as if she could always count on it being there.

Her parents were cultural anthropologists. Their primary research took them to Baku. They'd been working deep into the Caucasus Mountains, where they had just been hiking in Azerbaijan with shamans. But she would never learn more about the languages, customs, or shamanic rituals of that land they had described as a 'continent unto itself,' for there would be no traces to share this time. No images. No stories.

And they had been eager to share the world with Nell. "We can make the globe your classroom. You can learn the language and play with local children," they would offer, united in their child-rearing philosophy.

"We could create a cultural exchange for toddlers, Bradford," her mother had said. "Start them early on in becoming little world citizens."

Their daughter was a little girl who flourished in the soil close to home, though. They never showed their disappointment to her, and they tried to travel less, writing articles and giving lectures at universities. Being tethered gnawed at both of their souls and intellects, but Nell couldn't sleep, couldn't eat, couldn't thrive when they had tried taking her with them. They chose Nell over the world and their hunger to understand it and share that understanding with others.

When she was older, Nell missed them when they resumed their field work. But she also noticed how happy they were upon their returns, as if they had come to life again.

Besides, she had her own rhythms with her grandfather, to the extent that she couldn't remember how long their fateful final trip had lasted, whether three weeks or four.

When they died mid-air on the way back to Boston via Istanbul, Nell was waiting for them to make their photographs dance into life as they told their stories. She knew that Maman would open her magical camera bag after Thanksgiving, the quilted one that held her ancient Leica. She would disappear into her darkroom and emerge with fantastical prints. They would sit with the dried images and worlds would manifest.

"The son of the shaman was skeptical about the camera, but then I let him hold it, look through the lens. 'You can create a picture,' I said," Nell recollected her mother saying the last time she'd come home. Maman laughed and threw her caramel hair back over her shoulder. "These next photos were taken by the shaman's son. His name was literally translated as 'son of the shaman,' and look what an artistic perspective he had. I wish I could send them to him," Maman exclaimed. Nell shared her delight and giggled, clapping her hands.

Since Nell was ten, she had published a few stories about little-known cultures around the world in a popular children's literary magazine—put into her own words from a child's perspective. After they told her bedtime stories that only cultural anthropologists could tell, Nell would close her eyes and imagine stories of her own, albeit with the same characters and settings that her parents described.

But Nell would stop writing after they died.

Years later, she would even take Maman's camera to Paris, hoping to see the world as innovatively as the son of the shaman had, but she had never even developed the rolls of film she had taken of details that entranced her.

She had wanted to look up Maman's family when she was in France, but Waldo counseled her against it. He explained that her mother, Vivienne, had come to the U.S. with origins that were not to be unearthed. Maman had fallen into their family like the stork had dropped off an adult for them, Dad had always said. Privacy had long informed her life's borders.

Waldo cleared his throat and Nell came back from her reverie. She saw a fallen tree that had once been splendid in its girth and height. Beauty and death, such is the cycle of life, just like with Maman and Dad. She took solace in the sight of new saplings that had sprung up along the trail.

Enthralled, she followed behind Waldo until the light grew brighter. They reached a rocky clearing. Waldo didn't stop until they had achieved the pinnacle, where a small rock cairn stood. He looked lighter. Not as old as he had that morning. Nell wondered if she looked altered, too. Waldo opened the rucksack and handed Nell a thermos. To her surprise, it was full of hot chocolate. She sat on the damp rock and stared at the valley below in the direction that Waldo was looking.

Then she saw it: their home. As if they were in a wordless dialogue with the mountain every day, exchanging glances, they now saw what it was like for the mountain to look upon them. In the distance, the house with beams and field stone rock looked diminutive.

Humbled, she sat and chewed on the ham and cheddar sandwich on toasted pumpernickel bread with wholegrain mustard that Waldo had wrapped in foil paper in an insulated pack, so it would stay warm for her. It tasted like love. They didn't speak and Waldo didn't sit to eat. Nell leaned her head against his standing knee and sighed. Something in her had lightened on this hike.

From then on, they went hiking every day. "Nell's therapy," she heard Waldo say to one of his friends on the phone. "Big believer in moving it out." "Moving it out," she would learn later in Latin class, was etymologically inherent in the word 'emotion.'

The etymology of the word derives from the French émouvoir—to act upon the sensibility of something; to be touched—and the Latin emovere, *meaning to move. They would move their emotion out. The word's origins gave them a map for navigating their grief.*

Nell pulled herself out of 1994 and got up out of bed. Sitting on the edge, legs dangling down, she hung her head, staring at the floor. Her body felt like it had back then: old, heavy. She heaved her legs down onto the cool wood. Argos watched nearby, supervising her progress. She stood.

Nell drew upon their old map that day when the striated emotions of grief were more present than they had been in years.

It seemed important to use Waldo's old rucksack. She filled it with a Mylar blanket in case of an emergency, a whistle—although no one would be out hiking after a snowstorm—a first-aid kit, headlamp, and an extra bottle of water.

Grief killed her hunger, but Nell overrode it, adding apples, almonds, and salmon jerky in the front pocket. She filled Argos's new saddlebag for hiking with a baggie of dried chicken, a collapsible bowl, and a liter of water. Nell labored to lace her boots before they set off to retrace her steps with Waldo from long ago on Goose Pond Mountain.

* * *

The sky was dark periwinkle by the time she and Argos returned. Amelia was standing on the snow-covered stone steps with what looked like a crockpot in her hands. She set it on the top step and walked down the steps towards Nell.

"Nellcita! Mi amor! Arrrrgos!" she called, lilting the "r" as if she were speaking Spanish. "I wanted to check on you yesterday after the snowstorm, but after Fernando plowed, he said there was a truck in the driveway. I didn't want to bother you if you had company."

Argos ran ahead wagging his tail to greet her, and Nell quickened her step in spite of her weary feet that begged to be released from her hiking boots. Amelia's face widened into a smile that filled the yard. A loose bun gathered gray strands at the nape of her neck and she was wearing a down coat that covered most of her floral dress.

"Amelia! It's so good to see you," Nell said. "Please thank Fernando for plowing me out."

Amelia hugged Nell to her, and Nell felt enveloped by her soft strength. Picante spices lingered in Amelia's hair as if she had just been cooking.

"How are you, my dear girl? I made you black bean chili. Just plug it in, but it's already warmed up for you."

"You spoil me. We've been out hiking all day. You can't imagine how timely your dinner is. I'm starving, especially for food made with love," Nell said.

"I would do anything for Waldo's baby girl. Fernando and I wanted to give you some space since you sent the note about getting rid of the cell phone and needing privacy."

"Not privacy from you, Amelia. You and Fernando are family."

"It's an evil blessing, but I can't seem to live without my phone for five minutes," Amelia said, turning her palms up in surrender.

"Ha! Are we all squared up?"

"Yes. Mr. Holtzman sends me a check every month. I've been meaning to tell you we're going to spend Christmas back home in Argentina. Is that OK?"

"Of course. I'm happy that you two will be going to Patagonia. You must miss those awe-inspiring mountains. I'll be fine here," Nell said, reassuring her.

"You're not traveling? We worry about you all alone here."

"I'm good here. This is where I belong, in these woods." Nell stood up taller, like she was the embodiment of the trees she had passed on the hiking trails. Next to her, Argos whined for dinner.

She could see the other woman hesitate as if there was something she needed to say. "Nellcita," Amelia said, "I worry that you don't talk about it. That you don't talk to Fernando."

Nell shifted her weight to the foot that throbbed less. As she did so, she noticed that, for the first time, she had the resilience to hear Amelia's message. It wasn't the first time Amelia had brought it up. She nodded, meeting Amelia's steady eyes.

"Please think about this, dear. If you ever want to make a pilgrimage to Patagón to retrace the steps your grandfather took in Torres del Paine, let us know. Fernando has mentioned it several times. He would be your guide over the treacherous passes." Amelia raised her arm high as if to trace the steep mountains in the air. Nell kept nodding, attentive, respectful.

"He just says to tell you, don't wait too long. The climate is changing, the glaciers are melting, and he wants to share their icy spires with you. Besides, he's getting old." She laughed and patted Nell's arm.

"Maybe I'll take him up on that," Nell could only whisper, as if the poignancy of Amelia's message had coated her vocal cords.

"That's the spirit, my dear girl. Patagón is a healing place. You'll see. Adiós, Nellcita, Arrrgos!" Amelia drew out the "r," again, as if she had rendered Argos a Patagonian dog.

Nell turned inside with the crockpot. It was warm against her chest. She felt better, both stronger and lighter than she had this morning. *Have I moved it out of my body, my spirit?* She set the chili down on the foyer table, and plunked down to liberate her feet. As she massaged her damp soles, she thought about Amelia's offer. It sounded wise and generous, too.

She suddenly wondered if she was stunting herself. "Am I on the right path?" she asked Argos, who licked the dried sweat from her forehead in response. But the allure of chili overrode her intuition and drove her to the kitchen.

When Nell had stabilized, Waldo had taken to the mountains with his grief. He hiked it off in Patagonia when he was well into his seventies, claiming that he was as spry as ever, thanks to his daily hikes in New England. Nell had asked him not to go, pleading: "I can't lose you, too, Gramp," but he proceeded to grieve in the best way he knew. Her mother's best friend from college had stayed with her while he was gone. Nell could barely remember those days spent with Delphine, but she did remember the way she ran to her grandfather the day he came back. Sinewy and sunburnt from the wilds of the Andes, his vivacity burned as strongly as it ever had.

With a quiet fire set in the hearth, a bowl of black bean chili in her lap, and a bowl of bone broth and beef set on the floor for Argos, Nell felt like herself again. The mountains had absorbed Nell's grief once again that day, and she had found solace in the visit from Amelia, who always seemed to intuit when Nell needed her the most. The memory of Waldo's voice still tended to her as an echo of his healing force. Feeling Argos's eyes on her after they finished their meals, she looked up and met them. He was panting contentedly, looking at her with love. *Argos is my guardian angel sent by Waldo,* Nell thought.

"I have a lot of guardian angels, it seems," she said to her dog.

He looked as if he were laughing with knowledge she wasn't privy to. Knowledge she had yet to gain about herself. She wandered out to the deck to consult with the night sky. Argos followed her, and, for the first time in his life, he raised his head and let out an elegant homage to the swelling moon that shone low in the sky before them. It was so civilized-sounding that it could hardly be called a howl. Nell gasped at his budding wildness, at his own transformation.

"Hello, moon, am I charting your cycles with my momentous experiences falling on your fullest days? Am I in sync with your rhythms that are as old as this planet is?"

Argos was now lying on her feet, warming them with his resting head.

"I posit that psychological healing is the third stage of my lunar journey," she spoke to the moon as if it were her sage counsel. A surge of thoughts followed, and she hurried upstairs to her journal.

Chapter Fifteen

When Nell woke the next day, before she even opened her eyes, she could feel the vibrational hum in her heart, as if she had been reignited. She unwound from the bed to wrap her arms around a relieved-looking Argos. He brought her a ball to remind her they could play again.

After breakfast, Nell cross-country skied through the trails in a loop a few times while Argos bounded on and off the trail, moving out his own worries. When Nell glided through the hidden passages between the snow-laden conifers, she felt like she was in nature's private space. The dark-green trees made an outdoor hallway for her.

When she coasted into the clearing in the field, it was like she entered nature's public gallery. There, the deciduous trees lining the edge of the field were naked without their leaves. She could hear the Housatonic rippling in the background. The snow was already melting, slipping into the river and raising it higher. As they passed the hidden trail to the clearing Argos had showed her, he raced up it—as if to pay his respects to those Nell had lost—before retracing his steps to rejoin her on their way home. Nell still felt shy about going there, as if it remained Waldo's private sanctuary. The earth was calling her back to life, though, and she felt its aliveness tingling in her fingers.

Breathless from the ascent to the cabin using the herringbone technique on her skis, Nell made Argos's breakfast and poured a glass of cold water. Pulling a blank postcard from her bag, she sat on a stool at the island and started writing.

Dear Mrs. Hadley,

I think of you often, and I hope the Ephesus exhibit has been a resounding cultural success at the library.

Here, my solitary walks in nature have brought me to the precipice of my subconscious. I'm learning to soften my metaphoric integument, as I continue to seek my place in the world. Now there's a word I would only utter with you! Otherwise, Argos and I are thriving off the digital grid, and we have made friends. If you would like to write, my post office box in Stockbridge is 143.

Fondly,

Nell

With a satisfied sigh at the joy of reaching out to Mrs. Hadley, Nell stood. Giving Argos the job of guarding the house, Nell grabbed her messenger bag filled with library books and headed into town. She had largely phased out the 'Questions I want to ask the internet' sessions that she'd come up with as a compromise when she first gave up her phone. She limited herself to the most important questions she had. Now, unless it was too contemporary to find on the written page, she favored hard-copy research in the volumes and journals that the library housed. The older librarians found this amusing. The younger ones thought Nell was pedantic, like she was forcing a point, but they didn't say anything, knowing that Nell was one of their kind. She sensed all of this, yet felt as if she had matured beyond caring about other people's judgments. Like Willa's, she thought. She smiled with sympathy at Willa's exasperation with Nell's reluctance to digitize the rare book collection's holdings. Then she noted that she could think of Willa without apprehension now. She just wished Willa well. Nell parked and peered out.

Ignoring the cold, the old-timers sat outside in front of the coffee shop in their coats and wool caps, holding thermoses and mugs in their hands. She recognized most of them, but saw a few she had never met before. Maybe Mr. Butterfield would introduce her.

She stood on the street vacillating. The sky overhead was a metallic-gray.

It hadn't occurred to her that she might run into Xavier, but now that prospect dulled her legs and prevented them from moving, as she blinked from dread to hope and back to dread at the thought of seeing him. She looked for Xavier's silhouette in the coffee shop, but didn't see it (thank goodness). The old men continued talking, a background hum.

Then she heard it.

"I hate those Arabs. They need to go back home where they belong," a stranger said.

Nell's mouth fell open. She turned to see who had said it. He was wearing a baseball cap embroidered with the words: "TAKE BACK VERMONT." She had never seen the man before. The others seated out front looked uncomfortable, but the man went on, emboldened by their silence.

"It's one thing for them to be terrorists in the Middle East, but when they think they can come over here and spread their seed, that's another thing altogether and I won't stand for it," he said. Nell's chest constricted.

She pretended that she needed to rummage for something in her messenger bag, so she started pulling books out of it, while standing on the side. She knew exactly what Take Back Vermont was. It had emerged around 2000 as a protest against the state's legalization of civil unions between all genders. Signs with the three-word slogan had cropped up across the state on lawns and on the sides of barns. Her grandfather had been critical of the movement from the start. She could only imagine what he would say if he were here now. Nell looked up at the men. The conversation had lapsed.

Mr. Butterfield waved at her, gesturing for her to come over.

"Nell, this is my cousin from up north in Vermont," Harold Winterbourne said. Mr. Winterbourne had been a close friend of Waldo's, too. She knew they had shared the same values, that he was not like his cousin. She then realized that she could refer to him as Harold now that she was no longer a child.

"I thought Vermont was liberal," Nell said.

"You mean those folks that came up from the cities to be hippies in the '60s, not the old-timers in the back woods, like me," the cousin said.

"I see," Nell said.

"Nell, what do you think about the Iranians moving here?" Mr. Miller asked. He was an acquaintance of Waldo's, a banker who he had characterized as a fair man. She had never seen him in anything but a suit before, but he wore his retirement as casually as he did his faded fleece jacket.

Nell didn't pause, even though she didn't know any Iranians that had moved to Stockbridge. "Many of our families here in Stockbridge have descendants that came over on the Mayflower, but that doesn't make us Americans any more than anyone else. We're all immigrants around this table," she said, "not that that matters. But we tread on what was Indigenous peoples' territory once, don't forget."

She waited for the stranger's hosts—the old-timers from the Shires—to echo her, but continued when they didn't.

"If we can't be compassionate about someone else's circumstances that led them here, then we've lost our empathy. That's not the kind of country that I want to be a passport-carrying member of," Nell said.

"You're pretty audacious for a girl, aren't you?" Take Back Vermont said.

"Don't worry about whether I'm a girl. What counts is whether I respect my fellow animals and humans, and whether I'm a steward of the land."

"That's what I think, too," Mr. Butterfield said slowly. Some others piped up with: "I, too," and "Same here."

Nell looked up and saw a few people had paused on their way to get coffee to listen.

"I'm not the only one that thinks like this, you know. I'm not a lunatic. Not the only one that hates having a Black president," Take Back Vermont said, stubborn. He had crossed his plaid-clad arms and rested them on the tight paunch that met his upper rib cage.

He had a lot of gall to spread hatred like this, Nell thought. She prepared to raise her voice and then thought to lower it. She could nearly hear Waldo say gently in her inner ear, *"Cream always rises to the top. Speak with dignity. Maintain your moral integrity."*

"We all have blood coursing through our veins. That's our common denominator. All the rest is just details," Nell said. She suddenly felt as if she was channeling her dad. That had been his motto as an anthropologist who had made scientific studies on this vital fact; that all beings had more in common than difference. It was as if she had access to the lessons she had learned from him now that the scar tissue of her grief had been reopened.

The elderly men echoed her: "That's right, Nell."

There was no way she could go to the coffee shop now. She hurried to the library. As she did, a horrid thought came to her: *What if one of the people watching had a phone and taped the conversation? What if they posted it?* And she still hadn't figured how the newspaper reporter had found her. *My appearance in the paper after Bash Bish Falls has made me wary,* she reflected.

She pondered what was happening to her. She had chased Xavier away and then offered a soliloquy on her positions. Had she become an angry fringe person, the lunatic that she'd overheard someone calling her the day she threw her phone into Bash Bish Falls?

And that man, where had his hatred come from? Was this happening through the entire country in a swath of evil? Nell had tuned out the news because she didn't want to be force-fed from the media, force-fed a diet of angst for the world. She had never been so proud of a president as she was of the current one, though. He was an orator, an articulate man who spoke with substance, wisdom, and equanimity. Take Back Vermont's unfiltered violence shocked her.

And thoughts about herself were spilling over her mind's surface, too. It was time to find her own peace with the world, she thought. That was why she had returned home. She kicked her boot toes into the top step to brush off any remaining snow, and turned into an autodidactic armed with a library card.

Blinking her eyes as a greeting to the librarian on duty, she felt more at ease on her own turf. She went over to the nature section first, knowing just where to look on the Dewey decimal system. She found volumes on the subjects that interested her that week: animal tracks of New England, and Torres Del Paine, Patagonia.

Inchoate thoughts were trying to form, about how she had sheltered herself in libraries, retreated from being an active creator by cataloguing other's work. With a small stack in her arms, she climbed the spiral staircase to the main floor to check out.

An elegant woman with glossy dark hair caught Nell's attention. The vibrancy of her hair contrasted with the library's staid atmosphere. She was dressed in an emerald and cream brocade coat over dark jeans. She stood at the reception desk, setting a stack of books on the counter. Guides to studying for the SATs featured prominently in her stack. When the woman handed her card to the librarian, the librarian scanned it and said, a little loudly:

"Melika Parsa? Welcome to the Stockbridge Library. I see this is the first time you're using your new card."

Why does everyone blurt out names and betray privacy? Is that necessary? The innocuous gesture irked Nell, and then she realized that Parsa was a Persian name. She'd had an esteemed professor with that surname.

"It's very nice to meet you," the woman replied to the librarian.

"Hello," Nell said from the side. "Are you new in town? Welcome to Stockbridge, if so. I'm Nell."

The woman turned towards Nell, and smiled broadly, revealing one of the kindest faces Nell had ever seen. Her green eyes matched the Stockbridge pines.

"Who's studying for the SAT?" Nell asked.

"My son, Reza. His new school in Great Barrington told us he is very behind if he wants to attend college next year. And the SAT class at the library is full," the woman said, putting her hand in front of her face and closing her eyes, fleetingly. Nell had been looking for a way in, a way to be a contributing member of the community. Isolation was not the path forward.

"Melika, I have a graduate degree, and I could tutor your son. As a volunteer, not to get paid. I do know how to crack the SAT, and

I have some free time right now," Nell said, surprised to hear herself making this offer. She hoped not to sound awkward or intrusive.

The woman grasped Nell's hand. "Are you sure? We could try. My husband Cyrus and I are not equipped here with the tools we need, without the network we had in Isfahan. Beginning again at our ages is a humbling experience. I accept your help, Nell, at least to meet our son and see if you work well together," she said. They jotted their numbers on a sheet from Nell's notebook that she tore in half.

When her new acquaintance departed, Nell set her books on the counter.

"I need one more book. Where is your SAT section?" Nell asked. Unable to close her heavy messenger bag, the strap digging into her shoulder, her arms full of books on Iran in her arms that she had checked out on a final caprice, she returned home to Argos, grateful to have a purpose once again. *I've emerged from my sheltered life at the library. It oddly feels like I was hiding out in the library for years, and I'm stepping into a new life as an adult.* Although she couldn't chart where this new direction was taking her, it felt like it was coming at the right mile marker on her inner journey.

* * *

The following day Nell made lesson plans, assessment tests, and she researched Iranian customs so that she wouldn't make any grave faux pas at the Parsas' home. Melika hadn't been wearing a headscarf, or lengthy clothes covering her knees, so Nell surmised that the family was liberal—at least outside of the confines of the religious police's strict mandates in Iran. She memorized simple phrases to introduce herself in Farsi. A hum started to sound in her chest, a sign that she was enthused about the prospect of both helping and learning something new.

Nell remembered that she hadn't checked her post office box for days. Taking a break from her reading, she decided to walk into town with Argos since the snow was melting. Argos was relieved to be included; he didn't like it when Nell left him home to run errands. They were meant to be a pack.

When she scuffed her boots at the post office and left Argos sitting outside, she caught sight of Jack helping a customer. He looked like he was settling in well. She went to her box and retrieved the small stack of letters that had accumulated there. There was another postcard from Blake. A pang of guilt thumped her chest as she realized that she hadn't responded to his first card, apart from the letter she had written during the time when she had lost track of the calendar. Yet she had been the one to ask for an epistolary friendship. As she turned to walk out, she saw Xavier striding to the door. Argos had already spotted him and chose to greet him as a friend.

Should she look down and pretend she hadn't seen him? But they had never played games before. He didn't look like he had shaved or changed his clothes since she last saw him. He already knew that she was inside, for Argos didn't loiter at the post office by himself. She watched as he ran his fingers through his hair, lingering outside the door.

She put Blake's postcard and the rest of the mail in the pocket of her winter coat, saving it for later, and walked out.

"Nell," Xavier said.

She couldn't help but look down at his hand that held a bulky envelope in cream card stock addressed to her, with a return address that simply read, "The Apologetic Idiot." He paused by the royal blue post box.

"I didn't want to pester you, so I was going to mail this letter," he said.

She looked into his eyes, not unkindly, and said on a whim: "Why don't you post it, and then I'll write back to you once I receive it."

Xavier dropped the letter in the slot, as if it was the logical solution.

He turned to walk away without a word, as if to avoid adding an imperfectly spoken word to the perfectly constructed letter he had written.

Nell thought about pulling on the handle of the blue box just to see if the letter hadn't quite fallen in. She thought about asking Jack to open the box so she could retrieve the letter.

Xavier's presence had amplified the sound of her heartbeat. Nell thought of nothing but the contents of Xavier's letter the whole way home, and she scolded herself for not having accepted it in person. *Why am I so stilted? Why can't I improvise better in the present moment?* Now she would have to wait until tomorrow to read it.

The weather had failed to recover its late autumn pattern, with the sun heating the air to sixty degrees that afternoon—according to the sign on the bank downtown. The early snowstorm was more characteristic than the weather warming abnormally for the season. Nell paused to tie her winter coat around her waist. Still, her underarms squished as she and Argos kept their brisk pace, moist in the wool ski sweater that should have been appropriate in November after a snowstorm.

Scientists had reported that 2011 was one of the warmest years on record since 1880, she had read in the newspaper at the library. In the 1880s, when the Symbolists, like Xavier's Mallarmé, were writing poetry, they didn't have to fret about rising sea levels and the earth becoming uninhabitable as the thermometer rose inexorably. Mallarmé could write poems about chance, but in the twenty-first century, the earth's fate would be determined by whether humans could stop throwing the dice when it came to protecting their habitat.

Once home, she paused at the stone steps, covered in wet gray slush, and stripped down to her camisole. She threw her sweater and coat inside the door, then turned to look up at the azure sky and said: "We have to take care of you better." She imagined the heat from all the sleek metal devices, from phones to tablets, data servers, and computers exacerbating global warming.

Argos was panting from the sun scorching the black fur coat of his back all the way home. He couldn't discard his ever-present sartorial fur garment and looked up at Nell in misery. Bringing a bowl of water outside for him, Nell took the snow shovel and cleared the stone steps of slush, knowing that they would freeze overnight with the cold front blowing in, creating treachery for them come morning. Argos lay in the slush soup to cool off. She rested on the hammock, panting like Argos from her exertion, wondering if it was time to take it down for the year, or if the earth had more surprises in store.

The sun had disappeared except to cast light on the back of the rising moon. And the air had chilled again. After dinner, Nell took a thermos of mulled cider outside to contemplate. Zipped up in the winter coat Waldo had given her for Christmas one year, she felt like she was wearing the duvet from her bed. Leaving Argos inside in case the coyotes were roaming, she lay down on the hammock and sought answers from the night sky. What if she were to accept Blake's invitation to meet him under the Eiffel Tower in Paris? Or his second invitation to celebrate Thanksgiving together in Paris like they had in their youth?

The postcard she had received that afternoon modulated slightly from the imperative to one with a question mark: "Come to Paris for Thanksgiving?"

With the interrogative, she felt less like she was being summoned, and more like she had a choice. How would she cast her dice?

"Awwwhroooooooooo." One coyote's voice was joined by what sounded like two or three others. It rose in a not-too-distant chorus of variations with elongated syllables of "ah" and "ooh" with "r's" sounding out in a minor key. It sounded far more natural to her than the New York sirens had, and now she could see minute details in the night sky, too.

She stared at the seven stars in the Pleiades constellation as if the seven sisters for which it was named, the seven daughters of Atlas, could help her decide. The constellation had always reminded her of the Eiffel Tower's shape, and as she gazed at it, she tried to imagine being in Paris with Blake. Reason cut into her imagination swiftly, leaving her suspended in a plane just above the runway in Paris.

No. It would mean sacrificing herself. Her ideals. It would mean shifting from a long platonic friendship to becoming Mrs.

Blake Davenport. From above, the seven sisters whispered: *Yes, that's what he is seeking*. Her friends in New York had seen it, but she had always introduced him as her best friend. Yet when they met at museum exhibits, when she attended galas as his guest, and when they dined together, everyone from curators to UN officials and waiters assumed they were a couple. Blake rarely corrected them.

Blake was loyal. Blake was kind. *Weren't those tenets in the code of love?* Blake thought he loved her, but she knew that he loved a version of her that he wanted to tweak. It wasn't just that he scoffed at her rejection of the wireless version of Thomas Edison's carbon microphone that nearly everyone from the Amazon's rain forests to Bhutan's mountain monasteries held in their hands. It was also that if they were to marry—a life goal she knew Blake strived for—she would have to dwell in the city with him, reconnect to the cyber world, and leave the forests behind.

She wouldn't be able to hear this intuitive voice that was starting to help her along a healing journey that was heretofore closed off to her, buried under scar tissue. It was such a subtle voice that she wouldn't have known it existed if she had kept clutching the phone between her hands each time it dinged and beeped at her.

The answer was a resounding no.

The forests echoed it. The wind repeated it. And the choir of coyotes howled the refrain.

If he hadn't sent that card, with that wording, then she would have written to tell him that the specters had indeed come out, but that she was looking them straight in the eye for the first time. She would have written that because she was no longer seduced by the world's busyness, by the addictive attraction to her handheld metal device, she could hold the specter's gaze, boldly. And it was allowing her to heal. But she couldn't write those words in light of his imperatives.

She started composing a return message in her mind. She would write it on one of the watercolor cards she had painted of October Mountain at the sun's bedtime, as her mother used to describe it. Blake would never understand that the sun was setting on his romanticized notion of Nell. She would use the imperative, just as he had.

Discarding her thoughts of Blake for a moment, she returned to the stream of her imagination and the journey it was taking her on. Nell envisioned drawing a map to the secret clearing with a bench, and sending it to Xavier with an invitation for him to meet her there at midnight on the full moon. There, she would ask him to forgive her. She didn't know the words yet to the apology, she needed to learn them as these psychological epiphanies kept coming to her.

The wind raced across the back field from tree to tree, sending a bitter cold to the hammock that penetrated through her coat. Choosing her own adventure with the help of the seven sisters, Nell rolled out of the hammock onto the hardened ice-like snow.

Argos had been waiting at the window by the door, paws up on the windowsill peering into the nightscape, waiting for her return. He didn't trust Atlas and his daughters to watch over her like he could. She sensed his discomfort, and patted his head in soothing strokes. With him by her side, Nell walked up to her writing desk and sat down with her pen in the air above the card she had chosen. She edited the message in her mind: "Darling, I am not your Héloise," and rejected it. "Can't. Too romantic," did not suffice either. At last, her pen met the card, spelling out:

Don't wait for me.

Fondly, N.

The following day, Nell mailed the card to Blake and retrieved the envelope from her box. Jack was too quick for her as she tried to slip out.

"To be young and in love again, Nell. You two kids are awfully lucky," he said, chuckling as she waved, mortified. *Lucky until you hurled "Get out" at the young man in question,* she thought on her way back home.

Nell had cleared the snow and ice out of the fire pit to celebrate the full moon with Argos. She filled it with crumpled paper, kindling, and firewood before lighting a few matches. The kindling sparked and gasped before becoming infectious. Nell waited until the flames fed upon one another, and she could see the golden flecks in Argo's eyes before she took the thick envelope from her pocket. There were so many pages. It seemed as if Xavier had been writing his missive since she had last seen him. *What if he bids me farewell, disgusted with my sensitivities, my idiosyncrasies?* she fretted.

My Darling Nell, it read.

I have not slept since that fateful morning. I was not even on a quest for love, I was on a quest for discovering my own truth, yet I surrender to that gift that chance threw at us. And Argos.

Sitting outside our cottage at night with my insomnia, I see the moon rising and I remember the Mallarmé poem, "Apparition," that I was reading at your house that last weekend together: "The moon was saddened. The seraphims were in tears." (Translation mine.)

My rational mind tells me that I asked about your Thanksgiving plans out of love. Yet you had distinct boundaries. They were not nebulous, nor had you neglected to patrol them regularly, ensuring that the fence was erect between what you could divulge, and what you needed to protect.

I do not begin to understand your pain. I do, however, want to acknowledge it as Wittgenstein described in Philosophical Investigations*—which, by the way, I had to look up to understand the reference that you made so passionately.*

I trampled on something fragile that is irreplaceable, and that is the bond between you and me. I wanted to be your family, without even knowing that you no longer had living family members. I didn't need years of courtship to know that. I knew it intuitively, like you know what Argos is saying.

You frightened me with your departure, followed by your startling "Get out." I didn't know there was a tender place where pain lives within you and speaks for you, unkindly at times. But now I do, and I can only promise never to stomp on it again.

That morning at the diner, although I was stunned, I almost laughed at the sight of that old Volvo careening down the snowy street like a race car. Ed frowned at me when he cleared your plate, and I knew that laughter was not warranted. I asked him, "I wonder what's gotten into Nell?" But he shrugged his shoulders, and wouldn't say anything.

You should also know that when Harold Winterbourne came in, I even had the audacity of suggesting that he invite you to Thanksgiving dinner, since I thought you were too obstinate to go home. I'm ashamed of that now, but I want to be transparent, without harboring secrets about my faux pas that day.

Harold and Ed exchanged this stoic frown when I mentioned the Thanksgiving invitation, as if they were deciding what to divulge or not. I think they looked at me like one of the second-home owners, as an outsider. Harold gave me the clue I needed without meaning to, just as he was telling me that in the Berkshires, you protect one another's secrets. He said something like: "If she didn't tell you about Waldo's son Bradford, then I'm not of a mind to. I don't think she would appreciate you meddling." I felt so contrite, and that was all he would say, even though I argued that I was not a neutral bystander, nor an outsider. I said I had come to care about you a great deal. I guess I just want you to know that your Berkshire kin did not betray you. That's when I should have come to my senses, and waited for you to tell me.

If I had been less flustered, I would have remembered to respect your principles. It was like some animalistic impulse reigned over me that day, and I opted for the instantaneous gratification of the internet. Your nemesis, I know.

I nearly tripped on the mums under the snow by the fountain as I typed "Bradford Harding." My thumbs were frigid by the time the obituary loaded. I guess I was as numb as my thumbs, because I would have reminded myself that I didn't merit access to such painstakingly guarded information even if it was available for all to see.

By the time I read the obituary from November 24, 1994, in the Boston newspaper, my great violation was like an ugly epiphany. I felt nothing but shame. I wanted to drive over immediately, but it seemed like the refuge you shared with me just hours earlier was suddenly closed off to me, as if there was a newly erected sign that read:

"Do Not Enter if Your Name is Xavier." I cried for your losses. There were icicles on my eyelashes as I walked back to the car. I kept repeating: How dare I? I had never been so angry with myself.

I went home at first. It was a day that would have enchanted me with snow falling from the pines. But by the time I reached the cottage, I realized I might have lost you forever. I said out loud: "Soulmate." The gate opened and I just sat there in the car with thoughts shouting at me. It made more sense, your aversion to the internet. I respected you even more for pulling it off, and for taking a stand.

I tried writing you a letter that I was going to post—the rough draft of this one—but I couldn't wait for the post, for the chance that you wouldn't check your mail for days. The snow was falling in glops on my windshield from the great pines, and I almost slid off the road on one of those serpentine turns by the Stockbridge Bowl in my haste to get to you.

Then, my dad called, and said he had asked around about your family over the weekend. He said he was sorry for your losses, so the irony is that I would have found out anyway from my dad. Although he might have known about your family tragedy through his involvement with the land organization. I didn't ask him to clarify, and I just felt angry with him, as if he had violated your privacy, too. He asked me to invite you to Thanksgiving, too, and I responded: "Dad, do you have any idea how private Nell is? She is my girlfriend, not your project!" The wintry mix of snow and anger almost blinded me. I didn't realize I had overreacted when he was being kind. Then, as I left your house, I realized I may not be able to say that word about you: Girlfriend.

The only thing that gave me a modicum of solace was the way Argos took care of you that afternoon. I had asked myself on the way over to your house if you could endure what I had stirred up, and if Argos would be enough to console you. This is what he taught me that day:

One should never underestimate a dog's capacious love.

When you ran out, I started to cry, sitting there. I cried for you. I cried for your eternal loss. For the child that was orphaned at 12. I finally walked to the car with the song in my pocket that wouldn't be sung for you that day.

I do not know if there is a future narrative for us, or if the plot ends with this letter that I hope you are holding in your hands, those hands that I wish I were holding, too.

I dare to hope that love has not abandoned us, and I am willing to wait until you are ready. Even if it is a long time. I will miss you with the pain that comes from longing for what one has lost, that is to say, with melancholia.

Xavier

Nell pressed the letter to her chest and stared into the fire as if it would give her answers. Argos leaned into her. They left the fire together, and she looked up at the contours of the mountains that were illuminated by the light of the full moon. They had been there for centuries and knew patience intimately. It sounded like they were whispering: *Wait, wait, you may wait.*

Chapter Sixteen

On Friday, Nell dressed twice. In the morning, she was in Waldo's flannel shirt and her own leggings, romping with Argos and studying SAT strategies. By the afternoon, she dressed to look dignified while being lectured. Her sartorial rejections grew in a small pile on the dresser.

"Argos, you'll have to stay in the bedroom, so bring your bone," she told her dog, which was met with a groan and the sound of paws scratching against the door after she closed it.

The doorbell rang.

When Nell answered it, an impeccably dressed man nearing retirement age stepped through the door, briefcase in hand. She closed the door behind him. He looked every bit the part of the respected family financial advisor.

"Mr. Holtzman, you must have fought off a lot of bears to get here. Bravo," Nell said. She had dressed to match his style in an ivory silk shirt under a tweed jacket.

"I preferred coming to Gramercy Park and staying at that fabulous art hotel next door to you, where we could meet for a civilized Italian dinner, but the sticks will have to do. 'You must go to Nell,' they always stipulated. Come here." He dropped his briefcase, opened his arms, and brought Nell into his chest for a hug.

"You look like you're going to the Gramercy Park Hotel, dressed in a silk tie and suit like that. We wear flannel here," Nell said, jesting.

She ushered him into the living room where a coffee pot and two mugs were waiting for them on the coffee table, along with a plate of currant scones with orange zest she had just taken out of the oven. As they exchanged perfunctory niceties about the drive from

Boston, Nell's stomach tightened. The more polite Mr. Holtzman was, the sterner he was going to be, she knew.

"Nell, I am going to be candid," he said, coffee in hand. "I'm shocked that you left your job at the library in New York. I've asked around, and it's not easy to come by a job like that. The competition is fierce, and graduate schools take more students than they should at these elite institutions. You were lucky." His gray eyes showed his sense of responsibility for Nell.

They had always had a direct rapport, and she opened her mouth to respond in kind. Yet he was not finished with his outpouring: "Just because your parents took out a substantial life insurance policy for you—given the nature of their work—and just because Waldo left you most of his estate, doesn't mean that you should take license to be idle. What I'm trying to say is that no one in your family meant for you to be unemployed or a lady of leisure. These funds and resources, such as Waldo's house, were meant to bolster you, provide you with a measure of stability, not to permit you to check out," he argued.

In response, Nell said, "My family would be just as displeased about the modern state of the world as I am. I heard a child at the local coffee shop say that he doesn't like to play outdoors because there are no electrical outlets there to charge his tablet. A child, Mr. Holtzman.

"My parents would hate the cyber hacking that I suffered, and the trauma that ensued. Waldo would despise internet surveillance and this whole thing about cell phones being tracking devices,"

Mr. Holtzman frowned. "I fail to see the relevance," he said.

"I couldn't keep that life and challenge modern society. My family would be proud of me for going on this quest. I was raised to have a strong work ethic and I don't intend to be indolent. I just want to take some time off to figure out how I want to live," she said, sighing.

Mr. Holtzman exhaled. "Well, I'm relieved to hear that you don't intend to be jobless forever," he said.

"I appreciate your guidance as my advisor in financial matters, and I know that you are the executive of the trust, but my life is an act of protest right now."

"I respect what you're doing. I only want to make sure that you don't throw away your education and your chance of having an established career. That's my duty to Waldo. I promised him that I would look after you as he would have done. Please keep me apprised and posted as you make any new decisions," he said, taking a scone.

"My grandfather used to quote Emerson's (misunderstood, in his opinion) essay 'Self-Reliance,' and I think this line pertains to me right now: 'Man is timid and apologetic; he is no longer upright; he dares not say 'I think,' 'I am,' but quotes some saint or sage.' I want to be upright. And I am simplifying it for you. I seem to be confronting some stage of grief I didn't know I had to go through. And this 'experiment' seems to be taking me on a new path. It's like a delayed rite of passage from childhood into adulthood. I hope that makes sense. I just don't think the library is my future. When I discover a new future, I'll let you know."

Nell worried that she had stepped into territory he wouldn't want to enter with her, and pursed her lips as if to refrain from oversharing.

"When you put it like that, dear, then this is just what you need right now. I support you." And he reached over to pat her arm. "But you do realize that you, too, are quoting a sage."

Nell smiled, grateful, relieved, and then she clarified: "A sage who understood abandoning an old self in the pursuit of becoming." She added: "In the meantime, I think I have been frugal enough to sustain a period without working."

"The interest alone on these accounts will see you through with ease. But it's not about that. Your family wanted you to be a contributing member of society like they were, and I know you will be."

They went over her various accounts and investments.

"No pesticide companies, no giant internet engines, no pharmaceuticals that price gouge. Only ethical investments," she requested. "I can't afford to be a hypocrite. I have to be all-in."

Mr. Holtzman waved his hand to the side. "I know, Nell. You're like the female counterpart to Waldo. We won't make money from the bad guys, don't worry," he said, assuring her.

"What about the philanthropy side? I know we have the scholarships and Waldo's foundation. Do we have room to give more?" Nell inquired. "I want to do my part, especially now during the financial crisis."

"You're a true Harding, Nell. There is another possibility to help. Waldo's foundation is doing some very interesting work. I'm surprised that you never involved yourself as he wanted. I know it was painful when you lost him, but this may be a time to connect with it. Let's research opportunities and schedule another meeting. Actually, that could be part of your 'job' if you ever wanted it," Mr. Holtzman said thoughtfully.

Nell looked as contemplative as he did, and replied, "Just give me a little more time."

When he stood, satisfied that he had imparted his message and heard her counterargument, he said, "You know, I love dogs. You can let him out next time."

"That's very endearing, but you'll have to come wearing wool and fleece, then," she said, teasing.

"I'll do that. Patricia and I could stay and take you out to dinner. It's a holiday today, Veteran's Day, so I'm driving to meet Pat in Cape Cod for the long weekend, but we could make an overnight trip here next time. Talk about boys and all. You know, the Berkshires has quite a history of investment banking, but then you already know that. Goodbye, my dear girl," he said, leaving Nell with another hug.

With all due respect to Mr. Holtzman, who showed a kind openness to Nell's revelations, as if he were more like an uncle to her than a banker, his final tone and content cemented Nell in a space of childlikeness just as she was emerging into womanhood. But then, he hadn't had time to catch up to her growth as this narrator has. He hadn't witnessed the contours of her inner evolution, but he would see its fruition in time.

She walked him to the door and, after descending the steps, he turned to her again, calling: "Don't be an island, Nell!"

Nell closed the door and ran upstairs, unbuttoning her jacket as she went. Argos tumbled out of the bedroom, greeting her as if they had been parted for a week. When she was finally able to stop him from circling her and folding his ears back, they went out.

"No more confinement, Argos. I'm sorry," she said.

Standing out on the deck in bare feet while she watched Argos venture into the woods—a new freedom for him that they had negotiated—Nell thought about how the tedium of modern life was done for the year, with taxes and banking checked off from the list. She remembered to thank her ancestors for the abundance they had bestowed on her.

The night before, she had written a return letter to Xavier that she was eager to post. He had left his mailing address long ago on a sheet of paper by her rotary phone, during one of their dinners, and she had noted that it was among the stately cottages by the Stockbridge Bowl on the border of Stockbridge and Lenox.

On a weekend trip from New York once, a chalkboard sign in the bathroom of a café in the village of Pound Ridge, New York, had arrested her: "Build a longer table, not a taller wall." She imagined a dialogue with Xavier, in which they discussed that notion. Suddenly, she missed him and wished they could build the longer table together. But she needed more time to figure herself out.

When Argos came back, she sat down, armed with a fresh cup of coffee in hand, to read the letter one more time. She was feeling less than sure-footed with her words as she reviewed its content in her mind.

Dear Xavier,

I want to hear your song one day.

Please forgive me. I am not unkind. I am not given to hysteria. There is a tiny piece of me that is still frozen and operates from shock if it gets touched; you touched it without knowing it that morning.

I'm not a writer, at least not yet, but I like what John Greenleaf Whittier, who was also from the Commonwealth of Massachusetts, writes about forgiveness in a poem with that title:

My heart was heavy, for its trust had been

Abused [he goes on to write that visiting the graveyard awakened the following:]

Awed for myself, and pitying my face,
Our common sorrow, like a mighty wave,
Swept all my pride away, and trembling I forgave!

Trembling, I forgive, too. My heart is no longer heavy from the abuse of trust.

(I have been reading his writings on humanitarianism and social responsibility with much interest as of late, and I think they would resonate with you, too.)

Encountering you upon my arrival was surreal, for I've never experienced an immediate affinity like this with anyone outside of my biological family, apart from Argos. It was like a surge of knowing when we first spoke, knowing we could walk together in this life, with empathy for one another's spirits. But when I left Manhattan, when I left Bash Bish, I didn't intend to shift my gaze to another human, to meet "the one" immediately.

I wanted to live according to Thoreau's proclamation: "The most alive is the wildest." What I mean to say is that I needed to go on an inner journey, alone, with nature as my habitat. But I know this isn't the place to land. (And I'm feeling like Thoreau has mythologized solitude, but maybe we can talk about that one day.) I'm on uncharted ground, trying to create my own compass, Xavier.

Perhaps we have to forge our paths alone for some time before we can come back together again? We are two halves of the same eccentric mix, but as much as I acknowledge our rare connection, as if the stars hand-picked us to meet one another, I have healing to do alone before I can come together again.

Something is waking up inside of me now, like a yearning to fulfill a mission, to have a purpose beyond merely being able to read all day and hike with Argos.

I've designated a small section in my notebook to "Things of Import To Be Discussed with Xavier." Sartre is on that list. I posit that you, too, privilege what Sartre might call the authentic self. You did say you were on a quest to be yourself. Free from the pressures of society, I feel that I have escaped going down the road of mauvaise foi, as Sartre called it, or bad faith, but if I am free to make choices, I want to make authentic ones now.

I know our paths will converge again, and we can walk side by side.

Until then, please know that my heart contains unalloyed love for you.

Nell

She read the letter thrice. Then she paced around the kitchen island, before setting down her empty coffee mug to write a small addendum before she sealed the envelope.

P.S. We had created a sanctuary of honesty and love between us, of true intimacy, and I trampled on it. It wasn't symbiotic. You shared about your father and your struggles, whereas I kept my family's tragedy in a vault. Then I barked at you when you reached out with care and love. I didn't know how else to be, and I am humbled by my missteps. Can you forgive me?

She didn't care if there was some repetition. She had to get it right. It seemed there was more to say but she didn't know the words yet.

Popping into the post office to drop off her letter and gather mail, she overheard the lady at the counter say, "Would you be a darling, and fetch my parcel for box 128? I can't be back in New York because I'm gilding the music room in 22-karat gold. I'm here at my cottage roughing it until the artisans finish. Mail's on forward," she said, waving a diamond-clad hand. She was dressed in English riding clothes that looked like they had never been worn before.

"You got it," Jack said, polite.

Nell took a blank postcard out of her bag from a stack she had been using to send Haiku-like notes to friends. They were her creative solution to replace text messages. She wrote swiftly:

Dear Gilded Lady,

Did you know that Mark Twain coined the neologism "gilded age" as an ironic jab at the nouveau riche Americans that gilded everything in an ostentatious display of wealth? People in the Berkshires have a hard enough time keeping their oil tanks filled in the winter, let alone gilding them. Flaunting is verboten here.

Regards,

Your neighbor

Before she could stop herself, she slipped it into box 128, which was open with keys hanging out. Then she opened her own box, and began separating the flyers to be recycled from the letters.

"Gilded Lady!" the woman shrieked, reading Nell's letter.

Mortified, Nell picked up her small pile of mail and made for the door.

"The *nerve*," Nell heard as she ducked out the door.

Dropping down into the driver's seat and throwing the papers onto the floor beside her, she drove off. But such impish confrontations didn't suit Nell's autonomic nervous system. Hands trembling, ears feeling plugged, heart increasing its tempo, Nell's body responded to her mind's churning images, from the lecture on indolence to baring her heart in an intimate letter, from calling out injustice where she saw it to writing unsolicited advice.

Once home, Nell dragged her yoga mat and meditation cushion in front of the sliding glass doors. *Yoga for one, because I'm certainly not ready for group yoga yet at that studio. Too many emotions to process. Alone*, she thought as she prepared. She set the needle down on a record of Indian classical ragas that her parents had brought back from India, lit a white candle and incense, and settled down on her cushion. It was as if her body had craved the meditation cushion and all that it symbolized, for she felt lighter just by grounding her sitz bones.

Nell closed her eyes and inhaled from her root, incrementally yet purposefully. She started with a round of chanting "Om." The ancient vibrational sounds that had grounded many yoginis before her helped Nell find her sacred place of stillness in her body. The tension in her shoulders released upon each exhalation, like invisible waves radiating out. As she inhaled, she imagined breathing light into every area of her body, so that no tension could hide out in the crevices. When the light made her forget her awareness of her physical body, she turned to her next practice.

Nell pressed her sitz bones once more into the cushion and elongated her spine as if she were reaching the sky. She then put her hand up to her face to practice alternate nostril breathing that was known to calm the sun and moon energies in the body. She could hear her yoga teacher, Saraswati, whispering in her ear: "When you breathe in this way, practicing pranayama, you will balance the Ida and Pingala nadis in the body. All of life is a balance of energies between the Sun and the Moon, between the rational and the passionate. That's why we call it Hatha yoga. 'Ha' is the sun and 'Tha' is the moon in Sanskrit. We are creating a sun and moon union in yoga."

Nell gave in to her breath, surrendering her thoughts, until her body and mind stilled and faded out of her consciousness. The pranayama practice transformed her distress, and transported her into the etheric realm of peace. Argos sighed softly in the background, as if he were practicing with her.

She started to move incrementally yet fluidly, as if suspended from time, through a series of asanas she had created for when the world's churning stirred in her body and mind until she reached a storm state. Beginning with Tadasana, or mountain, she stood tall as if she couldn't be toppled. Imagining that her feet were tree roots pressing into the earth and that her arms were summits reaching into the sky, she took the mountain's strength through the sequence.

She was holding her edge in warrior posture, Virabhadrasana, calling up her inner place of resilience with her front thigh parallel to the floor, back leg extended, arms parallel to the floor, taut in all directions with strength when the phone rang. Just when she felt the strongest, she exhaled her body back to standing, fast-forwarding through all the exit cues, and jumped to the phone.

"Why not me?" Blake's voice blurted out from the receiver.

"Please don't be hurt," she whispered, still in her inner warrior.

"It's not because of the guy in the velvet suit you wrote about?"

"You're like my family. That would be incestuous."

"We're not blood relations."

"I love you like a brother."

"I have to go," Blake announced and cut the call.

After the call she felt unsettled. The warrior feeling had dissipated. Going to the window she tried to regain her concentration. She chose her favorite stately pine in the back woods to stare at as she grounded herself on her right leg. Once that root reached into the imaginary soil in her mind's eye, she brought the left leg up and folded it across her pelvis, stowing it there. She raised her branches, or arms, into the air. With a soft gaze, she grounded like the tree until her tucked leg tingled with a sensation that pine needles were needling it. Even her ability to sustain an asana, watch her angst melt with each deepening breath, and release her muscles was unprecedented in her history of practicing yoga. Her tension evaporated, and she could once again hear the quiet voice of wisdom inside her, rather than a loud maelstrom of anxious thoughts.

Time to let the body go. The moon shone through the windows as she lay down for her final asana, and she repeated what Saraswati taught her: *The moon protects, preserves, rejuvenates.* It felt true now, as her lived experience. Dropping into corpse pose, Savasana, she let her body go into the earth and rested deeply, releasing the week's emotional labors. Argos guarded over her, a sentinel.

Chapter Seventeen

Nell chose a long, mocha wool dress with care. Argos hadn't seemed to mind her scuffed hiking boots and flannel shirts, but as she prepared to step off from their island, she wanted to look respectable for this important first encounter as Reza's tutor. On the phone, Melika had told her how enthused Reza was about working with her. *This means as much to me as it does to Reza,* Nell thought.

She set her grandmother's wicker pie basket on the floor of the Volvo. Turning down the drive, Nell recalled that her parents had dreamed of traveling extensively through Iran but there was always too much political volatility for them to travel there. And they had promised Waldo that they would not go to hotbeds. No one wanted to place Nell's future in jeopardy.

As she wound through the woods on Jerusalem Road, she came to a home in the mid-century modern style: rectangular shape, flat roof, sleek steel windows, one story. She knew at once that it had been built as a second home. The Berkshires had been housing wealthy families since the aftermath of the Civil War, when an explosion of economic growth created vast riches that brought the Gilded Age to the Berkshires.

Nell parked next to a sports utility vehicle, which the Parsa family would need, living up on this mountainous dirt road when winter was in residence. Melika was already at the door, wearing slim black jeans and a taupe sweater, hair wound up in a messy bun that made her look like Nell's older sister.

"Welcome, dear!" she called with a hospitable smile.

"Sobh bekheyr," Nell responded.

"The professor has been studying. Please come in." Melika gestured. Nell could see two children peering from behind her.

When Nell reached the threshold, she removed her shoes as a sign of respect in a Persian household; she had been studying her library books. Nell handed the basket to Melika before she bent down to unlace her boots.

"It's an apple pie fróm my family's trees and my grandmother's recipe. She always made one for new neighbors. Welcome to the Berkshires."

She stepped inside to the offing of faint music with harp and unidentifiable string instruments. Silk carpets in rich palettes lay elegantly in the foyer, the kitchen, and the living room that she could see from the entrance. Mid-century modern on the outside, distinctly Persian on the inside, Nell assessed.

Mr. Parsa came forward, shaking Nell's hand, tilting his head to the side with a welcoming smile. Wearing dark gray wool trousers and a dress shirt with a cardigan buttoned up over it, he looked scholarly. Nell wondered if she would find out what their professions had been in Iran. Cognizant of her own fierce need to protect her painful past, she had already decided that she wouldn't ask a single question about their journey here.

"Az Aashnaayitoon khosh'haalam," Nell said, enunciating each syllable.

"You're practicing. Very good. Nice to meet you, too," Mr. Parsa said, nodding with pleasure, continuing: "Not very many Americans have tried to speak Farsi with us. In fact, you are the first."

A young man had been patiently waiting at the side, standing as tall as his father, and several inches taller than Nell.

"And this is why you have come, to meet our dear boy, Reza."

Nell repeated her greeting in Farsi, shook the boy's hand, and looked into his eager dark-brown eyes. This was a boy who was well-loved, she assessed. He was dressed much like his father, but he had his mother's enthusiastic expression, and his manners were elegant for a boy who couldn't be older than sixteen.

"Professor, my mother said you would be able to help. Thank you," Reza said nobly.

"Just Nell, please. I'm eager to get started. Where can we work?" Nell asked.

Nell must have skipped a few critical steps in Iranian introductions, for no move was made.

A radiant young girl came forward, wearing a dark rose dress with matching leggings. Her hair was neatly braided into a plait that fell to the bottom of her back.

"But you haven't met me yet. My name is Mansoureh, but I'm not ready for the SATs yet, they say. I'm only in grade school," she said.

"How could we have left you out. I'm delighted to meet you, too, Mansoureh."

"We'd like to offer you an espresso before you start working with Reza, and a little coffee cake Melika has made. We can sit here in the living room, and then we have cleared a table over there where you can work together." Mr. Parsa pointed at the table.

"Please pardon me. I have the old New England work ethic of getting down to work right away, and I was worried about intruding on your Saturday morning family time," Nell said.

They all laughed at this.

"Nonsense," Melika waved at the air. "We couldn't be happier to have you with us."

Mansoureh took her messenger bag and carried it to their work table.

"You don't have to wear a long dress next time on our account. We're very liberal Iranians from Isfahan. No need," Melika said, to which Nell laughed, pointing at herself as if she had come in costume.

"Do you like espresso?" Mr. Parsa asked, hopeful.

"It's my favorite beverage, Mr. Parsa."

"Then you've come to the right home. We Persians have an art to espresso. " He added: "And it's Cyrus."

"Like Cyrus the Great, the founder of the Achaemenid Empire, the king of the Persian Empire that became the largest empire in the world. You have a lot to live up to," Nell said, joking.

"Our professor has been reading. I'm not nearly as august as Cyrus, but I try to live up to my name and conquer foreign lands." He laughed.

Cyrus turned to make espresso with an elaborate shiny machine that they must have brought with them from Iran. It was far too intricate and grand to have been found in an ordinary department store in the states. Melika starting preparing a tray of coffee cake and plates for them, and Nell noticed how smooth and beautiful they were. The children brought Nell into the living room to sit down and wait with them. There was a sofa that looked used but respectable, and Nell wondered if the house came furnished. These were all questions that she didn't feel it was her place to ask, so she tucked them away and focused on the children.

"Your rugs look like they should be in palaces," Nell exclaimed, transfixed by the turquoise blue silk rug that was spread out under the coffee table, extending under the sofa and to the edge of the room where the massive glass window presided. It had square images of trees and landscapes with expertly woven silk threads in multiple colors. It was one of the most exquisite art objects Nell had ever seen. "How do you dare to walk on them?"

The children shrugged as if it was normal to have such a rug, but Melika came in bearing her tray and winked.

"It was quite a trick to bring them out of Iran. The silk rugs fold up very small, so you can put them in an old plastic bag at the bottom of a backpack. No one would ever think to look in there. They were in Cyrus's family for generations. We couldn't leave Iran without them," she explained.

Cyrus was calling from the kitchen: "Do you want a cappuccino?"

"Yes," Nell said, affirming, willing to break her dairy-free ways to accept his hospitality. She knelt and rubbed the lapis lazuli and turquoise silk rug between her fingers in awe.

Cyrus came in carrying a tray of coffees and two juices for the children.

"Reza already has so much vibrancy. I don't think he needs any caffeine to fuel him yet," Cyrus said.

"We make our espresso very strong in Iran. By the way, you have good taste if you like this rug. This is our most prized one," he said, setting his tray down next to his wife's.

"It's a cardamom and almond coffee cake," Melika explained as she served slices. "Made with almond meal, so it was gluten-free before the trend hit!"

Melika laughed and Nell joined her, knowing exactly what she meant. Melika's élan was so strong that Nell could not imagine her being oppressed under the Ayatollah's regime.

Nell was enchanted. She had stepped into one of the nicest families she had ever encountered in her life. She was a guest; they were her hosts. Yet, they were also her guests in the Berkshires. They each seemed to accept the doubled role of guest and host with humility at receiving what the other could offer, and with joy at giving what the other could not.

Nell learned that their city of Isfahan was the seat of Iranian culture and art. Cyrus was the head of the Department of Art History and Architecture at the university in Isfahan, and Melika had been his graduate student assistant enrolled in a Ph.D. program when they met twenty years ago.

"That's why your English is so excellent, from your academic research?" Nell asked.

Cyrus explained: "We were both avid readers of English and American literature, French literature, too. We had also studied abroad before the Ayatollah curtailed relations with the West. It's a complicated history. We thought it would be important to teach Reza and Mansoureh to speak English, so it's the only language we speak at home with them."

"You could tutor Reza for the SAT yourselves. You don't really need me," Nell said with a laugh, feeling redundant.

"We're very grateful for your help," Cyrus said, and his tone turned serious. "Neither of us had to take such an exam, and the intricacies of it should be explained by someone who took it successfully, as Melika said you had."

Nell hadn't shared her scores with Melika, but Waldo had taken endless practice exams alongside her, as if to provide her with steep competition.

"I had a good tutor myself," Nell said. "My grandfather. Thanks to his tireless work with me, I had nearly perfect scores," she averred.

"I overheard my teacher telling Mom that I'll never get into a good American college unless I can ace these exams. That we would need a very expensive tutor and college consultant. I have been getting very worried about my chances," Reza said, wearing his sentiments on a face that suddenly looked far older.

"Don't worry. Today we'll see where you are, and then we can devise a plan to achieve your goals. If you'll have me, we'll also spend some time getting to know your interests, so that I can think about a series of colleges that might be a good fit for you. There's an American politician that I admire. I have heard him say that 'a fine college education should be available to all regardless of anyone's socio-economic profile,'" Nell said, speaking to reassure Reza along with Cyrus and Melika, who looked like they mirrored their son's concerns. The parents stood up to clear the table.

"The cake was delicious, and that may be the best cappuccino I've ever had. But I thought tea was more popular in the Middle East," Nell said.

"There's a saying in Isfahan, which is famous for its coffee shops: 'Despresso without espresso.' I think it's time to let Nell and Reza get to work, but we hope this is the first day of a long friendship," Cyrus said. There were smiles all around the coffee table, and Reza and Nell moved to their workstation.

Nell administered her short assessment test to Reza, who took longer than she had anticipated, given his facility with the language. He sat up straight—ever respectful—as he worked. She wondered if he had been more meticulous because his teacher was sitting next to him, trying not to look over his shoulder. She decided to correct it with him out loud together as part of their first lesson.

The boy said, "I know what a lot of the words mean, but I don't know how to make the associations they want me to create. Also, the word problems in the math section are phrased as if they are trying to make me slip up. I am confident in my mathematical skills, but it's like a different language. Maybe the language of SAT?"

"That's very witty, Reza. I do think the test has its own language, and frankly, I don't recall ever needing any of its elements after I had taken it. It's like a rite of passage, though."

"Like entering adulthood?"

"That's right. We just have to undergo this test on our journey to attending college here. But we won't let it get the best of us."

They worked through the challenges of mastering the SAT into the early afternoon, until Nell's inner Argos alarm went off. She wrapped up their lengthy lesson with a series of assignments that included Reza timing himself on the reading comprehension passages, so he could increase his speed.

"Won't you stay for lunch?" Melika asked, coming to their table and placing her hand on Nell's shoulder, as if they were already becoming friends. The warmth inherent in Melika's gesture spread to Nell's heart. She missed having a close female friend.

"Thank you, but I have a very special German shepherd named Argos waiting to be fed and walked."

Melika and Cyrus exchanged glances.

"Bring Odysseus's dog with you next time, Nell," Cyrus said. "I had shepherds growing up, and we would love to introduce your dog to the children."

Nell patted her chest in gratitude. "I'm glad there will be a next-time, and I would like that very much. I promise, Argos will not destroy your priceless rugs," she said.

They planned to work together again on Tuesday night after school, and this time they extended a dinner invitation that Nell accepted with delight.

She drove down the road, buzzing from happiness at meeting

new friends and having a new job. She was smashing stereotypes in her mind as she bumped over every pothole. Iran was running rampant with terrorists, the newspapers reported. Iranians were religious fanatics, ready to kill Americans on sight. It was one of the most dangerous places on earth. Or was it all sensationalism? Nell wondered, thinking that she sounded like her parents often had. By the time Nell turned up the drive, the little girl in her that had written stories for children about distant world cultures had woken from a lengthy slumber. And she was awakening into adulthood, with a meaningful purpose and the prospect of having a sophisticated new friend. A friend who was intrinsically free in spite of having been so fettered.

* * *

She felt enlivened by her interactions with the Parsas, and wished she could share her afternoon with Xavier. Nell and Argos both seemed wistful for Xavier's presence, as if they missed their new pack-member-in-training. She thought of calling him, and then reminded herself that the timing wasn't right. Argos had felt her spark on their afternoon hike, too. He had kept nudging her hand to affirm this new change that he approved. Nell honored their old tradition of eating dinner together on the floor. She had crafted it from the box of provisions that had been left on the doorstep when she came home from the Parsas.

Jack had told Nell about a sharing program that a family with an organic farm was offering, and she had signed up. Every week through the winter—and beyond if she chose—she would receive a weekly box of victuals that included greenhouse-grown and foraged vegetables. Jack explained that they were biodynamic farmers who didn't overharvest or overwork the soil. Humanely raised cows were divided among many families, and her weekly portion of the cow was dinner for Argos that night. She found homemade yoghurt and goat cheese in the box, along with a vegetable stew and sourdough bread whose glazed surface still felt warm.

Nell thought their ingenuous idea was the way of the future. *This is what happens when you mindfully choose your own adventure*, Nell thought, raising her glass of freshly pressed apple cider that came from the box, and clinking it against Argos's bowl.

Although Nell had never felt quite so fulfilled as she had working with Reza, as if she could see the practical fruition to come, once she had sat down, she realized that the stimulation and company had tired her. She had become so accustomed to solitude that she had to learn how to be social again. After hiking and dining with Argos, though, she felt recharged.

As revolted as she would be with the following analogy, it was as if by retreating home to Argos, she had plugged herself into the wall like one charged a cell phone battery. Nell flourished on the meaningful company of others. Yet she needed time to be an introvert, or else her inner battery ran down.

Much later, clad in her flannel pajamas, she gathered all of the library books on Iran around her reading chair, eager to learn more. It didn't take a cultural anthropologist to perceive the discrepancies in what she had seen with the vulgar signifiers from the press.

"The entire city of Isfahan has been designated a UNESCO world heritage site for its Islamic art, architecture, and for its significant role in Persian trade routes throughout history," Nell read out loud to Argos. She had already traveled through the page. Nell was there in her mind, visiting the university in Isfahan where she saw a sculpture garden with busts of prominent Persian thinkers and artists. It was interspersed with roses and fountains that gurgled with the echo of Rumi's verses.

She strolled past an elongated reflecting pool leading to a pleasure palace where she ran her hands along its columns. She lay down on the cool mosaic floor to read the frescoes depicting the pleasures of music, poetry, wine, and love. She couldn't imagine anyone ever wishing to leave Isfahan. Her eyes blinked her back when she thought of the political regime that cast shadows over the dreamy aesthetics of the historic city that had once been the capital of Iran.

Nell set the unwieldy art history book down that had cut into her stomach. Her drifting thoughts on the associations between beauty and oppression led her to pick another book from the pile. This one was about the Iranian Revolution of 1979. As she ran her finger down the pages of the index, she thought: *I like the space and time between flipping through books to think about the previous things I have read, rather than typing out one question after another in the search engine, without pausing to think in between.*

The origins of the Revolution interested her the most; that's when the Parsa family's trouble began. Her readings led her further back in the twentieth century, when Iran was a liberal democracy until the Central Intelligence Agency of the United States led a coup d'état against the liberal Prime Minister Mohammed Mosadegh, inspired by British oil interests, and ousted him in 1953. This had set the stage for the Ayatollah to seize power in 1979.

The American empire strikes again, as clandestinely as the data thieves, Nell thought. *And here we are. We hate Iran. We think of Iran as a country run rampant with terrorists, and yet we ousted the democratic prime minister?* Disgusted, Nell closed the book and stood up, startling Argos.

She meandered the backyard with Argos in the dark, tracing the dog's zany trajectory. Xavier took her back to her parents. Yet, so did the Parsas. She suddenly understood why her parents had been so worried about raising a little nationalist, why they expounded on the importance of being a citizen of the world, not of one country. She looked up to ask the stars, but the sky was a murky gray that night. *Perhaps I am a citizen of the world, just not a precocious one*, she mused.

She had disappointed them by being such a homebody, she had always thought, but she liked to be grounded, not scattered across the world losing luggage and being crowded on a plane with strangers. Not for the first time, she thought that her parents would have been happier, or at least prouder, if Blake had been their child. He was the poster child for their platform on global citizenry, with his Peace Corps training and job at the United Nations. Perhaps that's why Nell had been attracted to him as a friend. Perhaps Blake had reminded her of Bradford and Vivienne, and that's why she could never leap from the platonic to the romantic plane with him. These thoughts would not lead Nell to peace.

"Come on, Argie, bedtime," she called out, and started chanting the beginning phrase of her new mantra: *There is peace within me today, even if I am dismayed by the world's injustices. There is peace within me today, even if I may not have been the perfect child. There is peace within me today, for I am grateful to be me.* When she walked upstairs, she sat down on her meditation cushion, and began to exhale the churning. She inhaled the light of peace, and she felt the inequities ebb out of her muscles and out into the ether as she exhaled, before she turned the lights off on it all.

Chapter Eighteen

Nell walked to the hardware store a few days later with a list, intent on shopping locally and supporting the small businesses that had held up Main Street for decades. She was still thinking about her place in the world, and she knew it was at least partly here in her little town with the people she shared history with. She was not a global citizen like her parents, but she was a local with cosmopolitan interests in world history. *Maybe I'm a 'glocal'?* she thought.

"Afternoon," Mr. Butterfield said as he walked out of the hardware store with a cloth bag.

"I've been hoping to run into you, Mr. Butterfield. In fact, I wonder if you would mind if I started calling you by your first name? I'm not ten anymore," she said, laughing.

"Ernest it is. And rightly so."

"I've also been hoping to ask if you heard anything about a reporter nosing around town asking about Waldo or about me? A pesky journalist showed up at the house a while back."

"I don't like that. You know I'm a steel trap, but I'll keep an ear out about it." They both frowned, and Nell nodded.

Ernest continued: "Been meaning to tell you that every single one of us agreed with you the other day about what you said to Harold's cousin."

"Is that so? I was terrified that a pocket of xenophobia had taken root while I was away."

"People like him worry me. There seems to be a whole contingent of people who think like he does. They've been going to rallies. I don't know what the future holds, Nell. Waldo would be out protesting if he could see this. I was proud to elect the president in office today. I thought it was a major milestone. But it seems to have brought out the worst in a lot of people. It's frightening to see what the true sentiments are under the veneer of what they call political correctness today," Ernest said freely.

Nell listened with great interest. She had never heard him give such a long speech before.

Nell confided: "I thought he was the one that sounded like a terrorist with his hatred spewing out. If there really is a contingent of people like him coming out of the woodwork to protest our president with a non-Caucasian surname and a glowing skin color, then we are in real danger of electing a dangerous lunatic next time. I'm worried."

Ernest nodded.

"How did anyone know about the Iranian family moving here, anyway?" Nell asked.

"It must have been someone at the post office who heard them opening up a box in a foreign name. Put two and two together, I guess. I'd kind of like to meet them myself. See if they need anything."

"I *have* met them, and I'm still in awe of their hospitality. It's the funniest thing. I was supposed to be welcoming them to the Berkshires, but they made me feel more welcome than I can remember," Nell said, marveling.

"All these light bulbs in my bag made one go off in my head," Ernest said, and Nell giggled. "Effie and the ladies at the Women's Fellowship could invite them to a welcome dinner. Do you know them well enough to ask?

"I do."

"Let's do it, then," he said.

On her way back to the car, she stopped to pick up her mail and found a note from Mrs. Hadley. Retrieving mail had become more interesting in the past weeks now that she relied solely on epistolary correspondence. Ripping the envelope, she walked and read:

My dear Nell,

I was delighted to receive word from you.

The Ephesus exhibit has met with great success, and has even been extended. Perhaps you could venture back into the city to see it.

Thank you for sharing an abstract account of your inner journey. It sounds like you have employed a heuristic process on this anfractuous path to being true to yourself.

Affectionately,

Mrs. Hadley

Nell hooted as she drove home, tapping the steering wheel with the joy of reconnecting with her old boss, now friend, even though she would have to write and decline the invitation to visit the exhibit. She was in her right place.

* * *

Now that Nell had a purpose, she found herself in a quiet harmony that she hadn't experienced since she was a librarian. Tuesday evening, Nell dressed in jeans and a sweater and brought a glass container of baked acorn squash with dried cranberries and cinnamon to the car. It would be her contribution to the Parsas' dinner. She had almost bought a bottle of Shiraz wine, but held back.

"Who do we have here?" Cyrus asked at the door, coming out to greet Argos, who sat politely for him. Melika relieved Nell of her squash, pausing to pet Argos.

"Nell, you leave Argos with us and go straight in to Reza. He has been working assiduously for you. How is that for a SAT word?" she said, delighted by her own joke.

"And I meet another logophile like me!" Nell clapped her hands and exclaimed with glee before she turned towards Reza.

"Reza, you are a model student," Nell exclaimed when he showed her that he had completed all of her assignments.

"I took another practice test, too, since I finished my homework," he shared, basking in her smile.

"Let's work on speed reading techniques so you can spend more time deciphering the nuances of the reading comprehension portion," Nell said, using her research on SAT strategies to hone in on his needs.

"You mean like this?" he asked when she shared a tip. They practiced on a few passages, and when he finished a section with perfect scores before the timer went off, Nell knew she had a special student before her.

"Let's move on to math," Nell said. Reza had discovered a way to map out the logic in the math word problems, too, and her strategies enhanced his ingenuity. It was as if they were meant to work together. Reza was a fast learner, and based on his work ethic and creativity, Nell knew that nearly any American college would be fortunate to count him as one of their own. She had started to ask questions about whether he liked rural or metropolitan areas so she could get an idea of what schools would be a match.

"Reza, do you have any particular area of interest in mind?" Nell asked.

"Reading is like a family sport," Reza said, "but I don't see myself as a writer or a college professor like Dad. The Persian buildings in Isfahan that Dad loves and teaches about, I would like to ..."

"Like to ..." Nell said, moving her head laterally to coax him into sharing.

"I have this vision."

"Go on."

Encouraged, Reza described his dream. "I think I could build a contemporary version of the Isfahan palaces and mosques with their azure-blue tiles, but secular, non-religious, and just reminiscent of the old grandeur. Sort of like this house is mid-century modern, but we made it Persian with our rugs and tiles," Reza said. His eyes traveled from his hands folded on his lap up to Nell's enraptured ones.

"That's brilliant, Reza. You already know what mid-century modernism is? I don't think I knew that until I was in college," she said.

"It would be half-Persian, half-Philip-Johnson," he explained.

"Where did you learn about him?" Nell asked, fascinated.

"Dad is an architecture professor. I have watched all of his slideshows when he is at home getting his trays ready. From the first time that I saw Le Corbusier and Frank Lloyd Wright, I knew that I wanted to be an architect, fusing Persian and European-American influences," Reza said.

"There's a private high school that's accelerated with college classes very close by. Do you mind if I reach out to them?" Nell asked. The boy's eyes sparkled as he nodded his head. Then she was called to dinner.

"The children have already eaten," Melika said. "I'm going to tuck Mansoureh in, and then we'll have an adult dinner. Reza, you may join later for dessert if you're still up reading." Leaving the room, Mansoureh reached to hug Nell. Argos followed them into the bedroom, smitten with the young girl. Nell had heard Mansoureh talking to him in the kitchen over her dinner.

The dining area had transformed. A satin embroidered tablecloth with gold threads and candlesticks made with matching mosaic tiles covered the table. There was no particular division of labor with the Parsas.

"So much for perceptions on how Iranian men might treat women," Nell teased.

With a warm laugh, Melika said, "We're a bit unique in Iran these days. But back when Mohammed Mosadegh was prime minister, young people were more forward thinking."

"And then the American government treats Iran like a hotbed of terrorists, when they are the ones that ousted the most liberal politician to govern Iran in decades," Nell said.

Melika and Cyrus glanced at one another.

"We had to put duct tape over our mouths in Isfahan, so forgive us if we are skittish when discussing risky topics," Cyrus explained.

"I understand skittish," Nell said softly. "How may I help with dinner?"

"Help? You are helping our son," Melika said with a laugh that sounded like bell tones.

"The two of you work very well together. I have been watching," Cyrus said, offering her a glass. "Would you like a glass of French pinot noir?"

"Thank you, but wine? I thought Iranians didn't drink wine," Nell said, raising the palm of her hand upwards as an inquisitive gesture.

"Only since the Ayatollah's rule. Iran has had prized vineyards since ancient times that he destroyed systematically. It's another great tragedy for our country," Melika explained.

Cyrus said, "In the 1960s, archeologists discovered jars with wine residue in the Zagros mountains that dated back to the Neolithic period seven thousand years ago, making the clay pots the oldest known wine vessels in the world. The Ayatollah destroyed a tradition that was a great source of pride to many Iranians throughout history. We have discovered some fine French and Italian wines in the local wine store that won't break the bank. It's the first time we have had wine in some time."

"To the vine's spirit that can't be killed by tragedy," Nell offered as a toast.

Melika, Cyrus, and Nell looked into each other's eyes. They seemed to recognize familiar traces of sorrow. They pressed their glasses together in solidarity, and drank together.

"À table!" Melika announced, clapping her hands. The table was populated with festive dishes. The cucumbers and tomatoes in the salad were the freshest she had seen in months. The mint leaves looked as if they had just been picked.

"I should be going to your grocery store," Nell said with admiration.

"We'll let you in on our little secret garden. We have a little greenhouse where we have been cultivating plants all fall," Cyrus laughed, passing a dish to Nell.

"I made this for you, Nell, a Persian delicacy: chicken marinated and baked in a pomegranate walnut sauce," he said, watching as Nell tried it.

"It's incomparably delectable." Her eyes widened at the wonderful bitter flavor of the pomegranate. Melika and Cyrus radiated pride.

"But it is so *symbiotic* with Nell's squash," Melika exclaimed.

"And that's one of my favorite words, Melika," Nell felt like they were bonding over sharing words.

Over dinner, Nell learned that their friend, a university professor, had lent them his weekend home in Stockbridge for the year, while he was on sabbatical in France.

"Where are you teaching, Cyrus?" Nell asked. But even that felt like prying because Cyrus's eyebrows squeezed together imperceptibly while Melika answered.

"Cyrus is a visiting distinguished professor at one of the most prestigious colleges in the area, about forty five minutes away by car," she said.

Nell noted the vague reply, having employed similar tactics when discussing subjects that she hadn't wanted to broach.

"You see, we're not undesirable immigrants. We're contributing to cultural capital in America through the partage of ideas," Cyrus said, joking.

Nell squirmed, not finding his sardonic wit as humorous as she would have, had she not overheard the hateful words spoken at the coffee shop.

"Even so," Nell said lightly, "there are misperceptions that blind people like a cultish mythology."

"Our awareness couldn't be more acute, Nell. We've seen the American television broadcast of Iranians chanting 'Death to America.' This world has manufactured much hatred. We're content to take refuge in these beautiful Berkshire hills," Cyrus said in a sober tone. Nell raised her glance and cheered to that.

"It may be hard to conceive, but I'm taking refuge here, too, from the loud world and its minefields," she said. When they acknowledged her as if that was normative behavior for a young woman, she felt encouraged to say, "I've even given up my smartphone and most contact with the internet to avert the cyber spies out there. I take the dangers of digital surveillance and its violations of privacy very seriously.

"But now I'm going beyond that initial action, because it revealed my inner landscape. And there is some gardening to do in there. I'm discovering a deeper set of choices to make about how to live in the world."

Cyrus's head was bobbing so much that she stopped speaking.

"The next time you do get on the pesky internet, look up the Iranian Cyber Army. They hacked into our elections starting a couple of years ago and stole presidential votes. That's when I realized that the next world war would be a cyber one," Cyrus said. He made Nell feel as if she had found people who might finally understand her iconoclastic proclivities.

"You left the internet, Nell, and I am just discovering a gleaming new world that has been largely banned in Iran!" Melika said, laughing, before adding, "But we agree on the point of resisting surveillance."

When their lively dinner discussion led them to Persian architecture, Reza reappeared at the table. "Papa, won't you show Nell some of your slides?" he asked.

With a slice of cardamom rose cake in her hand, Nell sat on the rug in front of the sofa, folding her legs underneath her in meditation pose as she would have done at home, with Argos nestled up next to her.

The slideshow began with images of the seventeenth-century Chehel-Sotoun pleasure palace that gave Nell wistful pangs for Xavier. She missed him because she didn't want to learn something new without him. She wanted to daydream about being at the palace with him.

From the reflecting pool to the innovative water features that cooled the palace in summer—as if there were indoor infinity water falls—it looked quite modern in a sense. Nell recognized some of the frescoes from her books. Their colors rivaled those of the Italian renaissance, and the water mechanism looked like abstract art. She was falling in love with Iran, just as her parents had. Cyrus's passionate lecture reminded her of Dad and Maman; they would have been kindred friends, she thought.

Cyrus became more animated as he clicked on an image.

"This is our treasure, the Sheikh Lotfollah Mosque, or Ladies' Mosque," he said, translating.

The blue mosaic tiles were the work of masters. Nell yearned to trace her fingers over their cool stones and crane her head to see how they rose high, perhaps higher than the Pantheon in Rome, her only point of comparison.

"Awheayaa," Reza yawned involuntarily, concluding the slideshow.

"Please excuse us; this young man must go to bed," Cyrus said.

"Good night, Reza. You deserve every minute of sleep after such excellent work. I'm just going to clear the table," Nell offered.

"Absolutely not," Melika protested.

"Hospitality is also about receiving the guest's offerings, so this is my gift to my hosts," Nell called out confidently, as they left with Reza, shaking their heads at her notions.

Nell rinsed dishes and started to fill the dishwasher, although the Parsas came back before she could finish her task.

"We don't like to talk about politics too much in case the children are eavesdropping. They've had nightmares over the years, like many Iranian children, and we're hoping that they find peace here," Melika explained, gesturing for Nell to join them again at the table.

"Reza was named for my best friend in Isfahan who was an outspoken political protestor. He lost his life fighting against the regime, though he had been a brilliant history professor in the pre-revolutionary period. No one knew more about history or Isfahan than Reza. We take heed from his outspokenness," Cyrus said, sharing.

"Thank you for trusting me. I'm eager to listen to your stories, but it's late and I can see we're all tired," Nell said as she saw the couple swallowing yawns. "Argos and I will bid you good night. Thank you again for the delicious dinner and the rich conversation."

The Parsas hugged Nell as she left with Argos, who had received his own bowl of chicken without the pomegranates and walnuts.

She had forgotten to mention Ernest's invitation, but when Nell brought it up the following Saturday morning after another successful tutoring session with Reza, Cyrus paced a bit in the kitchen holding his coffee, as if he was about to lecture.

"That's just the kind of thing that we like to avoid. I mean, drawing attention to ourselves. If someone from the library wanted me to give a talk on Iranian art and architecture and hosted a small reception afterwards, I would agree, but I don't want to be on view for the town as if I'm some curious specimen to behold."

"Exactly. It's like trampling on the flowers in front of the fence that reads 'Private.' It's a fragile line, and I don't think Ernest Butterfield meant to cross it. I'm sensitive to that, too, Cyrus."

The following day, Nell went to drop off a last bag of Waldo's clothes at the thrift store. She thought of looking for a heavy, winter coat for Reza, too. She had seen him shivering in his wool dress coat while he had taken Argos out on their study break. A motley collection of fall velvet was on display in the front window, adorning the center mannequin. Nell stumbled on the sidewalk seeing Xavier's plum velvet suit. She dropped the bag of clothes at the door, and spun off in the direction of the Great Barrington boutiques instead.

Had another woman encouraged him to shed his persona as a flâneur or had Xavier simply listened to Nell's talk of anti-nostalgia? He hadn't worn the velvet at their last evenings at home. Perhaps he had molted that skin. Nell's intuition—deepening with her time spent in the forest with Argos and on her meditation mat—whispered that it was not yet time to ask him, although she desired to feel his hand caressing hers once again.

She found a coat she liked in one of the shops, and went by the Parsas' to drop it off, even though it wasn't a scheduled lesson day. Reza was stepping off from the yellow school bus when she was standing at the door.

"Nell! We took a practice test for the SAT on the computers at school today, and guess what? ninety seventh percentile popped up on the screen when I finished," he cried out. Reza hinged over at the hips and swooped up, clapping his hands. Nell joined him, jumping up and down.

"My teachers could not believe I'd done so well. They asked me if I had a tutor, and I told them about you. I hope you don't mind," he said, suddenly frowning.

"Congratulations, Reza. We knew that you would ace it. This is impeccable timing, because here is a small gift to celebrate your success. It gets far colder here than your enchanting city of Isfahan does, I believe."

Reza hesitated, then caught up to his manners.

"Thank you, Nell. I did leave my winter coat behind accidentally when we left. But Papa wouldn't want you to think I am a charity project," Reza said.

"Oh, tell him it's a present from your teacher because you're so diligent," she said.

Reza hugged Nell in response. "I better start my calculus homework before Mom brings Mansoureh back from piano," he said.

"I'll see you Saturday morning. Why don't you ask your parents if you have Thanksgiving plans?" Nell said. "Maybe you'll take a weekend trip?"

"Everybody at school is talking about going to see grandparents, but no one asks the émigrés," Reza had a funny tone as if he were trying out sarcasm.

"Who's an émigré?" Nell asked. "You're just Reza, a very smart sixteen-year-old global citizen."

Reza smiled at that.

"Wait, Nell. I have something for you." He dashed inside and came back moments later holding a small cardboard box.

"I saw your face when Dad was showing you slides of the pleasure palace. I want you to have these postcards that I brought from Isfahan," he said as he held the box out to Nell.

"You are so dear. Thank you, Reza," she whispered, her throat caught with emotion. The circle of her parents' cosmopolitan world was folding her into it.

They waved farewell without a word. She wondered if they had come here as true émigrés in the sense of political or social self-exile, but a friendship was being woven, and it took time, as with the weaving of silk rugs.

* * *

Thoughts of Thanksgiving haunted her again. Nell donned one of Waldo's flannel shirts, with small checked squares of navy blue and Christmas red, and strode out for the second time since Waldo's death to his A-framed stone writing studio in the woods.

Argos trotted ahead, as if he already knew where they were going. As she stepped into the writing room that overlooked the field, she noticed that the secret clearing that Argos had showed her was framed in the center of the picture window.

"That clever old Gramp," she noted out loud to Argos.

Nell hadn't touched his writing desk since Waldo had passed, but Amelia must have dusted it regularly, for it was as clean as if Waldo had been writing there on the expansive walnut top that morning before sunrise. *Before the world is up making noise,* she could hear him say. She sat down at his wooden desk chair and ran her hands over his typewriter. He declined to switch to computers. Nell laughed, thinking how similar they ended up being in adulthood.

Nell opened the top drawer. There was a parcel wrapped in a dishcloth (Waldo had stopped using Christmas paper long before it was fashionable to 'go green') with a red ribbon and an envelope that read "My Little Nell."

As if in a state of dream-like wonder, she opened the card. There was a photo of Waldo standing in front of a gargantuan mountain with a trio of rocky spires jutting into the sky, glued to an off-white card. "Torres Del Paine, Patagonia," she read on the caption below. She thought he had forgotten his camera. How could this be?

My darling girl,

I may never have the opportunity to hand this parcel to you, for as I walk in the mountains this year, they whisper that I'll join them in spirit soon. These intuitions come to me stronger now, after having spent a lifetime in the wild. Intuition has been denigrated since the Enlightenment philosophers marketed their faculty of reason as the most important sense a human could possess, but I have come to learn otherwise, as I hope you will one day, too.

I know that my Nell prefers a den, like a safe wolf cub. There may come a day, though, when you hear the world beckoning to you as it has to me, Bradford, and Vivienne.

As I climbed over these glaciers with my guide Fernando, who has become my dearest friend, I see that they are autonomous organisms that crackle and hiss. They are made up of waterfalls and caves in variegated hues of white and blue that are otherworldly. The glaciers are calving rapidly. They are melting here, and they show me their diminishing mass as they do to others who care about this rapidly changing earth.

My darling girl, if you are reading this after I have gone, I exhort you to do your part in responding to climate change. Try to make a difference as I have done in the Berkshires and here in Patagonia. Speak to Fernando about his work. He is not just a caretaker with Amelia. He was a climate scientist in Puerto Natales, Chile, and El Calafate, Argentina, before he and Amelia came here to work on climate change with an American foundation that I started with him. I hope you will become friends with him, but he is just as private as I am.

Be the best you can be. You always have. All that I have cultivated in me has taken seed in you. Wherever I may be in the etheric realm, my love shall bolster you on the grayest of days.

Grandpa

Nell held the letter against her chest, and rocked back and forth in his chair with her eyes closed.

* * *

Argos put his head in her lap as she unwrapped the gift; he nestled against her thighs. It was a writing journal in cream leather, with Nell Harding embossed on the cover in dark red, her favorite colors.

On the first page, Waldo had written:

I know you say that in a family of writers, you are the reader, but readers write, too. At least, they participate in the great art of journaling.

Grandpa

It was as if he had orchestrated the timing for her to receive his gift only after she herself had gone deep in the woods. And she had nearly filled the journal she had started not too long ago.

As if making up for lost time, she picked up the other parcel—a thick bundle the size of printing paper—wrapped in brown paper, and undid it. "Lessons I learned from the Glaciers," Nell read out loud. "Waldo Harding." A posthumous manuscript? Nell wrapped it up carefully, stunned, and brought it back to the house along with her gift. She scuffed off her boots and held the door open for Argos, eager to settle into Waldo's book, when the phone rang.

"Ms. Harding? It's Grace from the Berkshire Botannical Garden. Thank you for continuing your grandfather's donations. We wanted to invite you to a workshop tomorrow. It's on pollinator pathways."

"I have been wanting to learn about that very thing. I'll be there," Nell said, astounded. Hanging up the phone, she looked around, as if Waldo might be around somewhere.

* * *

At the workshop the next day, Nell learned that people from Connecticut to Vermont were building corridors free of pesticides for bees and other pollinators to roam without being poisoned. She half-expected to see Xavier there, but to her surprise, on the flyer and handout, it said that it was sponsored by Lumière and Alden Enterprises. Had he something to do with this?

The thought of him stirred a primitive longing in her, but she was too intent on taking notes to let it linger. Nell wanted to create a native habitat on the land near the garden so the pollinators would cross-pollinate and fertilize the garden. She would help them move through the area in a poison-free zone.

When the speaker mentioned that larval plants were under attack due to climate change, Nell jotted down: "Leave bare ground for the bees. Leave some leaves for wintering eggs of pollinating insects." She added: "Nursery for native plants" and "See about converting the Volvo to vegetable oil," and lastly, "Solar panels" to the growing list in her spiral notebook.

When she was putting her notebook away after the lecture, she discovered that Reza's postcards were still in her bag. She took them out as she walked outside, and happened upon a fresco of two lovers entwined underneath the pleasure palace's innovative infinity waterfall. She had read about the engineering behind it, which still didn't make sense to her. She decided it was a wonder of the world.

Taking her pen out, she set the card on top of her hood and wrote carefully:

My dear Xavier,

Every time I see details of this iconic palace in Isfahan, I daydream of us being there together. It's as if these figures could be a mirage of us. I am still coming out of my unearthed past, still mourning the felled trees that I lost long ago in my tiny forest of humans.

Love, with a trace of nostalgia for you,

N.

As she pondered her gesture, she decided to add to it. She wanted to give Xavier a progress report on the choreography of her inner self, show him that she was becoming more capable of intimacy. Taking a fresh sheet of paper from her notebook, she sat down in the driver's seat and wrote:

I want to give you a more intimate portrait of my inner landscape. I couldn't do justice to an apology to you until I had worked through some stuff.

Our literarily minded Nell twitched her nose at the word "stuff," and then she decided to keep it. It felt most authentic unaltered. Any other word would have been pretentious, she decided. Even this narrator couldn't find a better one given the nebulous nature of psychology. She poised the pen over the page until the next thought came, and then she pounced on the page, steadied by the book she had placed under it. Black met white furiously, as if she had never been diffident about writing.

I didn't know, until I lashed out at you, that my childhood wounds had scarred over. Now, the scar tissue is uncomfortable. I seem to need to work this out on my own. I don't have the right words yet because I am in the thick of the evolution. Let's say that I am pre-verbal about it.

I can only tell you that given my level of psychological awareness, I couldn't have acted any other way on that fateful day. But it has awakened an intuitive voice that is guiding me through a sort of emergence into healing, into maturing. It's coaxing me out of my shelter … and I am ever hopeful that the path leads me back to you.

But I'm too unfinished, too unpolished to be in rapport with anyone else right now—even if it's someone who I think is my soul's favored companion. It wouldn't be fair to you, and I wouldn't want to take the risk of lashing out at you again. I couldn't bear to.

Love, still,

Nell

Suddenly confident, Nell folded the paper, located an envelope in the mobile office her bag had become, and swiftly deposited the postcard and the note in it before sealing it with gumption.

* * *

Later that day, she called Melika to make sure Reza had relayed her Thanksgiving invitation. The holiday was just days away. They discussed what the Parsas could contribute. It would be an Iranian take on Thanksgiving, with walnut pomegranate sauce for the turkey. Melika had even asked if Nell would join her for a girls' night out after the holiday. *My new community*, Nell thought, satisfied.

She picked up Waldo's manuscript of essays on Patagonia, and decided to sit in his womb chair to read it. He made the glaciers come alive for her, as if they were breathing beings with lives. She stopped to make a verbena tea to savor as she read.

Waldo had foreseen the deteriorating state of the planet as the sea levels rose and the ice caps melted at unprecedented rates. He made them seem closer, more relevant than how she had pictured them.

She would copy the entire manuscript tomorrow and send it to his publisher in New York. She made a note to call Amelia and ask what role Fernando had played in Grandpa's life, beyond being a caretaker. She seemed to be drawn ineluctably towards this foundation she had heard of.

She picked up the ringing phone to hear "Nell?" She sighed as she brought the phone down to the floor.

"Hi, old friend," she said softly to Blake.

"How are you feeling on Thanksgiving eve? I just wanted to check on you," Blake said.

"Serene and grounded. My new friends are coming for dinner tomorrow, and it's probably an in-person conversation, but it's very healing to be around them," Nell said. As she spoke, her jaw slackened and she realized she was back to being her vulnerable self around Blake. Their lengthy continuum could withstand such an interruption without being broken.

"Good. Listen, I am sorry for those cards. I feel contrite. I haven't been a very good friend to you lately, especially when you have probably had to confront old memories up there," Blake said. Privy to the craggy crevices of her past.

"I am confronting the specters this time, but I didn't even know they were still lurking until now. I couldn't have done it without these peculiar choices I've made to get rid of distractions. This is a good thing."

Her words were met with a positive grunt of encouragement, so she continued. "I just wish for you to find love, too. I know that you will."

"The bar's been set rather high, but I will," Blake said.

"It's thoughtful of you to call me tonight, of all the nights. Happy Thanksgiving, Blake. Come visit us soon," Nell said before setting the phone down.

Chapter Nineteen

Nell had decorated the house with pumpkins and gourds from the farmer's market, set the table with her grandmother's dishes, and made dark chocolate pecan pie for the first time since she was twelve. With the help of her grandmother's box marked "Thanksgiving Decorations," Nell had transformed the house with Amelia's help. They had ironed linen table runners with embroidered turkeys on them, and placed the cornucopia on the center of the island. Nell roamed the aisles of the co-op, gathering foods that she wanted to share with the Parsas. Pomegranates, acorn squash, and apples came spilling out of the wicker horn that symbolized abundance.

She had made pumpkin soup with carrot and ginger, cutting into her index finger when she peeled the recalcitrant skin. How had Eleanor peeled it every year? Hers went into the blender, peel and all after she failed to conquer it. She sprinkled the soup with extra cinnamon, nutmeg, and cloves. *It might not be Carpe Diem's soup*, she thought when she tasted it, *but it's rustic.* She dribbled olive oil and sea salt into the blender, and mixed it again, on a low speed.

The night before, she had chopped pounds of vegetables from turnips to brussels sprouts and kale. That morning she had washed the fresh Massachusetts cranberries, boiled them with water, and stirred a little honey with orange zest into them before dishing them into her grandmother's crystal cranberry sauce bowl.

Her hand hovered over a pumpkin pie at the co-op, but she pulled it back when she heard Waldo's voice singing. In those early days when their lives had been vacuumed of joy, he sang to her: "*Mourning may endure through the night, but joy cometh in the morning.*" Somehow, it meant that she should make the symbolic pie.

When Nell and Argos heard a soft knock on the door, the pie was cooling on its rack with a tawny flaked crust. As if it were a leitmotif, Nell surveyed her Thanksgiving scene in the great room while repeating: *the pie is cooling out of the oven.* It was the first time she had ever hosted Thanksgiving, and she had to reassure her subconscious that this narrative would end with a celebratory dénouement.

Nell opened the door and found her four new friends standing on the steps in holiday clothes, carrying various dishes.

"Welcome to your first Thanksgiving in America," she called out.

"Happy Thanksgiving," Mansoureh said first. Argos touched his nose to everyone's knee as they walked in. Their voices rose in a flurry of greetings.

As Nell went to close the door, she saw a tasteful ceramic urn with a potted echinacea in full purple bloom on the top step. That had been one of the native plants mentioned in the pollinator workshop. She hadn't heard anyone drive up besides the Parsas. Melika looked over Nell's shoulder at it.

"Nell has an admirer, it seems," she said, touching Nell's arm. Nell blushed, feeling hopeful that it had been sent from Xavier, but thinking one of Waldo's friends could have sent it to mark the anniversary of her parents' deaths.

Cyrus stared at the unadulterated view of the mountains and woods behind the cabin.

"It reminds me of going skiing with you in the Zagros Mountains during the early days of our marriage," he murmured to Melika. The children stood in front of the kitchen island peering into the cornucopia that stood there with fruit spilling out of it.

"We have heard this line in American movies: 'You've outdone yourself,' but without having been to Thanksgiving chez Nell and Argos before, we think you've outdone yourself," Melika said. Cyrus had migrated to the wall of bookshelves, but he came over and placed his arm around Melika's shoulders to echo her.

"I was going to wait for the toast, but our new friendship is what we are thankful for on this historic day," Cyrus said.

"I echo you, Cyrus. It's on the top of my list right now, too. This calls for an early toast," Nell said. She had already decanted a bottle of St. Émilion, and she poured the velvet burgundy liquid. She had juiced red grapes that morning in her juicer, and offered a glass in the same crystal to Mansoureh, who looked dazzled at being included in the adults' ritual. She handed a small glass of wine to Reza, looking to his parents for approval, which they gave.

"It's a rite of passage for you, Reza," Cyrus said.

They all looked at Nell to lead before imbibing.

"Thanksgiving didn't become a national holiday until Abraham Lincoln declared it to be so in 1863, two years before slavery was abolished in this country. But the treatment of others in the United States has always been a matter of concern. The Wampanoag Indians who hosted the pilgrims in 1621 were ultimately decimated by the settlers. Their ancestors think of Thanksgiving as a day of mourning," Nell said. She paused and then went on, "I, too, think of this day as one to mourn."

Nell hadn't mentioned her family to them before; she had merely come with good cheer to dinner and to tutor. The Parsas were attentive as she continued.

"It has always been a day to mourn, because my parents were killed in a plane crash on Thanksgiving when I was a little girl, as my grandfather and I were preparing dinner for them in this room," Nell said quietly.

Melika and Cyrus did not look stunned. They had lost many loved ones, both friends and family, in Iran; many disappeared never to return. They must have recognized the muted sorrow in Nell's eyes. Reza moved to hug her, but Melika wordlessly cautioned him to wait until Nell had finished. Mansoureh had tears in her eyes, as Nell thought she might. She was an empathetic little girl and had cried once when she accidentally stepped on Argos's paw and he yelped in pain.

"Yet, today, for the first time, I host Thanksgiving in my family home. As Dostoevsky's novel *The Brothers Karamazov* taught me, one cannot know joy if one has not known suffering. You have brought joy back into my life. Thank you. Let's all list what we are grateful for throughout the day," Nell said.

They placed their glasses down, and put their arms around Nell so that she was in the center of a multi-armed hug. They murmured belated condolences. Argos brushed up against their legs, walking around the circle, lending his affection. They broke apart but continued to console her with knowing looks, and individual hugs.

"Perhaps humor is in order?" Nell proposed, eager to modulate.

Mansoureh raised her empty glass of grape juice.

"I am grateful that a handsome fox gets to sleep at Nell's house," she said, solemn and funny at the same time, making them laugh.

"What are you talking about, Mannie?" Cyrus asked.

"There's a resident fox on Nell's lawn," she explained, "and I keep hoping to see him today." Cyrus looked to Nell for confirmation, and she nodded as they laughed.

"Let's gather around the island for hors d'oeuvres," Nell said. There was a tray of artisanal cheeses, olives, and almond rosemary crackers on a piece of slate in the shape of a pumpkin. It was borderline kitsch, but it was a day to break aesthetic rules.

Nell stabbed the turkey's thigh, and since it was nearly ready at the temperature imprinted in her brain's audio files, she turned the gas on underneath all the pots with water and vegetables that she had set out strategically before her guests arrived.

"I was a vegetarian in New York for so long after I adopted Argos, but here, one sees the circle of life. Coyotes kill deer and hawks swoop down to snack on field mice. My grandfather's friend Stanley dropped off a fresh turkey for us last week," Nell said.

"Melika went through a vegetarian stage in grad school after reading about Gandhi," Cyrus said.

"That lasted until our engagement dinner when our families set out roasted lamb. She didn't want to make a scene in front of my parents. That was the end of that," he said, laughing.

Nell carved Argos's portion first, ladling his broth on top. Melika and Cyrus were warming up the Persian sauces and dressing a salad from their garden as their contribution to dinner. At the table, Nell participated in the conversation, while observing that her revelation was like lifting a dam. Now that Bradford and Vivienne were no longer a verboten topic—a secret infiltrating all of their discourse—they talked openly about Nell's family and Iran.

"We had been watching for an opportunity to leave Iran since the children were born," Melika volunteered. This was the theme of the day.

"Cyrus's position at the university was prestigious, so we didn't want to jeopardize his career, or our livelihood," she continued, after taking a bite of squash and turkey.

Melika's tone was wry as she recounted their narrative: "We followed every rule under the strict Iranian regime, but when the academic offer came to teach at Smith College, Cyrus asked the head of the department to word it as a one-year guest teaching lectureship so that the authorities would not suspect he was permanently leaving his post," Melika explained. "We have no intentions of returning to Iran. It's actually a full professorship with automatic tenure, given Cyrus's history of publishing and his prominent place in academia." A worldliness infused her words, as if she had long been a cosmopolitan woman lying in wait to come out into the world again.

"That's why we were reluctant to state the name of the college at first. But no more secrets from the children, we decided," Cyrus said, "because it creates a burdensome atmosphere for them."

Nell nodded.

"Melika hoped we would land in France. She calls it her second home because she went to college there, but the salaries at certain American universities are incomparable," Cyrus shared. As dishes were passed, Nell paused to reflect on how similar she and Melika were—from their Francophilia to their nascent freedoms from restrictions—although Nell knew she couldn't compare her own sense of freedom to the liberation Melika was experiencing.

Mom and her best friend Delphine would approve of this friendship, she thought.

"I'm not much of a traveler," Nell said between bites of roasted Brussels sprouts with currants and harissa, "but I am suddenly taken with the idea of traveling to Iran. My parents were obsessed with studying anthropology in Iran, and I want to pick up their research, as an amateur. Do you think it would be safe for me?"

"Yes," Melika said in an emphatic tone. "Iranians separate the government from the people. They learned to do this by watching the Revolution at home. They don't dislike Americans. You would be very safe. As long as you respect the head scarf rule, and don't engage in public displays of affection."

"Maybe you could help me organize a cultural visit to Isfahan?" Nell said.

"We'll come up with a rich itinerary for you, Nell. We'll get our friend, who is a guide, to take care of you in Isfahan," Cyrus said. The conversation carried them into the plate-clearing phase of the day.

Cyrus walked with her to the dishwasher carrying a pile of plates.

"I found it at the library, Cyrus: *The Green Wave*," Nell whispered.

"And I've been thinking about your stance on it. It's just a drop in this vast ocean of cyber dangers," he whispered back. "The socio-economic ramifications will affect businesses that are hacked into, and nation states are at risk."

"You sound like a prophet, Cyrus."

"I'll babysit Argos," Mansoureh said, piping up, appearing at their elbows with her own dish.

"He'll consider it as long as you don't call him a baby," Nell said with a smile.

"I'm thankful that I don't have to study for the SATs today," Reza proclaimed randomly, and Nell raised her glass that she had set on the island.

"To our budding architect. May he attend the college of his dreams," Nell toasted. Reza looked at Nell fondly.

"To my kind mentor." Reza nodded.

Nell smiled.

"Have you ever played Autonomous Scrabble? It's like regular Scrabble, but everyone creates their own board." Nell shifted into post-dinner mode.

"We love word games; we're game," Cyrus quipped, standing to make espresso.

Amelia opened the door as they started a joint effort to clear the table.

"Happy Thanksgiving, everyone," she called out. Nell went to greet her.

"Would you like to join us for dessert?" Nell asked, hopeful.

"No, my dear, I just want to give you a hug and meet your new friends," she said, folding Nell into her chest. Melika came out to meet Amelia, and the two women chatted and made quick plans to meet for coffee one afternoon. Nell excused herself to prepare pie and coffee, saying: "Please send Fernando my greetings."

Nell told Cyrus about the last time she had made this pie as she was cutting slices. He patted her back. "It was courageous of you to make this today," he said. Melika overheard as she returned, and squeezed Nell's shoulders in solidarity.

"I lost both of my parents during the Revolution," she whispered. "They were close friends of the Shah." Nell nodded, patting her chest as she often did to show her empathy. Loss is universal. *It's a common denominator that unites us all*, she mused.

She wondered what it would have been like if she had just told Xavier, as she had told the Parsas. Would he be here with her today if she had? Or would she be in Boston with him and his family?

"I never tell anyone, Melika. You can't imagine what a pivotal day this is for me," she said.

"You keep your heart under close watch. Even Argos guards it for you," Melika said, leaning in to put her head on Nell's shoulder for a moment, as if they had already become intimate confidants.

"This is a breakthrough," Cyrus said affirmatively, "for all of us. It's cathartic."

Over espresso and dark chocolate pecan pie, they created "Pavilions," "Balustrades," and "Oenophiles" on their Scrabble boards. They relaxed the English-words-only rule to allow French and Iranian vocabulary, and the game went on for many hours until Mansoureh was snuggled on the couch under a blanket, and Reza looked like he was in a trance. Nell wanted to remember their impressive words to share with Xavier, if there was a future place for conversations with him.

Nell took note of the yawning Reza. "It's the tryptophan," Nell told him. "It's a property in turkey that induces sleep."

"Let's get our babies home, Cyrus," Melika said, tugging on her husband's sleeve as he was about to add more logs to the fire. He acquiesced.

"I'm on holiday all week," he said, chuckling, "so this is quite a treat. We have had the best Thanksgiving of all time."

"Le meilleur," Melika echoed in French to Nell. Nell packed leftovers for them in glass containers, as they pulled on boots and wound scarves around their necks. She extended a small cooler to them at the door.

"This is part of the Thanksgiving tradition: Leftovers," she said.

They looked surprised.

"Thanksgiving leftovers are greatly prized in American culture, and I would be a terrible host if I didn't send you home with some," she said, clarifying.

"It's the last gratitude for the day then," Reza said, accepting the cooler with an air of maturity. Melika glanced at the Echinacea plant, then turned back and gave Nell a wink.

Nell waved at them in the driveway as their taillights vanished into the opaque night.

Only then did Nell put Argos on a leash and follow his meanderings, for he may have followed his friend Mansoureh down the drive. Silently, she sent her dog a message: *My greatest gratitude today is for you. I recognize you as a great being. I am honored that you love me. I will always honor you.*

They had been communicating in this manner as clearly as Bell had with Watson during the first telephone conversation in history.

Nell just didn't share the contents of their dialogue with anyone. And he responded: *My chosen one, you are.* They weren't even making eye contact. Argos was following someone else's tracks on the ground with his nose, and Nell's feet were moving behind him but her head was craned towards the ceiling of white constellations. Her eyes were tracing the individual stars in the Cassiopeia constellation, but her inner ear heard Argos.

Their conversations had grown more frequent. Argos was easier to hear after Nell had dispensed with her phone. Conversing with Argos was a little bit like meditating, or like listening to the trees. He didn't shout. He could only be heard if she was not distracted. Argos had tried sending Nell messages in New York, but she could only hear truncated clips that she didn't trust, that she attributed to her propensity to daydream. So, he sent Nell mental images of the Berkshire hills she had only shown him one time, until she finally broke down and took him there for good. That was Argos's narrative.

The line had become clear and constant between them. Even their leash rules. Argos told her he wasn't going anywhere at night, but she reminded him that even though she knew he possessed a fine faculty of reason, she believed it could be overridden by animal instinct—which was not meant to be an insult, for she knew she possessed one, too. They turned inside to rest.

She had brought the plant inside, wondering how to nurse it over the winter before it could go into the softened spring ground. Was he thinking of her, too, so much that he gifted her with the Thanksgiving plant, as if he wanted to commemorate the anniversary of her losses? If only she could communicate with Xavier through her thoughts as crisply as she could with Argos. "Thank you, Xavier," she whispered as she lay her head down. The weekend would require a healthy night of sleep.

Since Reza had requested to take Saturday off to visit a few of the liberal arts colleges on the list they had come up with together, Nell continued a tradition that she and Waldo had started that Thanksgiving weekend long ago. She hadn't been able to uphold it in New York, but she had always gone elsewhere for the weekend, had always avoided invitations to friends' houses in favor of lonely beach walks on the sound.

* * *

The air felt quiet Friday morning. The cloud cover hung low, flat, as if it were pressing against the horizon. But it was the light at the edge that caught her eye. The oppressive gray sky couldn't keep those slivers of luminescence out.

"Hope, Argos," Nell said out loud to her dog, pointing at the sky, "in the wake of all that's been lost." She packed the car and drove north with Argos. She parked the Volvo by the Vermont border in a nondescript neighborhood with a tiny sign of a stick hiker figure and the AT symbol. She strapped Argos's saddle bags on, and adjusted her new backpack, brimming with gear and victuals. *Let's just see where we get to today. Are you on board?*

As they stepped onto the Appalachian Trail, they found their rhythm together. Their silent conversation helped set the pace. They hadn't been hiking for long when they came to a fork in the trail. An old wooden plaque welcomed them to the Long Trail, the oldest contiguous footpath in America that extended through Vermont into Canada. Nell reached for her phone to take a photograph of herself, and marveled that she still had that impulse. She had forgotten to pack a camera, so she put the sign in her memory and hiked on into Vermont.

Patches of snow lingered at the higher elevations. Argos traced the tracks of those species that had walked before him. He would call them out to Nell as he found them: *Bobcat. Porcupine. Bear. Deer. Rabbit. Human. Human. Human. Mostly human.* Nell was thinking that it was time to call Xavier when a cardinal's vibrant red wings carved a path in the air in front of her. She exhaled and continued to walk. The exertion of the uphill climb cleared her nasal passages so that she could smell the leaves composting.

They hiked until their stomachs protested. Nell looked down at the time, then sighed. "No phone. No watch. Brilliant," she scolded herself, hoping she could hold her own after the wilderness survival classes that she had taken with Waldo in her teenage years. She had insisted that he do so before he went to Patagonia, and she had merely accompanied him, not listening in as closely, not thinking she would ever need that knowledge.

As dusk began to fall, she discovered a flat area off the trail. It was nestled in a copse of conifers. It would provide a mattress of pine needles for them. They had encountered no one that day, to her astonishment and jubilation.

"We have the forest all to ourselves," she said to Argos. He sniffed the perimeters of the site while she set up camp, fumbling with the tent poles, until she nearly willed the tent to rise three-dimensionally. After she stowed her backpack inside, and unearthed the pot and stove, she stepped out of the tent with her headlamp strapped on to admire the sky fading from pale salmon to black.

Water filtered. Pot boiling. Mattress inflated. Hiking boots kicked off and light sandals kicked on. Argos was flopped inside the tent, all splayed out. Nell had packed frozen raw food for him that had semi-defrosted as she had planned. She had poured hot water on top of it, and stirred it for him. Fed and hydrated, Argos started to snore. Nell wished she could join him. She turned off the pot and carefully put it away as she let her hiker's dinner of black beans, rice, and dehydrated broccoli cool.

The moon highlighted the black skeletons of late fall trees. Nell breathed meditatively for a few minutes as she witnessed it. Instead of giving something to the forest, like sorrow, she was merely breathing with the forest. An unfamiliar contentment warmed her, as if there was nothing more to let go of.

Folding herself into the tent and zipping it up, she adjusted her head lamp, and stripped down to her base layers. Dinner appeased her primitive hunger after what Nell estimated was about fifteen miles of hiking. Argos had wiggled into his half of the bag, and she was quick to join him on a chilled early winter's night. She fell asleep to the night animals' concert.

Unzipping the tent at dawn, Nell breathed the pristine air, feeling at one with the wilderness. A Japanese forest ranger had called it shinrin yoku in the 1980s, or forest bathing, but it just felt like the woods had welcomed them. Argos ventured out and sniffed again, identifying the night's passersby.

Nell produced more turkey for Argos. She had wrapped it with an ice pack in a tiny insulated bag, and it was still cold. She boiled water outside to make cinnamon raisin oatmeal. She dumped some boiling water into her mug, and stirred it with a mildly disgusting instant coffee she had found. *It tastes better in the mountains*, she thought.

As she broke down camp, Nell marveled that there was little to move out on this hike, little solace to seek. As they hiked back down the trail, she thought that it was more about what was coming back to her. She broomed the thought away as best she could, but it kept swirling back like errant dust particles in the air: She wished that Xavier had been there with them, and the thought was in unison with Argos's.

It was dark before Nell and Argos returned home Sunday night. Dropping their gear in the foyer, Nell walked back to the piano. The mountains had gifted her with an epiphany that weekend. The lacquer cover slid open under her fingers. Nothing. No tears. No sorrow. "My parents never meant for me to be Sleeping Beauty," she whispered to herself, touching the piano for the first time since she was twelve. Gingerly, she pressed a C major chord, then played a chromatic scale, and then her fingers began to come home to the keys, as if coming out of a slumber and remembering discordant fragments of what they once knew.

* * *

They would be into December soon, Nell thought as she touched the days on the calendar Monday morning. She jotted a few things in her notebook that had come to her during their hike, under the heading: "My Quest to Become Self-Sufficient." One of them was a solution to her high electric bills. Nell called a solar company called Bee in the Light, which she had found in the book of yellow pages.

She thought she recognized Anne's voice, a former peer from her boarding school. She had seen her in The Hawthorne a few times.

"I'm glad to have your business, but I'm a little surprised that you wouldn't have used Xavier's new company," Anne said.

"What company would that be? I've been keeping to myself lately."

"His new solar company: Lumière."

Nell felt a jolt in her chest, almost as if something had rapped into the hollow place between her breasts.

"I always like to get two estimates. Would you send someone out to talk about putting solar panels on my roof?" she asked. That must have been the project he had been so shy about revealing. Nell hung up the phone wondering if they were going to mend the rupture. He had been hard at work since their cataclysm. *Perhaps he had forgotten her?* She thought that youth was idealistic about waiting, but it wasn't usually attainable in the face of desire.

Mr. Holtzman was the next item on her list.

"What a surprise. I usually have to chase you. I hope you had a nice Thanksgiving in spite of everything."

"The best in years. I hope that you did, too," she said. "But I'm calling to ask whether I could withdraw funds to take a trip."

"A trip?"

"A trip."

"I told you for years that your family had earmarked funds as 'Nell's travel education.' Each time I mentioned it, you looked sullen, said traveling had killed your parents and you didn't want to hear another word about it."

"Let's say that I'll be visiting Iran if you will allocate the funds," Nell said.

"Paris. London. Typical first trips. Iran? Like parents, like child. We can provide funds for this," he said.

"I'm going to apply for a passport and a visa," Nell said.

"You don't have a passport?"

"I was never going to go anywhere."

"I'll take this as a good sign, Nell," Mr. Holtzman said.

"I am cobbling together a life of substance, made up of scraps and fragments, like a bricolage," she explained, to herself as well.

"I'll accept that," he responded. "By the way, let's set up a meeting in early January with the foundation," he said in parting.

Having concluded her business for the day, Nell called Melika. Their joint anticipation of the girls' night that would take place that week rang through the phone.

Nell hung up and looked out at the mountains. How had she gotten to this chapter in the 'Choose your own adventure' narrative? Even though she was unemployed, phoneless, and single, she felt more content than she had in years. Still, she peered at the mountains' contours of blue and green. They always helped her to see what was intangible within herself. They heightened her sense of intuition, as they had done for Waldo. There were unfinished places. The contentment was more like a rest stop on a hike. She was writing it out, to her secret marvel, but she knew the journey still entailed a climb, albeit a metaphorical one.

Chapter Twenty

Over the next weeks, Nell and Reza prepared for his official SAT, which would take place on December 16th. They devised Plan A of a celebratory dinner at his parents' house if the scores that popped up on the screen following the test were exceptional. If the results were abysmal, then they would do Plan B: watch an old black-and-white French film that was playing in town over ice cream and popcorn, with no parents.

And Melika had her first American girls' night out, in the company of Nell. It was Nell's first time out since she and Ella had shared cocktails in Manhattan together, which seemed like another life. The two women met at a French wine and tapas bar in Lenox one early evening. Melika arrived first, and when Nell flounced in, her new friend's presence radiated through the bar. Melika's jean-clad legs were crossed at a bar table for two, and her hair shone in the dimmed lights as if she had just come from the salon. Her smile and wave gave her giddiness away, and Nell found it infectious. As Nell slid into her bar seat, she noticed Melika's black form-fitting cashmere sweater admiringly.

"Melika! What a pity to have covered your style up in Iran," Nell exclaimed, as they kissed each other on both cheeks. "You look so chic and beautiful," Nell gushed.

"I'll drink to that, Nell!"

The waiter appeared in a white linen apron tied at his waist, with a notepad in his hand. When his "Hello ladies," gave away his French accent, Melika ordered a glass of Sancerre in French.

"Deux, s'il vous lait," Nell seconded Melika, and they both giggled, as if they were engaged in some subversive activity and hadn't been caught.

"Nell, I have never been on a girls' night out before. I have never gotten to have a glass of wine in public since I was studying in France. Can you imagine?" Just as she finished exclaiming at this newfound liberty, the waiter set their pale-yellow glasses of Sancerre down. They beamed at one another and pressed glass to glass before taking a sip of the crisp wine that tasted like freedom to both of them.

Melika cooed in appreciation as she set her glass down gently, and looked at Nell with a mischievous smile. Nell noticed that Melika had an impeccable manicure with pale-pink lacquer and matte white tips.

"Although, I did have my micro-rebellions from the regime's religious police. I let my headscarf slide back lazily so that I could display my hair. I felt like Sampson and Delilah having to hide it under my scarf every day. You can't imagine."

Nell shook her head, intrigued, as Melika gesticulated with her hands in residual frustration.

Melika continued: "Of course, I was conservative coming from Isfahan, but my sister in Shiraz would let her scarf slip to the nape of her neck. She brazenly wore burgundy lacquered nails and didn't even pretend to care that she could get arrested for that."

Nell nodded, and said, "It sounds like a micro-freedom."

"But Cyrus's students would get checked to make sure they were abiding by the dress code as they entered his lecture hall. I know you're protesting cyber surveillance, so we both know what it is like to be horrified by surveillance of any kind, I think." Melika reached to take another sip and smiled at Nell, as if she had found their common angle.

Nell shook her head wildly and said, "My troubles with surveillance cannot be compared to what you endured, but I have empathy for you to the extent that I can imagine."

"Let's toast to that, Nell." Melika laughed and they drank deeply from their dwindling glasses.

"What's funny is that I have been seeking out solitude, Melika, retreating from society, whereas you were forced to retreat in Iran without being granted the agency to make that choice." Nell paused to take another sip, before finishing her comparative analysis. "So it's as if we are at antipodes with our experiences with freedom and rebellion."

Melika laughed, giddy at their quick verbal volley. "Antipodes, indeed. But we can be Nell and Mel with rapprochement!" Nell knew that she meant that in spite of the shocking contrasts in their backgrounds, there were similarities that brought them close.

"To the friendship of Mel and Nell," Nell proposed, lifting one of the fresh glasses that their perceptive waiter had placed for her and Melika. And they both cheered once again, becoming giddier with each sip.

"And what do girls talk about on these infamous cocktail nights?" Melika asked with a knowing smile. Without waiting for Nell to respond, she said, "Romance and young men." She gave the table a delicate thump for emphasis.

Nell sighed and crossed her legs in the other direction, looking pained. Their banter paused, as if Nell had fumbled her return, and she had gone off to catch the runaway tennis ball.

"Ahh," Melika murmured gently, "I see that we do have a young man to discuss." She patted Nell's hand. "There is a story to that Echinacea plant, after all."

From another table, discreetly, this narrator was warmed by the sight of the two women bonding. Two women who had been sheltered for differing reasons, who were burgeoning in their own rights.

"Mel, if I may use this endearing nickname, I have been cavalier with the heart of my love, I fear." Nell confided. "And now we are only speaking through letters, which makes little sense, I know." She covered her eyes with her hand and bowed her head, as Melika nodded with apparent sympathy.

Nell narrated her romance with Xavier for Melika, and as she analyzed her own role in their fateful last encounter, she came upon an insight that she had not yet thought of.

"And Melika, I was so guarded with him although he shared thorny details of his relationship with his parents, whereas I have opened up to you and Cyrus. It's almost as if I have been even more open with you to compensate for having been so closed to Xavier. But I can't go back and redo the narrative with him, I can just be more mindful going forward. You share, and I share, too, like friends should." Nell blushed, self-conscious about having rambled as this new psychological awareness surfaced in her conscious mind.

"If he is as extraordinary as he sounds, Nell, then all is not lost," Melika said.

Nell sighed and indicated that she hoped so.

"It's hard to forge an adult rapport, but this early struggle will strengthen your bond. All is not lost," Melika repeated.

Nell hugged her in response, grateful for her wisdom.

Later that night, once home, she felt that it had done her good to be with a friend. She padded upstairs to her journal, where Argos curled up under her desk and went back to sleep on her feet. Nell felt free to write, taking what this narrator would call excessive wine-induced liberty with her exclamation points.

I take umbrage with you, Mr. Thoreau! I feel as if you lied, either to yourself or to me, your ever-faithful reader. Solitude is not the greatest companion. I have seen through the illusion of solitude's allure, and no thanks to you, Mr. Thoreau. I have a budding friendship with a kindred spirit! At long last, a female friend with whom I can share my thoughts without a filter.

And the aching irony is that I had the opportunity to share my intimate thoughts that could run with free associations like a chain of signifiers. And I put an iron gate on it. Now there's a "y" added to that gate.

That opportunity's name was Xavier Alden. He was intimate with me in every way, sharing even his raw emotions. And I did not return the candid way he shared. It was only after I realized this, after I realized I had inner work to do, that I could rectify this in my friendship with Melika and Cyrus. I couldn't even do it with Ella. Pre-phone-flinging, of course, I couldn't! In another sad irony, Ella was a psychologist who would have welcomed it! She would have slid right onto a barstool tonight and found a kindred spirit in Melika, too. Both of them are sophisticated and carefree, which has always seemed out of reach for me.

From this point forth, I shall devise my own philosophy of life without your help, Mr. Thoreau. And the time is coming to voice these inner musings to Mr. Alden, and not just to these pages that don't speak back to me.

When she rose, Argos followed her, and he nestled his back into Nell's chest a little closer that night when they settled onto the feather bed.

* * *

The following afternoon, pencil and calendar in hand, Nell pulled a chair up to the telephone stand by the bookcase, and reflected. *Why haven't I called Fernando yet? He was Grandpa's best friend at the end. We have much common ground. It's a conundrum to all.* She closed her eyes to let go of the conscious control she held over her mind's content. Inhale. Exhale. After she surrendered to the meditative breathing, the wisdom came to her in the form of a sensation in her stomach, as if a gnarled tree root were lodged there.

Fear. *I haven't called Fernando out of fear of touching into that mourning again that could swallow me up.* Nell opened her eyes at once, bringing the fresh sagacity with her.

"Here I have been cultivating absorption, when simultaneously, I have an innate fear of being swallowed up. Absorbed by grief. Huh." She rubbed the place on her firm stomach where she had felt the fear, trying to understand the traces of trauma that had rooted inside her, so old that they were gnarled. Her journal was close by from the previous night's lucubrations, and she scrawled out: "I've been a fallible person. I'm just a work in progress, trying to heal my own girlhood wounds, now that I know I have them."

"It's time," she said out loud and picked up the black receiver to dial the familiar number.

"Nellcita, mi amor," Amelia greeted her at once. The element of a pleasant surprise has even been vanquished by technology, Nell thought.

"Feliz Navidad. I wanted to call before you leave for Argentina this week. I have some homemade gifts for you and Fernando," she said.

"Thank you, dear. We have been very busy on an important new project. We're coming back after Christmas to finish it," Amelia said, breathless.

"May I speak to Fernando? I'm ready to talk about Waldo," Nell said, suddenly shy.

"He has been waiting for you."

"Nell?" Fernando exuded calm with one syllable.

"I-I'm sorry that it has taken me so long to call. I was afraid of bringing the sorrow back," Nell said, as if she were a little girl again.

"I know the ways of grief. I miss him, too. I knew your call would come one day," he said.

"May we sit and talk? After Christmas when you come back from Patagonia? Just the two of us?" Nell asked her series of questions all at once.

"I know it will set Waldo's soul at rest," he said.

Nell set the phone down; the root softening inside of her.

* * *

The call came on a Saturday that Plan A was happening. Nell had intuited that it would. She had already wrapped a new Oxford English Dictionary for Reza, and tied a ribbon around a bottle of champagne for his parents. She dressed in her ivory wool dress, down vest, and riding boots to pay her respects to the young scholar who had achieved scholastic success in such a short time. He would be applying to the accelerated high school, now that he felt confident with his score. She went to tie a red ribbon around Argos's neck, but he shrugged against it, as if to say, *How could you humanize me?*

After a celebratory dinner with the Parsas, Nell wasn't ready to go home. She dropped Argos off against his will, and drove down to the Lion's Den to unwind. One could count on live music at the Den seven nights a week. Nell thought she might toast to her own success as a tutor. Her first job had gone well and Nell was gratified by the work. Reza's confidence and scores were her reward, with a glass of wine thrown in.

It was bustling, but there was a tiny table left for one in the dark basement bar. The artist must have gone to the bathroom before the set started.

"A glass of pinot noir, please?" she flagged the waiter passing by. The artist cleared his throat in the microphone without sounding out a word yet, but it was that tenor voice infused with honey.

A low hum rose from her pelvis as Nell looked up. Sitting cross-legged on a stool, slightly slouched over his guitar, Xavier was wearing a gray T-shirt under a flannel shirt with jeans.

"Good evening, for those of you that don't know me, I'm a half-breed local boy, Boston boy. But my better half was bred in the Berkshires."

Everyone laughed in the bar.

"Let's start with a coming-of-age song."

He sat up straighter, inhaled, and began to sing.

"*Let it go into the old river. Nostalgia flows away in the current. Let it go, let it go, let it go. O river, teach me your ways … O river, wash away my stagnation.*"

He was good. It was undeniable. His chord shifts were flawless, and his picking style showed off his classical background in guitar. Nell sipped pinot noir as she listened, pondering.

What had she done? Had she driven away about the only man that got her? Was she destined to be Waldo's eccentric heir out at the old Harding place who shunned love along with the conveniences of the modern world?

"*They told me that you come of age, as a man, by the time you are thirrrrteen.*" Strum. Strum. "*But I aint' no Holden Caulfield, uh uh. I ain't no boy in the Lord of Flies, nah nah. Ya have to make your way in this peculiar world on your own terms. Ya gotta make your own way on your own terms in this minefield of a wor-huh-hurld.*" He brought the crescendo down to end with the spoken words: "*You can love yesterday, but try to live in today.*" His lyrics—unique to him—drew her in. Zavs paused for a sip of water, and she knew that he was staring straight at her.

"Thanks for coming out tonight to support a shy musician with a fresh batch of written songs. This next one is about a girl I met here in these Berkshire hills we all love."

Nell looked around the tables to see if there was another girl Xavier might have written about. Her stomach suddenly felt empty and pained. *Had he met someone?* The crowd looked pretty typical Berkshires, which meant retired locals, tourist couples, and a few random loners like herself.

Xavier started out softly: "*She was a gossamer girl that shimmered in the moonlight. On a dark night. When the world went to sleep, she danced to the ligh-hi-hight of the luna. The luna. Her soul was as light as the creamy moonlight*," he sung.

Nell knew it was her. She was gossamer girl, and she felt longing coming out in the tears that made her face glow.

He paused and started speaking as he strummed.

"*This girl made me realize that good fences do make good neighbors. Even Robert Frost didn't get that because he thought fences were just about keeping cows in place. But I found out fast when I bust through this girl's fence.*" Then, he started singing again. "*I got zapped.*" He rapped the guitar, moved from side to side, and made a staccato plucking sound.

"*Zapped by her electric fence. Shoulda known better. Shoulda respected her fence.*" Then he modulated into a major chord, resolving the dissonance as he sang the happier refrain:

"*Cause' good fences make good neighbors, good friends, and good* lovers, *too.*"

She listened to every chord change, every lyric, stunned. In a reversal, she was the one feeling melancholic for lost love. The audience adored him, too, Nell noticed. She found herself in an odd state, and she had been the one to put herself there.

At the end of the last set, when the clapping was finished, Nell dropped enough money on the table to cover her bill and tip. She rushed out of the bar and up the stone steps. She leaned against a short pillar, deciding whether she should wait for him to come out.

With her face covering her hands, she heard the door open behind her. There he was, chasing after her when she should have sought him out, she thought. His forehead looked moist from the performance, he'd been sweating, and he brushed his dark brown hair out of his eyes as he looked at Nell.

"Zavs … I … You're very talented. I had no idea you were playing tonight," she stammered out. Why couldn't it come out automatically in an articulate manner? She wondered.

"Thanks for coming out to see me. I have to go get my gear." He spoke in his familiar tone, as if there had never been a lapse between them.

"Are you free? Will you please come over after?" Nell asked, trying not to sound plaintive. He stared at her with those molten chocolate eyes that reminded her of Argos's, and nodded his head before turning around to skip down the stairs again.

Nell drove home, surprised to discover that it was past midnight. She stood outside with Argos, pleading with the stars to lend her the eloquence she needed. The other Hardings were skilled with words, but she had merely alphabetized them, or so she had thought until the words started coming to her, too. They empowered her. Now she could never go back, for it was as if she was channeling some greater force, guided by a muse that had been dormant since her early successes publishing children's stories. Argos nudged her thigh as if to say, *Yes, you are worthy. You'll find the words. You're a writer. Just look at those journal entries.* Nell was so tuned into his frequency that she barely heard a car drive up. When Xavier's car door closed, Nell and Argos jumped, and Argos barked quite a little. He ran to welcome Xavier back into their pack.

Shedding self-consciousness like an ill-fitting coat, Nell ran to meet Xavier, too, chanting inside: *Act and say how you feel.* Argos had jumped on Xavier—knowing full well that jumping on others was unacceptable— and he was licking his face while Xavier was stroking his head, saying: "I missed you, Argie."

"Please forgive my foolhardiness. It's contained in my surname," she said, "but I will never be so careless with your heart again if you will forgive me."

He extended his arm to her, drew her in, and the three of them embraced all the way to the door.

"Would you please wait here?" he asked, adding, "Come with me, Argos."

"Yes." She stepped inside the foyer, staring at what Xavier would see. There was the line of crystal Christmas trees she had put out for the holidays. Cloth bags of homemade Christmas presents were lined up, ready to be sent. Envelopes with donations to the local food banks and homeless shelter were stacked up. New York seemed like another life, another reincarnation, she thought as she waited.

Nell folded her hands across her chest, thinking that when she bade farewell to New York and surrendered that life, she started in the Berkshires with a smudged slate, not the blank one she had wished for. Her secrets were in the smudges, in the traces of old chalk. In wanting to separate the private from the public, she hadn't accounted for the secrets that were in the space between. It felt good to be honest about her heart. Keeping secrets was tiresome, she realized.

Xavier came in and took Nell's hands, looked over at Argos, and said: "When I cue you, Argie. Let's do this."

"Nell Harding."

"Xavier Alden."

"I don't need another two years of courtship to know what I know. I hereby commit to you. I'm not asking you to sign a contract," he said, motioning to Argos.

Argos tossed a small box to Nell as if he were throwing his tennis ball to her. She stooped to catch it. Nell observed them both with a wrinkled-up face as she took in this improvised scene.

"You had this in your car?"

"For a long time," he said. "I brought it back from Boston the day of the conservation party."

Nell opened the box: an antique sapphire ring set in velvet. Her forehead was still wrinkled.

"I'm not going all conventional on you. I just want to be your family. We don't need a document for that," he explained, confident.

"Xavier, you are a lunatic. A real one," she said. Xavier waited as she peered into his face. Nell wondered if she was a character in an absurd play, but the candidness Xavier wore on his face was compelling. *Act and say how you feel*, she chanted inside.

"I am with you, Xavier. You're the human I can align myself with. If it means wearing your ring, I can do that. Maybe on a random finger?" she said.

It was so late that one could debate whether it was still night or early morning, but Xavier held her by the shoulders. "Are you up for a quick adventure?" he asked. She nodded, and they took Argos with them in the Land Cruiser. He drove halfway to Great Barrington until they reached a hand-carved sign painted in shades of yellow that read, "LUMIÈRE."

"I've been busy." Giddy, Zavs led her up the front steps to a glass box of a building with a flat roof. "All solar-paneled," Xavier explained proudly. "I started this before I met you, but I wasn't ready to share. You do understand," he said as he flipped the light switch up.

Nell gasped, holding her hands up over her face. She was inside a miniature version of a glacier. It was an exhibit comprised of digitized images on the walls.

"This is the climate change museum that Fernando Garcia helped me with. He's going to be the director, even though he's retired. He's a scientist from Patagonia that lives locally," he explained. Nell stared.

"I basically take people through an entire overhaul of their lives so that they can be efficient from A to Z from the way they drive and consume, heat their homes, and even how they eat and compost their food waste. There are also exhibits for children," Xavier explained with passionate sweeps of his hands in each direction.

Nell was looking at him in the oddest way, because behind him, on the illuminated panels of glaciers, was a digital image of

Fernando and Waldo in full climbing gear. Waldo looked hale, but he was at least eighty in the photo.

"Gramp," she whispered. She caressed the glass Waldo's face was imprinted on, standing on tiptoe to press her cheek against it.

"What? That's your grandfather? Wait, on your mom's side? Fernando said he had permission to reveal that it was Raymond Sebond. The reclusive famous writer?" Xavier asked in stops and starts.

Even the obituary had failed to make the connection, but hearing his innocent questions, Nell could be certain that Xavier had never been a fan befriending her to get closer to the words of her grandfather.

"Yes, he wrote most of his works under a pseudonym, and he refused to give public appearances," Nell explained for the very first time in her life. "That's partly why I was so worried when the pesky journalist from Georgia showed up. I was afraid he was going to dig up Waldo's identity."

Xavier gave a deep nod. "Fernando told me he worked with a writer until the end of his life, and when I found out it was Sebond, I almost fainted. He's one of my favorite writers. But I had no idea. Wait. You don't even have his books at home," he said, trailing off.

"That's all part of our guise," Nell said, laughing at how private Waldo had been. She continued: "But you asked one night who Waldo's favorite author was, and I said Montaigne. You were a French literature major. I was worried that you would get the reference."

"Montaigne's essay on the apology of Raymond Sebond. I am obtuse. But how can you not know this about the foundation? Fernando heads up the Sebond Foundation for Climate Change, and they funded a major portion of this," he said, gesticulating to show the scope of Waldo's clandestine involvement. "We are so connected, you and I."

"And we shall be. Let's just say I've been disconnected for a while. You have used your family resources in the most meaningful way possible for the planet." Nell took his hands into hers.

"Your family resources, too, apparently. I hope you'll be part of this, Nell."

"I've been keeping a journal since I got to the Berkshires. It wasn't intentional, but reading back on the last three months, it's extraordinary to see my post-phone thoughts. I scheduled a meeting with Professor Gupta to talk about my trajectory in person at his office in Cambridge. I may turn it into a memoir. I'm still eluding the digital panopticon, but it's not even a focus anymore. I might be able to use part of that here if you want," Nell said, looking shy about her own work.

"If it's anything like your letters, it will be a literary success. Truth." Xavier said. After a minor hesitation he added: "But I'm still questioning the notion of you being post-phone."

Nell quieted her thoughts and decided to sound them out, try them out for the first time before she took them to Professor Gupta.

"I looked up your Photo Gram at the library. The way that people post is indicative of the smartphone-addiction culture. I mean, it's all about theatricality. Putting yourself on the stage, or on display. You can't have absorption and theatricality at the same time. That's my philosophical argument. I choose the former." She shrugged her shoulders, and Xavier stood staring, as if to absorb the meaning of her thoughts in a way that he didn't through her spoken words, so she shifted back to him, to his new life's work.

"But I do have one way I can be part of it right now that involves Waldo. I discovered a volume of essays in his desk recently. I've sent it to his publisher in New York, and I want it to be published posthumously under his real name. It's like we're communing, because he even typed his real name on the front cover. He doesn't have to protect his privacy anymore. I never even made the connection between my fierce need to be private and his cultivation of privacy," Nell said. She was stunned by this epiphany. She felt like she was becoming more like her beloved grandfather. Her shoulders dropped, as if she could finally be at ease with all she had been carrying on the inside. She could be seen. She no longer had to hide. Coming out of hiding brought a fresh idea.

"Perhaps we could host a reading here, and I could read from the essays?" Nell asked. She turned up her face to catch his glowing eyes.

"I'm in the soft-opening phase until mid-January—building a client base and getting feedback—but how about doing the reading on the grand opening celebration?" Xavier suggested.

"I'll call the publisher and see how quickly they can be printed. I don't know how posthumous editing is done, but knowing Waldo, he wouldn't want a word to be changed."

Xavier was turning off lights and Nell was walking beside him around the perimeter of the museum space, reading quotes painted on the wall. One gave her pause. Written by a famous scientist, it said that climate change would have more of an impact on people's lives than the advent of cyberspace.

"No one can believe it now," Nell mumbled. "It's been displaced while everyone hangs out on Photo Gram, absorbed in a place that doesn't exist."

"The permafrost is melting. Greenhouse gases are permeating the air. Vector-borne diseases like Lyme disease are increasing as ticks spread rampantly …" The scientist droned on like a poet giving weight to each word at a reading.

She paused to touch an interactive display on the wall labeled: "Will the Seas Cover Your Hometown?" She typed 'Boston' on the keyboard attached to the wall, and watched the map of Boston's coast creep inwards towards the city. It corresponded to incremental increases in global temperatures over the course of the twenty-first century. Xavier took her hand to watch with her as she gasped.

"This will get people to look up from their phones," he assured her. "Come on, it's already tomorrow."

They were on the threshold of the door. Nell raised up on tiptoe, and curled her arms around his neck.

"It was only by happenstance that I wandered into the Lion's Den tonight. What if I had missed you?" Nell said, musing.

"We would have found each other again, Nell."

There was no grand narrative, Nell knew that, but this was the story she wanted to be part of. She took his outstretched hand, reached down to touch the top of Argos's head, and walked out into the Berkshire sunrise. Leaning her head against the head rest, half closing her eyes, but not wanting to miss the scarlet rays beginning to paint the sky, she mumbled:

"I'll invite you to visit Iran with me when we wake up later, and then I'll take you to meet my friends, the Parsas."

Xavier heard every word and found a wool blanket from the back seat to put over her.

"Ha. I'll accept the invitation to visit Iran later on—one of the greatest ancient civilizations of the world—and I am pretty sure I caught a glimpse of the Parsas when I was leaving the echinacea plant at your house on my way to Boston Thanksgiving morning."

"I knew that was you, at least I hoped it was. I alternated between knowing and hoping," she laughed.

"It was to commemorate your family. A native plant."

"So kind," she mumbled.

"We'll plant it together," Xavier whispered.

"I have to go to the Andes alone, though," Nell mumbled, eyes closed now. "And then I will have years of photos to develop. More about that later, too."

Argos felt the hum in their chests. He rested his paws on the console and licked Nell's closed eyelids.

"Argos has probably masterminded all of this," Xavier said.

"I would believe that," Nell said before sinking into sleep.

Chapter Twenty One

Nell woke to see that Xavier was still in the land of sleep next to her, where even Argos remained. She walked on the tips of her toes over the wood floors to the bathroom, splashing her face and dressing for an early morning winter walk. She left a note for Xavier on one of her postcards, announcing that she would return soon, and slipped out the door with Argos.

"It will be your great return," she heard the echo of Blake's pronouncement on their last night in New York, as he thumped the top of her yellow cab. And *it has been a great return.* Nell parked by the trail where she and Argos had first met Xavier.

The year was nearly through its last chapter, and she wanted to take stock. Gingerly crossing the icy suspension bridge with Argos, she turned onto the same trail they had taken upon their arrival. *Be a good steward to the land. Till the land. Share my harvest. Be faithful to my aesthetics. Cultivate self-reliance,* she continued, enumerating the tenets of Nell's Manifesto for 21st Century Life. *Give back to the community in a meaningful way. Heal.* Pondering her journey from New York, Nell walked, looking down at the fine crystals of freshly fallen snow, noting that her tracks weren't the first human ones that morning. *Foster an atmosphere for absorption to cultivate space for intuition.* As she turned onto the loop that would bring them to the tail of the circular trail, she heard dry autumn leaves crush under the weight of a footstep on virgin snow. Looking up, she heard Hugo's words from their first encounter: *"I humbly challenge you to do so."* She had become fond of the tall man in the camel hair coat with a burgundy silk scarf since the walk they had shared during her period of intensive solitude upon her arrival. It was his shock of unruly white hair that she recognized. She put celerity in her steps to catch up with him.

"I accepted your humble challenge, Hugo," Nell said from just behind, so as not to startle him, and then stepped into stride with him on his right side.

"Ah, so you have gone back in time?" he asked, looking pleased that she had remembered. He was carrying a book under his arm again, and it happened to be Nell's favorite novel.

"My very last thought before I heard your footsteps in the snow was 'Fostering a sense of raptness lends itself to profound epiphanies.' That's what I have been doing, Hugo," Nell said.

"Name one profound epiphany, if you may. I'm curious to hear what your experiment has yielded."

Nell nodded. "At first, without the phone, without the internet being omnipresent in my mind's eye, I found myself in a state of enthrallment with my object at hand—whether it be a book, an idea, nature, etcetera—that enabled me to concentrate for prolonged periods. It reminds me of what a famous art theorist I read in grad school wrote about absorption, and the way that it's in diametric opposition with theatricality. For me, the smartphone culture and these social media applications that are photo-based—in which the photographer puts herself on stage at all times—is the modern version of theatricality. The obsession with theatricality obviates the ability to be absorbed. To see inside. You can't be theatrical and absorbed at the same time. I was trying to explain this to my partner, who is an advocate of social media and smartphones. I told him that I choose absorption over theatricality."

"But without the voyeurism implicit in viewing the painting of a subject absorbed in an object, therefore privileging privacy," Hugo said, stipulating for her.

"Without the outside gaze, of course. But that was only the beginning of the experiment. And with that—ignited only by a period of solitude—I was able to do some inner work I long needed to do. Epiphanies started coming to me that allowed me to heal from something like scabbed-over grief that I had been hiding behind. Then, with the help of my strengthened sense of intuition, I found a deeper purpose in life without being distracted by the fray and the static noise that came with it. I started writing and confronting what lay in the shadows behind me."

Hugo nodded at her as she spoke. "It looks like you answered your own question, Nell, the one that you posed to Dr. Gupta what seems like an eon ago: 'Is absorption possible in the age of distraction?'" Hugo said, reminding her.

"Yes. I needed to live through this to know I was answering it." She flung her hand into the air as an excited gesticulation. "And it became far more profound than I had ever realized it could. So, you see, I'm not one of your sleep walkers after all, not really suspended between a vanishing world and an emerging—let's say technological—one," Nell concluded.

"Good girl. I never thought that you would be," he said, an enigmatic glint in his eye.

"Never?"

"Edward Gibbons. I don't forget a first book," he announced with subtle triumph, or, rather, it may have been understated delight.

"You don't mean to say ... You couldn't possibly ..." Nell clapped her hands and clasped them in front of her. "You remember me reading Gibbons at the Café Musil. My first time at the café?" Nell stopped. She started. She looked as if she had just met a family member that had been deemed lost in a war.

"I happen to own the Musil," he said, revealing their complicit solidarity at last.

Tears spilled over her eyelids.

"I inherited the café from my Austrian father, and it will be our seventy-fifth anniversary this week. I read the *The Man Without Qualities* at the end of December every year to mark it," he said, smiling as he held the book up in his black-leather gloved hand for Nell to see.

"*Der Mann ohne Eigenschaften*," Nell whispered the title in its original German, and quoted: "'His life had been a series of convulsive experiences from which emerged the heroic struggle of a soul resisting all compromise.'"

"Walter, yes. Don't be like Walter either," he advised with a stern countenance, as they shared a laugh.

"That explains why you read these iconic Austrian authors," Nell exclaimed.

"Write to me at P.O. Box 212 and we'll talk about it over lunch, Nell."

He turned around to cross the bridge. Nell sat down on a snowy bench and went back in time for a while.

When she stood—urged by her own stomach and Argos's, and the thought that Xavier was surely awake—she walked back to cross the bridge with Argos. It felt like the bridge was graduating her into mature adulthood. On the bench, she had her daydream about New York at long last. It was fleeting, with no trace of nostalgia. Then she had started writing in her head, as if momentum had gathered around an idea.

In her head, she was responding to Emerson's essay on experience, which she had just read. It had come at the right place in her autodidact's syllabus that year. Emerson posited that people would find sanity and revelations in solitude, and those epiphanies, as Nell called them, would be carried into new worlds, presumably of ideas. Emerson thought that if one could carry out such a missive, it would mean the transformation of genius into what he called "practical power." But in the same essay, he scoffed at people's ability to do that: "Many eager persons successively make an experiment in this way, and make themselves ridiculous." Nell could quote it in her head, since it had lingered with her, as if she were having a conversation with Emerson.

I haven't made myself ridiculous. "I have to write my own philosophy within a twenty-first century context, and it does involve solitude," she voiced to the silvery trees whose winter coats were laced in snow. *But not as a means to an end, rather as a means to the stillness required to investigate one's inner landscape. Only once one has eluded the seduction of the digital world can this percolate. Then, the lived experience with sustained concentration leads to the cultivation of intuition. It's an intuition-based philosophy, but it has to keep evolving,* Nell concluded, writing in her head, and eager to put it on the page later that day. "And, Argos, I mean 'intuition' with its Latin etymology intact: to have an insight that is like a spiritual perception, a cognition that comes while contemplating. *Intuicioun.* You have always had it, and I'm learning from you."

As they walked back to the car, she felt a lightness of being that was authentic now.

On the drive home, she turned to other thoughts. A sentence floated in her mind: *Build a longer table with Xavier.* That was the last tenet on Nell's draft of her manifesto that she had been contemplating since Thanksgiving. "How about hosting a New Year's Eve party with Xavier, Argos?" He shared the glint in her eye, and he knew that it would fall on the full moon—a cycle he had been tracking alongside Nell. She wrote a mental guest list on the way to the car: the Parsas, Amelia and Fernando, Blake, Rose, Saraswati, Jack, Harold, and the Butterfields, of course. Perhaps Hugo would attend? *"Don't be an island, Nell,"* Mr. Holtzman had called after her. And she wouldn't be.

This narrator would no longer have to recount a misguided narrative that Nell herself had insisted on, based on a faulty mythology of what solitude would bring. Yet perhaps it was through those sustained periods away from society that Nell learned that being an island was nothing one should aspire to. Nell's sheltered island had spread its landmass across continents. She had found her community, and it had nurtured her into becoming.

About the Author

MICHELLE B. SLATER is the author of the memoirs *Soulmate Dog* and *Starving to Heal in Siberia. The Lunatic* is her first novel. She is a former professor of French and Comparative Literature, and holds a Ph.D. from Johns Hopkins as well as Masters degrees from University of Paris 8 and Dartmouth College. She spends her time between New England and Switzerland.

MIX
Paper
FSC® C100212

Printed by Imprimerie Gauvin
Gatineau, Québec